Praise for *Killer of Crying Deer...*

"This journey into a history whose legends and myths still shape our present is a dreamlike yet realistic portrait of two disparate worlds in contact and collision. William Orem paints an Impressionist canvas using prose of gemstone precision and brilliance. Readers will not soon forget Henry, shipwrecked, reborn and spiritually awakened on the shore of a brave new world, nor Speaking Owl—the Native American girl who touched and changed him. *Killer of Crying Deer* is an extraordinary book that captures the felt change of consciousness, the recognition and estrangement of a time when two worlds met and mingled but did not fuse."

—Verlyn Flieger, Professor, Department of English, University of Maryland. *Pig Tale*; *Splintered Light*; *Interrupted Music*; *A Question of Time*; editor, *Tolkien Studies*

"Far more than a historical romance, *Killer of Crying Deer* is an unflinching look at the naked human creature, a rousing tale that asks moral and existential questions that are urgent and contemporary: What does it mean to be civilized? What do human beings owe each other? How are we to know ourselves in a time of violent upheaval and cultural collisions? In a very real sense this is not only history understood as the past, it is history understood as precursor, as our history. Mix A.S. Byatt, David Mitchell, and Umberto Eco together, add a dash of Hilary Mantel, and you have something like the storytelling genius of William Orem. Bravo!"

—Richard Hoffman, Chair of PEN New England. *Half the House*; *Interference and Other Stories*

of

eer

m

oks

Killer of Crying Deer

Kitsune Books
P.O. Box 1154
Crawfordville, FL 32326-1154

www.kitsunebooks.com
contact@kitsunebooks.com

Printed in USA
First printing in 2010

ISBN: 9780981949550
Library of Congress Control Number: 2010927525

Cover photo: David Roy Urquhart

First edition

For Lauren:

When the hot sun had descended among the trees
they came out of the woods once more
and stood at the gate to the World

Preface

The manta ray is diminished; the manatee, the sublimely graceful Key Deer all but extinct. September is still the season of squalls, and the tiny pieces of land on which these creatures depend are at all times threatened by modern men and modern ways. Their existence beside us is testimony to the profound beauty at the heart of nature's process; the question of their continued presence a reminder of its final fragility.

In writing this story, my gratitude goes to the authors of the true, first-person narratives of shipwreck and survival among new cultures to be found in the 1575 *Memoir of Do. D'Escalente Fontaneda Respecting Florida* as well as the marvelously titled *God's Protecting Providence Man's Surest Help and Defence In the times Of the greatest difficulty and most Imminent danger; Evidenced in the Remarkable Deliverance Of divers Persons, From the devouring Waves of the Sea, amongst which they Suffered Shipwrack. And also From the more cruelly devouring jawes on the inhuman Canibals of Florida. Faithfully related by one of the persons concerned therein; Jonathan Dickenson, 1699.*

Another acknowledgement goes to Janet Raloff, senior editor at *Science News*. In the quotation at the beginning of part six, she is referring to the work of Lenes, Prospero et al., in *The American Journal of Limnology and Oceanography*, September, 2001.

—*William Orem*

Contents

There be three things which are too wonderful for me,
Yea, four which I know not:
The way of an eagle upon the air;
The way of a serpent upon a rock;
The way of a man with a maid;
The way of a ship, in the middle of the sea . . .

—*Proverbs*

Part One: September, 1699

So I alone became their prisoner.

—*Hamlet*

1

There was a pounding across the water. The gunpowder colored man raised his head once more and looked eastward at the sound, straightening to full height with the long shovel in one hand. His skin was not the uncertain blackness of mixed-race men—the midway, conciliatory hues of Afro-Indians or Anglo-Africans or Franco-Hispanics—but true black, deep blooded and shining almost purple in the sun. Shirtless, he was a man-shaped exclamation on the narrow beach, hot ash from a recent cataclysm.

"*Les canons*?"

The captain did not rise from where he knelt, his broad red hands making a tracery on the ground.

"Thunder," he said, after a while. "Up north. Two hours, three."

Cautiously the African walked to the edge of the channel. The muscles in his back were awake with recent use, vibrant and sweat-fringed. In front of him, like a mirror that displays the soul, the shallows swam with angry color: aquamarine shifting gradually to hot fields of blue, themselves diffusing farther out into emerald patches and, farther still, the deep, ruby-blood shadows where the bottom sloped away. At the limit of vision stood the thin, fishbone-like barrier of the reefs.

When the African was satisfied he splashed out to the jollyboat and tossed the shovel and chain back in.

At their clatter the boy jumped. He was crouched down in the square end of the hull, his entire head wrapped in cloth. All that was visible of his features was the round chin underneath and, above the crude wrapping, a crazed looking upshot of blond hair, giving him a ridiculous resemblance to a potted plant. One hand came up instinctively but the African made a hissing sound.

Eventually the captain rose. The eye, on encountering him, registered nothing at first but profound *physicality:* his body was massive, not only in its actual dimension, but in its spiritual implication. His bulk somehow insulting, its very presence an imposition on the world through which it moved. He wore tooled leather boots that climbed midway to his knees where the stuff had been tied cross-wise by hand. The shirt, frilled and flowered so that among the pavilions of London it might have belonged to a dandy, swung open as he moved to reveal a thickly haired chest marked by two looping, whitened scars. These met in the general region of the captain's heart, as if his entire person had been singled out by some divine and sinister hand.

With a meditative gesture he picked up his greatcoat from where he had laid it and presented his tongue to the wind.

"*Ehh-h-h,*" he said, shaking his head fiercely once and spitting. The thick maroon hair swung past his eyes and he made no effort to remove it. "*Ehhhh.* What's this world but a pity, P'ter? What's a man but a joke."

The African made no reply.

"Now we sail."

When the jollyboat found its water the captain came forward, his motions the slow, explicit ones of a dominant animal. The African pulled at the oars with one foot pressed on the blinded child and he, the captain, balancing his excess weight at the prow without looking back at the little unremarkable island with its low line of hills on which he had spent the last three hours in such torrents of emotion.

"Boy," he said, when the schooner loomed over them once more like a doom.

"I'm here," answered the blindfolded child. His arms were spattered with oar-drip, the fingers of both hands flinching to ward off what they could not see.

"*Oi*, art there," the captain rumbled. "Art there."

When evening came the cook lit the brick stove and the sharp scent of food drifted up from the galley. Near-starvation conditions were regular onboard *Arrogante*, as were their opposite: the riotous excess of eating, orgiastic bacchanals leading to temporary madness as the confused, desperate tissues took in more protein than they could handle. Like materializing specters the shift men came down from the rigging, their faces at once joyous and bitter, the fierce pain of hunger drawing them close.

After mess the captain still had not appeared and the boy was given two full bowls and some cabbage to take to the rear cabin. It was one of his many minor duties onboard ship: the transporting of raisins or bean mash or salmagundi to the great room at the stern, like the keeping of a dangerous animal. He went carefully through the companionway with the foodstuff balanced against his chest, the hot smell rising to his nostrils and eyes. He was a handsome child, in the way of youth, with the awkward limbs of adolescence and frank, startled eyes. Unlike the other sailors he was dressed in what had at one time been formal clothing, the narrow vest and dyed breeches broken now at both knees.

There was a grunting sound and the boy entered. The captain was perched over his desk where a thick roll of paper had been spread, held down in two corners by his pewter cup and by the skull. Next to him stood the African. He leaned hard over the parchment, seeming to consider.

"What a man needs," the captain muttered, low and irregular. "You see, P'ter? A flame below, hot air to buoy you up! Up, like a sounding corpse!"

The boy lowered the wooden load cautiously. He had made it to the cabin door again before fingers gripped him by the back of his shirt-collar.

"*Look then, sneak!*" the captain bellowed. "Ye'd spy on my plans and say nothing?"

With a twisting motion he thrust the boy's head to the paper. An enormous balloon had been drawn on it in lead pencil, ropes leading to a depending basket from which stick figures were dropping an anchor.

"*Airships* are what we need now," the huge man hissed in his ear. "We'd ride across the sky in such a device, lad. We'd sleep in a cloud then, *eh*? In a cloud!"

The captain's body was sour, each bubble of sweat pungent as if the Frankish wines had filled him like an overflowing pitcher.

"*What is there then we could not do, my P'ter?*" he cried to the African. "*Eh, my blackamoor*? Strike a Dutchy outpost from above, hop fortress walls? Drop fire on your Man-o-War? What think ye, boy? Eh?"

The boy's arms were spread trembling against the scarred table. The entirety of his strength was required to keep his cheek from touching its surface.

"You'd better speak now, Roojman," the African said.

"What ..." the boy tried, blood knocking audibly in his ears. "What...keeps it up...sir?"

"Up? *Up*?"

The captain drove the boy's cheekbone down and released him in one motion. The push of his own muscles unopposed now the boy stumbled backward and fell hard under the couch, one hand splashing in the hot stew.

"*Up*," the drunken man mused, turning away.

He took the golden skull quietly in his fingers and walked over to the windows with it, stroking its surface meditatively, like a cat.

"Up."

The captain's voice faded to a whisper. He looked out the cross-hatched glass at the stars.

After a minute the African jerked his head and the boy scrambled a second time toward the cabin door. Outside the cabin he felt suddenly the pain of the burn along his arm, putting the hurt skin to his mouth and tasting food taste. As he pressed against the swaying bulkhead he could hear the captain making a quiet, high pitched noise from within. It sounded like the man was crying.

On deck the unoccupied crew sat around a drum fire, cinders vaulting through the empty rigging and toward the stars. The drum had originally been part of a Dutch whaler's tryworks and was secured now in a small indentation in the quarterdeck, flame-light shining through it in multiple points. The boy huddled just outside the glow, feeling the cold night air and the perpetual rocking of the ship, feeling the keel slip through invisible waters.

"Whitepaul give you what you like, monkey?"

The crouching sailor laughed, showing a mouth marked here and there by worn teeth. The boy said nothing; the captain had never used him in that way.

"Why don't ye sing for us, lad?"

"Let's have a pipe dance."

"A fancy reel."

"Leave Roojman be."

The sailor slapped suddenly his own neck. A small, luminous insect glowed bluish for a moment before he flicked it away.

"Too close," he grumbled, his expression going foul. "Too close for night sailing. We should be taken out, or strike canvas."

“This is no night for deep waters. There’s a blow in the offing.”

They were not men but voices now: mouths, foreheads catching firelight only when they leaned toward the flames. When they spoke they had faces, squared or round or stunted, expressions mirthful or brutish or simply empty. Then with silence they fell back into the immaterial world, the place of shades.

Something shattered below and the captain hollered after it, a long, tuneless rage. The voice of the African could be heard following him, his own words steady.

“At his dreams again. His cloud riding.”

“Extra lines want to be below deck. And your shop, carpenter. Look to your tools.”

“Oh aye? Has the man given order?”

“The storm gives the order. The sky bled at morning.”

A cigar tip opened and closed, lit against the iron edge of the tryworks and passed among the faces. From somewhere high in the rigging a line caught the wind with a mocking cry.

“Now my lady banshee has found us. She howls for her food.”

“*Oi*, for Whitepaul’s soul.”

“Hear the damned witch sing.”

The shadow-men listened to the cry that rode with them, a draped, trailing thing fixed to the heart of their craft.

“With her above.” A bitter laugh. “And him below.”

“Here’s blood and water,” Angel grinned, stepping out into the light. He passed the bottle with a cracked lip, the not-men turning it carefully to drink while avoiding the edge. The boy crept aft away from the ghost light and worked his body into a space farther back between the gunwale and its railing. The spray was cool and faint across his skin as they broke through the unseen waves. He had stayed there, wedged tightly and swallowed in darkness, on nights when hammocks and shot lockers and other sleeping places were a danger. Without seeing his hands he took a cloth from his breech pocket, unwrapped the stolen salt beef there and chewed it with animal feeling. When he had cracked the thin bone and sucked also at the marrow until all the sweet was gone he pitched the bits over the side, staring exhausted into the absolute blackness of the sea. It seemed that, just for an instant, he had seen an arc of lightning fall.

Henry Cabbott Cote had been abducted on his thirteenth

birthday. His father was a Cote of the London Cotes, his mother a York woman named Foe who had been related to the London Cabbotts and so at her husband's wishes had publicly fashioned herself a Cabbott. She died birthing his sister Amelia Lordsgrace Cote whose middle name was a prayer, inserted by his father and meant to propitiate whatever God had overseen the difficult labor that for almost a week kept beginning and ending without issue. It was September and his uncle sailed with a Virginia Company trader. Though the family line had dissipated into more name than influence the generation before, his father was still a reasonably wealthy man and wanted his only son to be raised near a plantation where he could learn the trade of factoring.

Henry was a gentle boy and had been deeply afraid of the voyage. He was afraid of the separation from the children he knew at Sunday's School, from the circle of older boys he had just been allowed to join that summer, though one or two of the oldest had already gone to the colonies themselves. He did not want to leave his sister and the memory of his mother's voice. But his father was an unapproachable man and Henry had said nothing when the old patriarch, sliding his oak chair back one evening after the family meal like an orator rising to a public address, told him of his decision. Instead he had simply filled two leather trunks with clothing and several cloth-bound books that he held to his face tightly before packing them, wanting to force in the reassuring scent of home.

"To be master is as much labor as to be slave," Henry's uncle said. "You have inherited much, but one does not inherit character. This one cultivates like the smokeweed itself, starting when it is young, green. One cares for *character* as one cares for a planting, each day bringing some measure more into existence, nurturing it, finally weaning it, when all is made right and fruition is achieved. Look at them."

His uncle indicated the workers who sailed the merchantman.

"They are not slaves, but I am indeed their master. What the midatlantic grows passes through me to the crown. The captain of this vessel receives twelve and a half percent cargoes; for twelve and a half percent, I am his master. Now look at me. Look at *me*."

Henry's uncle swelled out his chest so that the belly, a yellow mound under his thin silk vest, protruded against the buttons. His emphatic lips were turned downward.

"Life has not been easy for me, not as it was for your father. *Prima geniture* is a Latin phrase. You have Latin?"

"Yes, sir." Henry blinked against the sun. It was a windy, fitful day on the Atlantic, and though the weather had been fine for weeks the crossing had amazed him with its length. "*Arma virumque cano—*"

"*Ames parentem, so aequus est,* Syrus says. The second son must create himself out of the lees. Bestir your understanding: I bear your father no ill wish when I say that he has been less of a man…less of a man because he has not had to *forge* himself in the paths of commerce."

"Yes, s …"

"The paths of commerce," his uncle repeated, liking the phrase. "With us the world is on the edge of a new dawn. Nations have been found to be mutable. The reins of power have been seen to change hands. Yet *commerce,* belonging to no state, will remain. It is the single greatest engine of our time.

"I have dined," he stressed, and straightened unnecessarily the hem of his jacket, "in the company of eminent persons. But tomorrow will say of me that the greatest of my companions was *commerce.* Let me ask you something."

With one hand Henry's uncle led him to the rail as if their conversation were now taking a more intimate turn. For a moment the stiff hair on his wig was troubled by the sea breeze, several strands coming free and pointing upward as if in mock astonishment. Henry concentrated hard so as not to look at them.

"Do you know what I see when I look across these waters? I see the *future.* And I see myself in it. A landowner, moneyed, a new man of the colonies. Do I see *your* future in this changing sea, Master Henry? Do I? Do I?"

For a moment the elder man seemed actually to be looking.

"You have read my pamphlet?"

"No, sir," Henry said, startled by the unexpected turn. "I have not had that pleasure."

His uncle did not hide his disappointment. He had written for public instruction a folio on the recent appearance of the comet, holding the strong opinion that it was to be explained by means of Reason and on no account to be taken as justifying violent dissention against the Popish. Henry listened carefully, waiting for and failing to find the association that had led to this juncture. Then the bosun wanted to speak to his uncle and when his uncle returned he had something small and white in his hands.

"Your father wanted me to give you this," he sniffed, uninterested. "As we were to be at sea on the actual day of your birth. It belonged apparently to your mother."

"Yes, sir. Thank you indeed, sir."

Henry began searching the box for an appropriate place to unwrap it without tearing the gossamer paper in which he felt he could sense his mother's delicate touch, but when he noticed a strange silence around him and looked up again the crew were all facing starboard. His uncle was looking that way too, on his pinkish face an expression Henry had not seen before. A schooner was approaching them swiftly from the west, rising out of the afternoon like a dark spot on the sun. When it came aside an enormous man in a greatcoat crossed the distance between ships, stepped over to Henry's uncle and, drawing a flintlock, shot him in the head.

The crew stared mutely. Henry was unable to stop looking at the man: barrel-chested, huge, his maroon wash of hair blowing like a torch around his features. His right ear was loaded with coppery gold so that the lobe hung low and distorted. He looked like a pagan tree set fire and come to life.

"That your father, boy?" the man roared.

Henry looked down at the package in his hands. The white tissue was spotted in places with red.

"Parents, boy," the man muttered, confidentially. "They are a damnation and a curse."

Then he turned to the crew.

"This vessel is hereby confiscated for her majesty's god damned *you pisshole whores stand down or die!*"

The giant paced in front of the crewmen in a fury, his stride bringing him to a head-on charge toward each figure followed by a last minute reversal. While other thieves began appearing over the companion ladder he stormed wildly across the quarterdeck, looking each sailor blank in the face as if they were shouting insults at his soul.

"*Who's in mollygrubbing charge here?*" he hollered finally, stabbing two fingers at Henry's uncle. "Him?"

The captain of the merchantman made no sound. When the navigator started to speak the huge man struck his jaw lengthwise with the copper butt of his weapon. Following on his question the gesture was nonsensical in the extreme.

When his men had finished tossing boxes into their longboat and dumping what they apparently did not like the flame-headed figure walked off without a word. He was about to step over when Henry heard a shirtless man wearing two antique swords say, "Any of them?"

"None of them," the great man answered. Then, as an afterthought: "The boy."

Two men grabbed Henry and lifted him physically off the deck. He cried out in wordless alarm; for an instant in his swaying field of vision he could see the merchantman captain standing silently and watching him go. It seemed to him more important than anything that he keep hold of the package in his hands.

The *Arrogante* was one hundred and odd feet long, long enough for a full minute to pass on Black P'ter's watch before Henry could hurry from bow to stern completely with his leg irons on. For days the African had not tired of the game: striking at Henry with a pike and watching him try and run with the short chain between his ankles, so that he was forced to keep his legs straight and use them like wooden stems. Henry said nothing, his fear welded shut inside, emerging only in little gasps. Eventually he was granted a longer chain, which the blacksmith affixed with a damp smile that seemed to be offered in some kind of recognition. Looking at the old bits of metal spilled randomly on the deck something flashed unexpectedly in Henry's mind and he suddenly became cognizant, not just of the thrumming, incessant terror of what was happening to him, but of time itself—how it had continued to wash past since his abduction, unoffended in its course. Peering down at the broken chain his own life, what he had always implicitly taken as the central fact of the world, appeared as a linked series connected to nothing.

The schooner had three masts of which the foremost were of equal width and stretched high into the salty air like pines, and a third much narrower mizzenmast that had foot pegs but was difficult for a grown man to work. With the new longer leg chain freeing his movements Henry could ascend all three, his small body going from footholds to ratlines to a series of improvised hand-grips that led, eventually, to the towering crowsnest itself. He was sent aloft often, to cut loose material or run up lines, and as often he was forgotten there, the quartermaster having used him as a man uses a tool and then turned blankly to something else. Gripping the swaying pole with his heart triphammering, a primal feeling of escape grew inside him, the flight into trees from predatory earth.

The smaller canvases came down frequently and several of the crew set to checking them for ruptures or strain. At the blow of hands Henry learned the art of re-crafting a sail, of recognizing the shine on fabric that had not torn but was likely to tear; of working in thicker, resin-washed patches of stuff around the rope holes for a more certain hold. No one asked him his name, where he lived, what his life had been like before the abduction. He came to know the toeholds, the bucket, the beam; he came to recognize the meaning of the different whistles the quartermaster used; and when he was not racing to follow a shouted order there was abruptly nothing for him to do. At these times Henry would find himself simply watching the enormous mainsails, having forgotten himself completely, forgotten under what conditions he drew each breath. It was *they* who belonged here, out in this blue-black stretch of water where man was a stranger and this moving caravan of men an absurdity; they, the great sails, as primal and true as the wandering sky or the dark ocean face itself.

Always the smell of resin was there, below decks where it mingled with sweat and boxed meat, above where the breeze blew it somehow both cold and hot at once. A slow brush was used to work it between planks, the remaining caulk sanded down afterward by hand. One day the Irishman showed him how to lay a thin length of rope between boards, cutting a shank of Henry's hair to sprinkle some in before gluing the whole into place. The man shaved his own scalp flat with a bodkin and stained what was left with colored ink, yellows and blues crawling over his skull in strange array.

"Grace O'Malley be blessed," he spat.

Always there was work. Henry pulled on the lines he was given with no gloves and after a while a thin sheet of skin peeled agonizingly from each palm. After the second occurrence a tall, jocular fellow with a prominent goiter lifted Henry bodily and planted him on the tryworks, holding his hands up by the wrists and showing them around and laughing and saying something in a language Henry did not know. The man slapped Henry's back as if they two had a joke to tell, and poured grain alcohol across the raw flesh and tied two thick squares of sheep's skin over each hand with strings, holding the knot in his teeth as he pulled the new coverings taut. The pain, a blinding wind at first so that Henry's jaw dropped and he feared he would faint, faded almost immediately into numbness and in the astonishment of his relief Henry had to tell himself that he was not going to cry, never in front of these men; he was not ever going to let them see him cry.

Always there was work. The gathering of rain in the harness casks; the operation of the pumps, done to the rhythm of a broomstick knocked on the bulkhead by a thick-limbed New Mexican who was either mute or never cared to speak. Always there was work: and Henry watched as he labored, examining, taking in. After a time beneath the current of his terror a quieter eye was forming, something distant and unaffected that he could use. His body, pregnable at first, grew stiffer and more resilient with the rod and the jeers and the slaps. He began to *feel less*, as if his soul too had been worn down and coarsened. Something less touchable inside him began to grow.

Every man wore something in his ear: a small silver hoop for those who could afford them, tin stakes for those who could not and fishing weights to bring the earlobe to a point.

"The hoop pays your burial if you wash up in some Christian land," Angel said, pulling the thing over to his lips and kissing it. "Captain Whitepaul wears many, on account of he has many deaths in him."

He swabbed something from a glass onto Henry's left ear and stabbed it with a thin needle that flashed in the sun. Then he tied through a wire attached to a tiny blue feather that had blown up on deck.

"The hoop you earn," Angel said. "Like your right to die."

Benjamin Oldham was a prophet. He was in the tradition of the great mages of the past—Asclepius and Merlyn and Zarathushtra; Hermes Trismegistus and the Albertus Magnus, known to his pupils only as The Great.

Like bar-Joseph, I ride the waters. Don't think you I could not sail by night in a storm, in a cloud. If I choose to be present among you now, it is still in my power to be a gull, a spray, a barnacle.

Oldham had been a miner before *Arrogante* and had tattoos wide as five fingers and stretching from elbow to shoulder, images of Egyptian gods, their heads adorned with rising moons. In the cool Caribbean evenings he wore a cable sweater made of wool and nothing underneath, so that the gods and heroes peered out with their strange hawk faces, like dream fish trapped in a net.

In a lighter mood he debated the usefulness of the Irishman's slingshot. The weapon was a thick wooden Y with a loop that anchored it to the wrist, the drawing arm pulling the strap back entirely before letting a projectile fly. With it any object became lethal, shot pieces, pottery shards; but could he do more than knock pins off the rail? One day in a bright sea shine and with a small wind the Irishman crouched on deck and brought three gulls out of the air, their bodies landing each with a confirming splash.

"Grace O'Malley be blessed," he spat, crossing himself. Then, to the magician: "Do that with your kelpie spirits."

Oldham carried always a bible in a sack roped over his heart. Before each attack he read prophecies, removing with immense seriousness the fragmented text and laying the bits out on the quarterdeck. With legs folded he passed his hands over the strange collection and twitched at the air, feeling for its runic energies. At some point the sensate fingers came decisively down and he intoned:

Hell from beneath is moving for thee
To meet thee at thy coming:
It stirreth up the dead for thee
And the worm is spread under thee
And the worm covereth thee.

Captain Whitepaul grinned out of his shaving lather and pronounced the omen good. *Thy coming* was your fat Spanish trader, he explained, loaded with mule train from Vera Cruz and

Peru. *Arrogante* was the hell that yawned for her.

They came astern of the West Indiaman before it had time to respond, staying away from her flanks where the nine pounders were. It was a bad design for cannon, the gunner explained, and filled the gunrooms with gagging fumes when used; but the trade off was worth the inconvenience, for even a single volley from such a load could bring irreparable loss. The Dutch captain fired once, making it apparent that if he were challenged he would have no compunction with fighting. Seeing the enthusiasm with which Whitepaul accepted the challenge, however, he went about quickly and tried to run.

"To the last minute, the last second," Black P'ter smiled, holding his timepiece high.

Onboard there had been no real battle. The Indiaman was already carrying all her canvas; *Arrogante* merely closed from behind and flung grappling hooks into her rigging. The Dutch captain, seeing armed men vaulting his stern, panicked a second time and simply stood at attention. His crew, several of whom were West India Company guards in swallowtail coats but boys still and not yet shaving at all stood furious in line, awaiting the undelivered order to fight. The *Arrogante* had lashed herself completely so that the spars of the two ships clattered, the hulls gripping each other in fierce embrace. When the looting was finished P'ter went and stared in the captain's eyes.

"*White man*," he said, leaning in until his pupil was only inches away. The Dutch captain's gaze remained fixed on the horizon, descrying some trembling point only he could see. "If I told you to shoot yourself, you would do it, no?"

The captain did not move.

"You have one minute," P'ter grinned at him.

The Dutch captain stood immobilized for a long moment before Henry, watching from *Arrogante's* ratlines, realized his hand was stirring. The hand itself was thin and white, like a doll's hand protruding from the red linen cuff. His face too was a doll's face, oddly clean with hair that emerged from under his cocked hat in little curls. As if acting of its own volition the hand moved to the flintlock tie, drew the barrel, the thumb moving over the wide iron heel of the hammer to set it in place, the forefinger touching gingerly several times at the fanciful trigger guard before finding the trigger itself. It took almost the full sixty seconds for the captain to raise the gun to his temple and fire.

When the powder went off the guards who were standing in line cried out as if they themselves had been hit. One boy with an outraged face grabbed up his musketoon and discharged it at P'ter without leveling the end. The shot went wild and P'ter slung his boarding ax out and impaled it in the boy's sternum.

"*Courageux!*" P'ter cried, coming over to the boy who knelt on the deck as if offering the weapon back. "*Le brave garcon!* This one had spirit, *n'est-ce pas*? Now you! You!" P'ter shouted at each of the remaining guards in turn, painting their shirts with the bloody head of the ax. "You! Fight us! Don't go like a dog goes, yes? Pick up your guns!"

Tears were streaming down the faces of the boys.

"*Pas de larmes!*" P'ter barked. "No tears for your mommas! Fight us now!"

As if at a given signal the company lifted their musketoons and held them, the bayonet ends quivering defensively, like spears. P'ter spun toward his own men and raised his hands happily.

For a long time he had no name. When he heard himself referred to in English he was the whip, powder-monkey, he was *the boy*. After the incident with the hands he became *mains rouges*, Roojman.

Always there was raiding. Whitepaul had no discrimination, almost no strategy. They struck tiny English sloops and island traders, high Spanish galleons when they sailed without escort and immense, hundred-gun *galliots* like floating cathedrals. They stole sugar and clean barreled water; they stole tins of flour; they stole tobacco and timber, filling the ship's stores with the rich smell of uncut leaves pounded into crates. At night Henry listened to the rats pulling at the mash, a wet, toothy sound that entered his dreams.

After a month the blacksmith removed his chain altogether.

"You're what we are, lad," he said. The smithy had one eye that was milked over white and unseeing, and the eye stared off disinterestedly into the clouds. "Still if you run." He gestured toward the dead pupil with his thumb and made a slicing motion.

They stole rum and deerskins. They stole ambergris and soap, the latter breaking open from its papers and the men all soaping their limbs and body hair in the gentle surfless waters of coves just off of the trade routes. Surrounded by water, bathing happened only rarely, and many straight-razored their chests and their pubises to avoid infestation. Henry managed to obtain a cake left floating when two sailors began punching each other once in the small waves and he scrubbed and tore at his scalp and his groin and the pits of his arms until it seemed that, like his newly toughened hands, the old self was rent off and gone.

They stole ivory beams and clean packed clothing, emptying holds entirely and tying men and laying them out flat on their decks like stripped meat. When there were women the men took the women two or three at a time and Henry did not watch, staring instead at his ridiculous buckled shoes or the unquiet sea but not at what was being done to the women and not at the faces of their husbands, their lips tense with dignity, who were forced to stand seeing and not seeing the image that was before them.

They stole porcelain and oranges, pork and molasses. They stole men, Africans and Indians and some poor whites, their eyes like lamps in which the wick has been pinched tight. Black P'ter made always a point of looking the Africans over when they came aboard, his expression backlit by contempt. When Captain Whitepaul had shown him the head of his former owner P'ter alone from the group of indigo slaves of which he had been a member had laughed. Then, laughing still, he had taken a stake and sharpened one end of it and gone into the eleven-bedroom house of his master and tied up his master's whole family and pierced their hearts and, laughing still, gone out and pierced the hearts of the neighboring French families for three plantations around, over thirty five murders in all; and with every purple-grape rush of heartblood his laughter grew greater. In other versions of the story the number killed had been fifty or higher before the laughter was sated.

They stole rundlets of wine and fat balls of chocolate, a great glass case holding six pounds of butter. They stole other children, younger than Henry himself, who had been taken off cobbled streets or from under bridges where they lived and then sold and resold as indentured servants in eight-year blocks that stretched together into perpetual slavery. Indeed the presence of children on the ship was a regular feature of its life, though Henry never made contact, often fearing their broken faces as much as those of the men. When a brother and sister were onboard once who it was said had been upper class Britons Henry went to them but they were animals, not even human things, and were tied to a berth with cloth ties until they could be taken to a landowner on the coast.

When they stole, Henry watched the flag called the *Jolie Rouge* fly up the gaff of the mizzenmast, long, longer than a man, and broad, unfurling like a splash of blood, and despite his horror something inside him wakened. When the signal was given and the *Arrogante* tensed for attack he clambered into the rigging and watched, safe and high, higher even than the men who would balance the soles of their feet on the ratlines and fling over home-made grenades and stinkpots like avengers born out of myth. Henry watched and when the two ships were approaching each other and the *Arrogante* crew stayed low to the rail so their numbers could not be seen and there was still question as to whether the other side would drop colors or flee them; in that minute or two of approach before the fighting began, seeing the men's' sweating shoulders bright and tense, seeing the tops of their sweating heads, he felt something inside himself quicken; and after the fighting when the surgeon's table was slopped clean of blood and coins were spilled out on it and the gambling began, always the gambling, he would hold on to the mast where he clung until sunset and look at the stars appearing like luminous sand overhead and feel that something inside himself, he did not know what, but something he carried like a discovered treasure of his own.

Whitepaul did have strategy. It was to double back on his own wake, staying close to headlands and bays that were not yet mapped and watching the shipping lanes, like a caged animal pacing. Once a season his predatory course took them past the tiny unnamed island where he kept a hoard greater, it was said, than a ten thousand ruby chest. It was after his ritual anchoring there one year during which the entire crew was required to wait blindfolded that the captain had returned with the skull: child-small, dirty and crusted in sand, he carried the jawless thing onboard with the delicacy of a man holding a sacred item. His drunkenness had been the worst Henry had ever seen it that night, continuing with undiminished intensity through all the following week. He stayed in his cabin and took wine straight from clay bottles set in square wooden holders to keep them from sliding and Henry, taking in and out the uneaten food, had seen him lifting the entire collection of wood and clay in one hand and tipping the wine back into his throat with his eyes wide open, like a man screaming.

At week's end the captain emerged from his quarters, went to the forecastle and urinated over the side and then crossed himself and began bellowing, calling on God above to leave him the *shite frick alone*, taunting the Divinity with every manner of obscene imprecation. He said he would *shag the Virgin in her hot fricking hole, he would frick the Christ child up his tiny pink arse and the wise men one at a time and the manger animals too, and he would frick God in his God-hole and if he had a Peter Quince big enough to reach heaven he would frick heaven too and everyone in it.* Then he leaned over the bows and vomited explosively into the air, protecting the little brown skull in both hands as if to shield it from so unsightly a vision.

After that he was well again and in a fierce humor. They raided all the way north to the Carolinas, and at Charles Towne the captain left the ship with something inside one of the wooden bottle boxes and was gone an entire day. Crew members who had legal knowledge took charge of the bargaining of goods with the governor's men on shore and when Whitepaul returned the skull was plated in gold, all but a small square on the back where whatever the metallurgist had used had been insufficiently wide.

The crew were released into town that night and at midnight the captain emerged from the room always kept for him at an inn called the *Dovecote* and, his arm around Henry like a mentor, challenged any seaman there to arm wrestling. A cutting block was carried out from the back. Henry watched as both men, Whitepaul and a stranger from a different ship, were stripped to the waist and their wrists knotted together, and when the game was begun Whitepaul reached over with his free hand and punched his opponent square in the face. The stranger, astonished, kicked out his seat and the two men's torsos collided over the table like clashing stags, both striking freely and Whitepaul using even his head as a batter. A group gathered in a semicircle around the contestants, knocking the money down under the portrait of the King. When the other man's arm finally went flat Whitepaul would not release it but leaned all the more heavily in, knocking the bone down again and again as if to drive it through to the ground. Then he untied and walked to the bar and filled a grog and then, without sipping it, returned and took the stranger's smallest finger in one hand and twisted it out of its socket.

"Rhapsody on his cat," Hooker said, bringing down Thins from his perch. They had been sailing all through the spring, and with the hottest months beginning once more the *Arrogante* lulled in southern waters like a well-fed creature. "Now you and I must immortalize our fellow traveler here, young Roojman. Must we not?"

The cat was lean and brown with unpatterned spots on its sides. Familiar with the ship, it could disappear for days at a time, like a wraith for whom material existence was merely optional. "But it must be fresh, in image and word. Did they teach you no poetry in your fancy life before us?"

Aside from the captain's strange affection Hooker was the only member of the crew who addressed him kindly, with almost an avuncular air. Henry tried to think. He remembered a poem he had memorized for the Sunday School pageant, something about *the water waxeth clear* and her *lovely scattered locks*, but the work was unreal, so far from him now that it might have been some element in a dream.

"No sir," Henry managed. His face and his arms were covered in grease, from where he could not say. The buttoned shirt he had been wearing on the day of his abduction was tatters, its formal blue now a mild gray-green. "Not that I remember, sir."

"I'll deliver you one, then, my lad," said Hooker, warming to his love of performance. He said that *when April with his showers sote*

The drooght of March hath pierced to the root,
And bathed every vein in such sweet liquor
Of which virtue engendered is the flower;
When zephy's blow, with gentle breath
Inspires in every wood and heath
The tender crops, and the young sun
Hath in the Ram his half-course run;
And small birds make melody

That sleep all night with open eye
So pricks us nature with her courages
That men long for pilgrimages.

***

When Henry awoke the world was on its side. He grabbed spastically for hammock but found only slick wood: remembering where he had gone to sleep then he wrapped one arm quickly under the brass rail and gripped his own wrist with the other hand. A gray wall was approaching him; he heard himself make an involuntary sound just before the wave hit.

When he came up again he was in slashing rain. There was light—for a moment he could see morning sun just stepping up on the horizon—but all above the *Arrogante* was charcoal sky, wind firing through the disorganized sails. Then the rain seemed to bend its course and he could feel the true force of the blow: wind such as he had never witnessed or dreamed, crazed, explosive, like something conscious and abruptly unleashed. Henry held on to his slick wrist bone as the *Arrogante* rose, firing him into the air like a rider on a lunatic horse. His elbow slipped all the way under the rail and when his legs came free it was his only point of contact with the ship, and he cried out again as he pulled hard at the root of his shoulder, feeling the muscle tear. The *Arrogante* heeled once more and Henry forced himself to inhale before he was dropped a second time into the froth.

He was under long enough to hear his released breath bubble and then the ship righted itself violently, his own form unrecognizable in a current of spume that came off him like a white river. As Henry watched a crewman in an ankle-length oilskin skidded the entire deck before coming to a violent halt against the gunport, his rag-like body sliding to and fro among spilled lines.

"Topsail!" someone was shouting. "Topsail! Out and lay... !"

Henry spat against cutting grains of ice that blew from somewhere and the whole deck pitched sidelong, jumping in one direction and then another as if the hull had been rammed from below. He could see the scuppers belching like gargoyles.

Somewhere male voices were singing a song of lashing and courses, but their motions were comically futile, like dancers imitating distress. One crewman came clawing his way toward Henry but a twisting column of air played across the deckwood and the man grasped at his own face, dropping backward. The ship listed down deeply once more, impossibly far into the trough, plummeting until Henry could see the steely edge of the next breaker mounting like a canyon wall. He was in the shadow of that watery doom: he was being deposited in a deep well in the sea.

A vibration ran through the body of the hull and all at once the mainmast loomed sickly over him. A vertical line was drawing itself in white against water-blacked wood and then at the same moment as Henry understood the mast was breaking a splinter twice his body length burst free, gyrating over him like a projectile. The foresail tipped at two different angles and a bundle of thick iron chain, released from its hold, came looping almost gracefully toward him through the air. Henry let go.

Part Two: Los Martires

He who hath known the bitterness of the Ocean
shall have its taste forever in his mouth.

—Joseph Conrad

2

Comandante Marces Mene'n Albenix spotted the gray discoloration of smoke just south of the river mouth and ordered his men to drop anchor even though they had just spent the better part of the month at *San Augustin* drinking and eating well with the friars there and had only just restarted their southward trek. Albenix was in a good mood: the small cabin boy who sucked on his penis had done his particular job well, so much so that it had not been a shameful experience for either of them but simply a necessity between servants of the crown who understood their respective positions in life. The result had been a far superior orgasm for Albenix, so much so that he had been thinking of returning to his quarters for a second experience when normally it was his practice to wait a solid ten days to two weeks before requiring the boy's assistance. The boy, Albenix thought, had enjoyed himself too: normally he closed his eyes tightly as if only waiting for the *comandante* to finish but this time, he noted, the eyes had been open. Bright startled eyes, like a girl's. Always the boy said nothing unless he was spoken to but Albenix thought he had seen something in his little brown face this time, some hint of a womanish satisfaction. He would return early to his quarters, he decided internally, after inspecting the settlement.

At the little village they found a scattering of *Inglès* among the larger number of Carib. The lime-plaster houses spoke of Spanish presence but had been abandoned for some reason and reoccupied later by natives. After a brief interaction the Carib who were unwounded were placed in the hold; then Albenix returned to consider the whites.

The British were offered the holy bread and then a prayer was said and they were offered the sacrament a second and final time, two of them seeming to think better of their positions and coming free from their peers in a little torrent of hisses. The old woman, however, was a different case. She would say nothing and was sitting on the floor with straight white hair that hung limply with the brass holder still dangling from it. Her expression was rebellious and she had a fleck of something by her lip.

"*Tome el pan de vida, madre,*" the eucharistic minister said. The eucharistic minister was also a soldier. The old woman spat and Albenix stepped forward and shot her in the eye. He turned to the others.

"You see what will come," he said in English. The scent of the exploded charge was rich and sour inside the little room.

All but three professed the faith then, explaining that they did not mean to be living in Spanish territory but that they had been cast here by fate when their vessel with supplies bound for Cambridge foundered on a bar. They were Quakers and not residing among the heathen at all but only this afternoon had come to trade with them for food, the merest procurements. One man hurriedly repeated some Spanish words he knew, moving from soldier to soldier, as if the single capitulation were not decisive. At the back of the room a woman who was evidently his wife looked on with derision.

"God bless your soul, Jirah Bond," she called out.

"These are indeed blessed," Albenix answered her, loud enough to be heard. "Take the repentant outside."

The wife would not look at her husband as he passed. The husband, tears assaulting his face, stood in terrible indecision by the door and then flung himself back, going down on his knees and speaking frantically to the woman's legs as if her legs and not her face were the actual center of her being. The wife simply looked away, her partner's frantic entreaties a stiff but irrelevant wind.

When Albenix came out of the building a few minutes later the husband was seated on the little stone steps, the other Britishers standing around in a hesitant group. The husband's unshaved face was chaotic red and he conversed silently with himself, as if practicing an explanation that might some day be put to use. Albenix patted the man's skull.

"Give them each the sacrament," Albenix said to his soldiers, turning aside and kissing the small crucifix that hung inside his shirt. "Make sure it's swallowed before they hang."

3

The boy lay in quietly shifting water. There was no sound, save once the far off questioning of a sea bird, answered by its mate. In the great stillness his mouth brought slow, half-choked breaths, drawing bubbles.

Henry Cabbott Cote, known among his captors as Roojman, felt fingers move across his skin. He had seen women in the Carolinas whose faces were painted white like the white rounds of eggs, women who leaned out of the top rooms of public houses all along the quays and let their breasts show down to the nipples around which painted fish swirled and called to the men who were coming in on barques. The waterways there were shallow and good for seclusion, difficult to give chase in and the Royals never tried them for fear of becoming mousetrapped. Once inside the houses those same women sat in the laps of the *Arrogante* men and laughed without feeling it, an empty practiced laugh like the ringing of a bell; the men laughing also in a darker, more serious way with on their own faces a strange look like hatred and starvation. One day at the *Dovecote* when the men were laughing their no-laughter one of the women had suddenly come over to him, to Henry—behind the thick whiteness her face was surprisingly young, a girl's face, on her small brow a rope of false tangerine hair—and stared at him before reaching out to touch the skin next to his eye. For a moment she looked like she might cry.

Henry had never forgotten her, that barefoot girl in women's clothing who had walked across the sawdust floor and put her finger out to him as if he were an unreal thing. In the days and weeks afterward he had examined his own face in cabin mirrors, touching the tiny place she had touched, looking for some trace of what she had seen.

Now again he was with her, that girl, only her touch was fading and being replaced by the sharper fingers of the others: women he had seen from India who were as dark as Africans but with white women's noses and mouths; Italians with thick blue glass beads hanging between their cleavage and beautiful serious Jewish women and deep-skinned, deep-eyed Greeks. In his dream the women were touching him now with their fingers, touching him and working him like a newborn child or a bread loaf. Only their fingers had sharp long nails and as they plied his skin he could feel the fingernails more and more, they were pinching and stabbing now teasingly into him, he was trying to push the fingers away but the women were pinching and hurting him, their eyes turning from amusement to insistence and from insistence to something dark and cold.

Henry rose up and the tiny crabs scuttled away from him in a tide. Water streamed off his body and for a moment he held himself on one elbow, turning confusedly then to his right arm where it hung limply at his side. He could feel nothing in it at all.

After a minute he looked around. He was in thin, bright water, hardly an inch deep but running on seemingly for miles in a glittering, unbroken sheet. Wild sparkles played in his eyes. The sand beneath his hips was clean and firm.

And there were objects in the water, scattered about: small, whitish and straw-colored and sun-colored; their undersides purple and ochre and dancing with silent living nubs.

Starfish, Henry thought.

And then: *I am alive.*

The conjunction of ideas seemed a rational one, and he listened to himself as he might have listened to a formal speaker at Bristol Hall to catch some difficult but central thesis. But the words seemed to have exhausted him and Henry lay down again in the trembling water, backwards this time so that his face stayed entirely in air. Silently the star creatures pulsed around him, sensing, feeling.

Someone was there. Henry opened his eyes: a figure, small, made of blue shadow, coming between him and the sun. A girl was standing before him, carefully poised, as if balanced on the water itself. She held up a glistening starfish in one hand like a symbolic gesture.

Henry looked at her and wanted to tell her he had remembered her always; had remembered her and wept for her life at the *Dovecote*, and dreamed of escaping the world into which he had been cast and returning to take her free. But the vision was gone, the shining expanse around him empty once more. Somewhere far off a slop of water passed into a rock cavity, washing out in a noisy gurgle.

I have to get on shore, Henry thought. *On shore.*

He rose and made his legs walk, finding himself unable to lift his head and staring instead at the streaking white flashes through which his feet passed. Looking at the reflections shattering and reforming all around him he had a vague sense that he was walking in the sky; he was made of ephemeral stuff now and was stepping through a bright star-clustered heaven.

On shore. Yes but tide.

Then the fatigue came on him again and he fell with a hard plash, the sand cold and abrasive around his body. He began to shake. Half his nose was crusted with something solid and with intense effort he kept his face turned so the unclogged half could draw air. The sun was good now, warm on his terrible coldness; the sun was warming him through his shirt and pushing away the icy feeling: it was good to think on the goodness of the warm sun slowly moving farther and farther through his body, drying him like a fish flung on a dock. He vaguely understood that hours must be passing.

The snorting sound of his own choking brought him back. He wanted to lie still but some panicked voice deep in his consciousness was telling him if he did not move he was going to catch fire and burn. Henry forced his sticky lids open and the light was coming from an entirely different part of the sky; he was now not in the bright submerged field that had gone on forever but lying on a mass of parti-colored pebbles. He tried to move but the hanging arm dragged strangely again, the fingers seeming to dawdle with a blue shell. The skin along his shoulders and back cried out as he felt the immensity of the burn he had already sustained. His sleeve had come down off one shoulder and one entire side of his body was a fresh, tender red.

Henry stood, fell ridiculously on his buttocks, rose slowly again. His legs remained difficult to control but he staggered them in short motions the way he had once learned with the chain, though only when long sharp blades of grass began dragging against his bare ankles was he was absolutely certain he had come any distance.

When he was convinced that dry plants were underneath his feet he sat and, for some reason, held the longest blade of green in his good fingers and slumping once more to his side placed it in his mouth, not to pluck or eat but to hold it there with his teeth. He had the faint notion that his body itself was getting longer, that he was changing somehow, perhaps taking on a new form or shape. He wondered what shape he would have, what kind of life would be his in the new body when it came. Vaguely he hoped he would be a bird.

Three stars were visible when Henry woke. His body was returning to him now: not the arm, which he feared confusedly he might do damage to if he could not remember how to use it, but his legs and the soreness and beaten ache that were the muscles all along his hips and his spine. Several times his strange emergence from the field of sunlight had begun replaying in his mind, he kicked his legs out clumsily and his lungs began clutching for breath. But the dream receded and he was lying in cool grass, quiet and unthreatened. It was twilight.

Henry's mother had taught him to read when he was five and by his tenth birthday he was able to spend time in *Histories of the Reborn* and *The Whole Duty of Man*, copies of which he had found on a forgotten shelf in the cellar next to scented cranberry preserves with wax caps. His father was a literate man but not a bookish man, preferring exercises that had worldly results—barring, later on, his single, fixed obsession—and looked at his son's enthusiasm for literacy as something unfocussed and vaguely epicene. Thus Henry had learned both his reading and his languages from his mother's tutelage, and when she had died the daily pleasure of these experiences was taken from his soul.

So it was quite by coincidence that he had come across in one of the three small barns a copy of the Taverner translation of the Bible, secreted like a guilty object behind a beam of wood. Half swallowed by the earth the text was a riot of mold, the near-colorless cover from which he plucked individual bits of hay having become degraded until it had the texture of silk. The barn like the orchard around it had been unused since before Henry's birth. Opening the book he found tiny flowers growing through the pages, and rather than plucking these he read through them, as if the green shoots were an intentional and elaborate ornamentation.

He did not tell his father about the book, as bibles and prelates alike had become forbidden after his mother's death. Instead with a pleasurable guiltiness he began spending his unoccupied time in the barn, working his mental faculty on the thorned, thick-sounding words. He remembered the Rector, a dust-colored man who had instructed him in catechism, saying how *God's eye is ever critical*; yet in the Biblical tales he did not sense a God of blood and retribution. Rather they were passionate stories about a loved people, about individuals lost and yearning to be found.

When his mother died Henry's father had stopped attending the Rector's suppers, and then religious services of any kind, withdrawing from parish society as his metaphysical speculations became more and more the focus of his strange mental life. He came to believe the true Word had been stolen by Papists, deliberately altered, and that the hydra of their conspiracy included the modern vernacular print. A year or two into being a widower he announced to the village that the secret to the gospels' meaning resided in an accurate understanding of the Zodiac. Christ he understood as The Sun, dying and rising perpetually, while the Apostles were twelve signs *Through which that orb passes*, as he titled the long treatise he was composing in which he would expose the obscurantist plot.

One afternoon in summer Henry had been reading his book when the creaking paper revealed a separate sheaf worked carefully into a hole that had been knife-cut into the pages themselves. With astonishment he inched out the tightly folded parchment which bore the still-legible heading *Spiritual Testament of Lucy Foe.* Much of the Latin was beyond him but the English lines, penned in-between the others like a commentary, asserted that this note would be sufficient on the Judgment Day to satisfy the Lord's requirement that one Lucelia Foe had in her heart retained her family's true teachings and been all her life secretly a Catholic. It took Henry a full minute to understand that the woman being described was his mother.

For several days he had returned to the secret note, reading it over and again as if reading a missive from a forbidden lover. On the last day of the week he had only just returned the paper to its crook when his father strode into the barn. Horrified, Henry sought to conceal the book but the old man went into a kind of fury.

You creep out here to imbibe their distortions? The true Logos is writ in the heavens, not in clandestine reading.

Grabbing Henry's coat lapel he demanded submission but Henry would not kneel. It was not belligerence; yet how could he degrade himself with cowering in the presence of his mother's bravery?

After a moment, pale under his careful beard, his father had stalked coldly from the place.

Now Henry lay, his spirit quieted by exhaustion. He knew he was already fully conscious and that soon he would have to rise, rise and to think; yet for a moment longer he lay doing nothing, remembering for some reason only the look of hurt on the old man's face when his son had driven him inadvertently to defeat.

When a falling star made a rusty arc from one cloud to another he came to his knees. His first clear knowledge of his condition was thirst.

"Lord," he whispered, understanding fully only now what it was that had happened to him.

He turned toward the sea, which was calm and untroubled, as if any notion of hurricane squalls were a thing from storybooks for children, as if the earth were a blessed place and vessels might travel upon her with an absolute trust. There was no ship.

Henry scanned the purpling horizon, finding the last husk of sun. There was no ship, anywhere.

"Lord," he repeated senselessly, as if he had witnessed the swallowing of a world. Vaguely he understood that he should say something better, something with dignity and purpose. But nothing came; he looked at his sleeping fingers.

I am free.

In an uncertain gesture Henry reached down with the good hand and drew a cross in the sand, mounted by the letters that had been inked on the first page of his mother's bible: I H S.

An evening wind began passing over the beach.

Somewhere in the middle of the night Henry came to. In a crazed state he searched out a clear patch of soil, clawing at it frantically until water appeared. The whitish fluid he managed to swallow for only a few seconds before it came back up in a roar.

I am full of salt, he thought, his throat clutching at the taste of his own bile.

The sensation was crippling, overwhelming. With the slow return of awareness had come the mounting knowledge of pain, of burned skin and spent muscle. But above all was the salinity, filling his blood, incinerating palate and gum. His clothing crunched faintly as he moved, dried in hard patches against his belly. And the vinegar taste of the sea would never be out of his throat; the thirst illuminated his body from within, it crusted his lips and his eyes. Henry began to gasp.

Night air filled in the little canopy of branches under which he had huddled, the brilliant point-lights of constellations shining down through their fissures like the imperfections in the drum fire on *Arrogante*. Peering through the waxy leafwork Henry forced himself to look for, and recognize, three: archer, southern cross, the water bearer. They were the only things familiar in his world.

At first light he picked and ate berries that grew on a straggle of nearby rocks. His thirst was awakened only more strongly by the tiny pulses of capsuled juice, though, and he sat down groaning over the buds. After he had scraped clean several branches and chewed the greenish inside of the bark as well he leaned over heavily and vomited again. The sand pack that had filled half his sinuses broke free in a rush of bright blood.

Don't leave me, Henry thought, slumping backwards against a log while the air danced and spun. He sat motionless until the dislodged clot began to draw flies. *Don't leave me here.*

He tried to come up on his right side and fell; in senseless shame he gripped furiously at his numb hand, the cool and flexible and terribly unfeeling part of himself, and then put it gently down as if repenting and arranged the hand in his lap and rocked soundlessly over it. The whole arm had no feeling now, from the mid-shoulder down. He wanted to hide it, even from himself.

For minutes Henry sat watching the edge of the ocean, unaware of what he should do. It was as if any time he stopped actively pursuing the task of cognition his mind slipped into the same numbness as his arm, a mute, swollen-feeling torpor. The horizon shimmered before him and gradually he understood that the morning heat was so intense here that the air over the beach was beginning to waver like a curtain, the deep-set blue of the water seeming to leak upward into the pale sky.

He was on an island; other than that, he knew nothing. When he turned toward the interior all he could see was the wall of trees, densely grown. In the other direction was cloudless horizon.

Henry forced himself up, sliding through an expanse of palmetto fans and into the underbrush. He had no plan, nothing more solid than a vision of interior streams, rainwater perhaps, pooled inside bent leaves and glimmering and unsalted. But once inside the forest proper the creepers and sloping trunks were tangled together, and passage was painfully retarded. He doubled back twice, losing his orientation. After an hour he struck at the curved bole of a palm, feeling the resistant solidity of the thing and knowing the whole of his universe was resisting him. The very air repulsed him, growing thick with insects and more ovenish with every hour that passed. Henry slumped on a tangled root pile and sat, panting like a sick man.

For a long time he rested. He had survived so much that the possibility of dying of dehydration in an unknown place, at no criminal hand, seemed somehow incredible. But he had no choice: he knew nothing, his mind was like an infant's mind, helpless and unknowing.

It was several seconds before he realized that he had already been staring at the thing that was before him without understanding what he saw. He had come to a small, rounded opening, a natural clearing in the scrub. The tiny space, no wider than an adult's body, was indented into the ground. In the center of it was an arrow.

Henry leaned closer to the wooden shaft, moving his eyes along it as if to persuade himself of its reality. At the sharp end something white lay submerged in the grass. He parted the green blades cautiously: the point of the weapon had been driven through the skull of a small animal. The fleshless contours of its face were wide-eyed and strangely expressive.

With astonished care Henry passed his good hand along the grass. The whole carcass was here, or had been: the bent neck, the spine like a long, curving gesture from which narrow ribs depended. No part of the animal had been eaten, no element removed. Curled down here to die in its secret place it gave the odd feeling of submission, as if bowing its head.

Henry backed out of the grotto and found his way stumblingly back toward the water. The noise his feet made clattering through the foliage was unendurable. Every sun-shadow announced him, in every dark hollow was the bowing animal head. When the undergrowth turned to sand again he stopped at the forest edge and hid. Even the blistering sunlight felt cold.

Father, he thought, not conscious of the thinking. *Don't leave me here.*

He came to again with the smell. A deep impulse inside his being reacted, and he believed for a moment he was going to fight. An image of the arrow shaft, descended from a cloud and entering his own heart, dissipated like spume; the smell was more intense, more exciting than anything he had sensed in his life.

Henry shook the blackness from behind his eyes. He had spent an entire day hidden and dreaming in the little well, sucking on berries. After darkness fell he had come out and tried to look around but the moon had risen, stitching the terrible bowing head once more into every shadow. Somewhere in the depth of the night he had snuck down to the water to wet his flaming skin and out of the blackness a shining devil had approached him. Astonished he had watched the ray, its horns trailing a luminous green, cruise silently along the ocean's edge.

With absurdly cautious movements now Henry inched his way out of the leafy retreat. His skin was scratched and bitten, his tongue felt swollen in his mouth. He could feel his heart beating slowly, thickly, as if it were burdened with sleep.

There was a wide palm leaf in front of his hiding place, several feet long. On it sat a lump of brown paste and a squat, yellow gourd.

Henry grabbed the hairless gourd first and felt its sloshing weight: it was filled with what looked like a mixture of milk and fat. Without thinking he drank, swallowing so quickly that his innards attempted to reject the invasion. With a surprised gasp Henry clutched frantically at his own lips, squeezing them closed with his fingers. After a moment the next swallow remained where it was; and the next; and then he picked up the smelly bean-patty in his hand and ate without remembering it, only knowing he had finished when he found himself masticating some sour fish skin that had been inside.

Almost immediately with the water a part of his mind he had forgotten about leapt into focus. Henry was more startled at its return than at the discovery of the gift itself: the thing that had re-emerged was cool and evaluative and capable, and had never been gone, letting him suffer while it simply gathered information.

"Thank you," he said, this time making it come out aloud.

The trees were silent, considering.

On the third evening he saw her. She was moving quickly across an exposed space between two palms: Henry himself crouched against a small cliff he had found that had been gradually carved out of powdery stone. He had discovered the hollow that morning and spent several hours climbing down into it, learning to suspend himself well enough with one hand to pull the thumb-sized creatures that clung there off their splashed walls and gnaw them out quickly from their shells.

She was there, a form standing among the higher rocks; then she was gone.

"Hey!" Henry cried, grabbing by mistake the ledge where he had piled the empty shells and falling entirely backwards into the water with a boom. He scampered stupidly out of the hollow. "Stay!" was the word that came. "Stay…!"

At the high lip of stones he stopped short.

A man was there. Around his loins he wore a skirt made of some kind of woven grass, the same material as was bound on his feet. His hair had been cut away so that the skull showed in stark outline, the remaining mass of black knotted behind his cranium and transfixed with two stakes. His skin was the color of brick.

Henry stood voicelessly. A slow, damning finger was raised and held accusingly at him.

"*You…Jesus*?"

"Ah …" Henry answered, backing up a step and realizing that the sound he had made was only an astonished release of breath. "I…my ship …"

"*You*," the man repeated, the hot close eyes looking at Henry the way a hawk might look at an opening in a barn door. "*Jesus*?"

"My name…my…" Henry tried quickly, and a terrible loneliness opened inside him at the words. He wanted to explain his name to this impossible creature, to explain it in all of its injustice, all of its consequence.

The man had nightmarish markings on his face and chest, a series of circles and lines, including one solid blue ring in each cheek with a line down the center, like an icon of cat's eyes. The double set of eyes examined Henry in silence, tracing every aspect of his person, as if committing him to some lethal account. Henry looked down at his own scratched naked feet, the torn breech-cuffs draining water onto the rocks.

"I'm hurt," he began.

But the other man had turned without comment and started back through the trees.

4

The village had been built in a clearing that had once been natural, though human work had both extended and solidified its boundaries. Met on one side by a high wide shelf of mangrove and thus sheltered against the abrasive wind, the unexpected flatness of the area had left it ideal for habitation. Its most notable structures were round constructions that seemed to have emerged, as if by natural sympathy of kinds, out of the background growth: blunt, brown-green huts, the supports of each one covered in waxy palmetto with the slant turned downward in a way that gave them a dolorous look.

At the center of the huts was a wall-less roof whose wooden beams had been fleshed out with knots of tightly rolled leaves, hundreds or possibly thousands, each one bound and worked into place by hand. Scattered around this centerpiece like children around their mother were several open-air structures; and then the lesser dwellings, arranged in a rough spiral and each with a cleared space for gardening in front.

"Hello, London Town."

Henry spun. The man who had spoken was European, wearing a loose dun-colored shirt Henry realized after a moment had been fashioned out of a sail.

"I'm quite comfortable with English," the man added, grinning at the incongruity. "I was raised in a house where several languages were spoken, at my father's decision. He was a traveler of sorts, a businessman. He believed a citizen of the world must know its tongues."

Henry swallowed.

"You're Spanish."

"By origin." The man bowed, a precise bend, surprisingly graceful. "You might hear something a bit like Castilian when the People speak to me."

There was a pause. Henry had followed the native man back here into the heart of the island, the other walking quickly and, after their initial confrontation, seeming to care not at all whether he was seen. He had more of the dark red tattoos in bands around both ankles and after a while Henry had chased only the bands, focusing on them like a swaying beacon. The weirdly adorned figure picked trails rapidly out of the same tangle that had been so impassable to Henry, as if the colorful feet carried with them the power to establish passage wherever they landed.

Then he had simply disappeared. For a terrible moment Henry was lost in deep forest; then, coming through an upward tumble of butterflies, he stopped dead at the sight of two shirtless women carrying baskets on their heads. The women had skin the color of milked coffee and their nipples were heavy and large. Beyond them was a gate-like entrance and more people, wearing clothing cut out of a brownish moss. The women had passed him by without breaking the flow of their talk.

"They tell me they thought you might be a friend of mine," the Spanish man said, bringing Henry back. He had black, soft hair and an accent, but only slight, like a delicate scenting to his words. Henry had only spoken with a Spaniard once, an orphaned child in Bristol whose own earth-colored skin meant nothing until his father struck his walking cane hard against Henry's shoulder for *fraternizing with the idolater*. Later, boys at school told him of how Spaniards drank blood, were in league with Germans and with the devil; how they kept orgiastic rites in their churches, splashing their statuary with viscera and worse.

This man, however, was not that. His lips were thick and kind under a slight moustache. His expression was open, with a smooth, easy feel to it, absurd in this world of dangers.

"Apparently you left some kind of a mark in the sand. A… hmm?"

The man drew in the dust with his foot.

"I saw it," Henry said. "In a book."

"Symbols everyone here associates with me. They thought you might be a friend of mine. Are you?"

Henry stared.

"I don't know where I am," he stammered out. "I don't know… I don't know anything."

"I understand that," the Spaniard answered softly. He put a hand on Henry's elbow, so easily Henry failed to withdraw. "But the first question is: are you my friend? Will you be?"

Henry, unspeaking, looked at the dark Latin eyes.

"Good," the man smiled. "That is good."

Inside the large central structure he ate a combination of fish pieces and finger-sized clusters of root that tasted of something he almost recognized but could not place. Several times he had to stagger into the trees and exhaust himself diarrhoetically, returning in shame to the several campfires that the natives lit in the central space when twilight came. No one reacted. Each time when Henry returned the natives would without looking give him a bowl of water and when he had successfully washed his moving hand someone would put food in front of him once more, the mixture of the same fish parts and berries and roots that he now recognized had the ruinous taste of death in them.

"They're drying you out," the Spaniard grinned. "Later on I'll show you where to *shite* more politely."

After meals the Spaniard stayed in lengthy conversation with the natives, wishing Henry a formal *buenas noches* and then not speaking to him again, not even looking in his direction, with an utterly peremptory conviction. During daylight he, Henry, slept on a reed mat in a tiny raised structure built on a pile of shells, breathing shallowly and watching papery insects rotate on the inside of the shelter and thinking, sometimes for hours, nothing at all. In the evenings he ate the strange bitter food given him by strange hands, its consistency thickening and becoming tougher each meal, and slept again, more hours than he was awake. The sibilance of unknown language was around him always, like trickling water.

Eventually—he did not know how long—he began to experience something more than simple endurance, felt less the necessity of leaving the central fires as soon as food had been taken in either to excrete it or to re-enter the sluggard unpleasantness of sleep. He found himself wanting to remain, the curiosity about his surroundings growing gradually loud as, and then louder than, the call of physical recuperation. He began to notice the weirdness of the people around him, their body markings, the ornaments on their upper arms and woven into their hair, even the men's hair; and to realize that they were becoming stranger to him now, not less strange, because at first he had taken them for nightmare visions.

Different odors of smoke entered his sick hut at various times, men with bowl-cut heads drawing pipes around the opening as if to cast something into it, or cast it away. He saw them also chewing something that looked like bread, wadding it carefully with their tongues and then passing it to others who chewed it as well.

Other times he was ignored, and in his changing state Henry came to understand that there was a life here, a communal activity that had preceded him and was not interrupted by his appearance. At meal time a woman with thick wooden bolts in both her ears said something to the Spaniard that produced laughter and the oldest man at the gathering rose and walked angrily into the dark. The Spaniard came over to Henry, amused.

"He doesn't like it when I joke with the women," he explained. "He says fucking a woman who laughs at the table is as bad as fucking a man. How are you feeling?"

"When I first washed up," Henry said; but the words had come too spontaneously.

"You remember that."

"Yes."

"It's a good sign. The People have brought bodies in from the sea before, even a European once. To leave them floating poisons the fishing. But you're the first living thing I've seen come up."

"I couldn't ..."

The Spaniard looked at him and his eyes were limpid. Abruptly and for the first time Henry realized the extent of the other man's intellect.

"You can't feel it, can you? The arm is cold."

"No," Henry admitted, though that had not been what he was going to say. "I can't feel anything. It's as if my arm is gone."

He looked away at the clapping fires, the faces surrounding them, grotesque, as if he had descended into some lower circle of the world.

"Can you move this hand at all? Try now."

Henry tried, but even putting his mind in the numb thing was frightful to him. He thought of the men eating fish eating men.

"Something," the Spaniard mused. "But not enough. I think you may be going to lose the arm."

"To what? What did you say?"

"The People can remove a limb. I've seen them do it."

"*No one's going to cut off my arm,*" Henry shouted, standing up. The whole scene tilted weirdly before him. He saw the marked, brick-red faces fall silent with his outburst, saw them witnessing his difference, his unutterable alienness. "I don't know where I am! I don't know who you are or what you are! Am I in hell? Is this hell?"

"You're on an island," the Spaniard answered, carefully. "My name, in Toledo, is Juan Batiste de Daylaylo." He pronounced the three names slowly, his accent showing most in *Hoo-wan*. "Here, however, I am *Man-in-Tree*. This tribe ..." —he gestured slowly around him—"doesn't have any name. They call themselves *The People*. Just as they call this settlement *The World*. But these are just words. Like *Belgian*, like *Dane*." His thick eyebrows lifted a little. "Like *Englishman*. Yes?"

Henry sat again, trembling.

"Yes. Bristol."

"And a little blue feather in your ear. I wonder how you got that."

Henry said nothing. He would not look at the faces, would not give them the merit of his recognition.

"Let me ask you something," the Spaniard said finally. "Your spirit is *hot*, as the People say. You have fever in you, bad fever, not just in the arm. But there is something else as well. When I look at you, I see fear."

"No one is doing anything to my arm."

The Spaniard nodded, as if respecting the words. Henry felt shock: never, even before *Arrogante*, never had his voice been *listened to* with that level of intensity. Then the man rose and went back toward the fires. Having cleaned his fingers in a water bowl he ate for a while, speaking to the natives, digging carefully into the flesh of bluish shrimp and setting aside the thin carapace after each. Eventually he returned.

"*Ahora bien, al que sea culpable de que una de esas personas...*"

"I don't know Spanish."

"Some feel it possible ..." the Spaniard said, choosing his words with deliberation. "Some feel it possible...to become closer to God... while missing part of ourselves. An eye. A hand."

He rose again and began walking away.

"*Que savez-vous de Dieu,*" Henry said bitterly.

"*Nada*," the Spaniard answered, not turning. "Not a thing."

The People grilled fish and filled them with herbs and unshelled nuts, stretching the lean headless shapes across wooden frames high enough over fires to simmer but too high for the wood, which had been painted with some kind of dull sap, to ignite. Three of these structures existed in the main area and always at least one of them was in use, the fresh surprising odor of sea life crossing and re-crossing the air. There were perhaps seventy-five dwellings altogether, perhaps twice that number of natives, and different groups took turns minding the fires in a mutually understood pattern whose outline he did not know how to read.

The People ate oysters, clams, unfamiliar bivalves that they split quickly along the hidden inseam in a fluid motion that brought the flesh yellowish pink into the light. Each evening when they gathered they crouch-sat in small circles, their knees deeply bent and their buttocks not touching the ground. Henry tried the posture, alone inside his hut, but fell over so completely that he collided with the leafy wall, bringing humiliating laughter from outside.

The children of the People went naked entirely; their job was apparently to skewer stony crab-creatures that walked across the land and pass them to the adults to cook over open flames. Henry laughed a little to see the crabs, which as they moved resembled portly gentlemen in shirt-fronts. Indeed, the island underbrush in which he himself had seen nothing was now revealed to be plentiful with animal life. From the abundance of it Henry realized the noise and commotion he must have made on the beach had driven the host of creatures away, his clumsiness creating his own circle of abandonment. The image seemed potent to him, like something from a morality play.

As the courage to walk among them grew Henry found that the native settlement—*The World*, he remembered—was in fact scattered throughout with European items. Among the seemingly endless collection of shell tools he found a bidet with tin handles; some dressing elements that had been hand-cut for ships' quarters; two washbasins with whalebone ends, being used now for collecting stones. The men most often used palm-sized shells resembling abalone to cut driftwood, but some he had seen working with gunner's knives, their copper lengths tinted green in degrees that told how long each had lain underwater. One older native he witnessed inscribing bark tablets with the end of a boarding pike, holding it by the edge so that the handle stuck upward and turning the whole thing as dexterously as a quill.

The juxtaposition did not cease to surprise him, even as he walked more than he rested and began to feel himself less of an absurdity among people who pierced not only their noses and ears but their foreskins and the brows of their eyes. More than once he started as a native man passed by in an English peacoat, or with a greasehorn belt buckled around his waist; or a woman, once, nursing two infants on a blanket that Henry, looking twice, recognized to be the remnants of a wedding dress washed empty by the sea. All—the useful, the foolish, the merely coincidental—all of it came from wrecks, and his spirit ruminated strangely on the idea of Empire casting itself gradually on disparate shores, its artifacts presented under the ambassadorship of dead men.

Yet among these hundred or two hundred natives were ten and a hundred times as many objects about which he knew nothing, objects made of sandstone and bone and shell, while gestures and disagreements and reconciliations took place among the People whose nature he could not even guess. The effect built inside him to a nausea that mirrored the rising and fading sickness and he felt himself a creature out of time, existing in a beach-wash of pieces and fragments. He remembered walking the quays one Sunday morning at home: a merchant ship had been grounded by a small collision in port and the bulk of her lay against the pylons like a creature come up to die. No one had been injured but the cargo was being quickly sold off, there on the piers, to any offer. As his mother haggled over a throw-rug he and two other boys had run down the docks, dodging between china cases and tea sets and, he remembered, a hollow brass tube on a tripod. Now he felt himself gathering for a second time his own wreckage, feeling the want of guidance to reassemble in himself all that had been so violently strewn.

One morning Henry was taken to see an immensely old man. The man lived in one of the three central buildings; he had his meals served to him, the native women adorning his food with flower trinkets and berries and using their front teeth to puncture the little thumb-length bananas so he could more easily digest their meat. His face when Henry squatted down before it was a chaos of lines, the skin over his eyelids bluish and mournful.

"The Caffekey welcomes you on my honor," Daylaylo said loudly.

The old man held out a hand and Henry recoiled as the bunched fingers touched his face, exploring his brow, his nose, the edges of his lips.

Not blind, Henry thought, *no. But the world is nothing to him now but soft hazes.*

The Caffekey sat with his wife, an old woman also but not of her husband's great age. She had a proud womanly face, marked only by two wavering lines on the left cheek. As the hand explored Henry she looked at him unabashedly.

"Welcome here," Daylaylo translated when she spoke. "She says you are strange looking." The old man's whispering tongue moved and the woman leaned toward him. She spoke the old man's voice and Daylaylo translated her voice.

"The Caffekey asks if your arm is not well."

"It will be all right," Henry said, feeling odd shame. The man had not touched his arm, nothing more than with the faintest drift of the fingers.

"The Caffekey asks if the arm is rotting."

"Tell him it will be all right."

Daylaylo translated and the old man nodded before he was finished.

"The Caffekey will sleep now," Daylaylo said.

Outside it was a warm, vibrant day. The sky overhead was a simmering green, as if the relentless vegetable health of the island were passing its energies upward into the heavens as well.

"The hand …"

"I don't want to talk about that," Henry said. He slid the arm into his shirt where he had begun carrying it, feeling almost disgraceful in the act. Daylaylo was quiet.

"How old is the …"

"*Caffekey.* It's a Tekesta word, I think," Daylaylo said. "But the languages run together. I don't know how old he is. He has been here since I arrived."

"What happens…when he dies?"

"Then she becomes Caffekey in his place."

"A queen."

"Not truly. The People say a Caffekey is male and female both. Kings and queens they are learning from us."

Someone was there. Henry saw her just at the moment before she let the door- cloth drop: small, thin-bodied, her head a round clean surface in the moonlight. Shaking the thickness from his eyes he rose and pushed open the flap.

The center of the World was empty. All three fires were quieted, their ashy surfaces glowing. He could smell the cinders.

Henry walked through the central part of the village, out past the gate and into the softly blowing darkness. He could see nothing; the blackness there was absolute, total, the island outside the perimeter an uncreated world. Far out in the hills something *whoo-ipp*, *whooo-ipp*ed.

He started back. But felt again the eyes: and, turning, saw her there. She stood at the far end of the trees, bathed in sudden moonlight. Her hands were on her middle as if feeling something intense and even difficult, something painful to her. And her face, quiet and alive, was watching him with expectancy.

5

In the afternoon Daylaylo showed him a way through the denser trees. Made of nothing but the gradual impress of feet, the path was soft and accommodating, one of the almost invisible footways the People were able to use and the using of which to Henry still had the character of a magical act. The walk on it was long and as he followed the Spaniard Henry felt his consciousness beginning to stir, some part of his awareness he could not directly name. They passed over ground covered in clasping roots, so intricately woven they resembled a fantastic carpet. The light that came through was softened by the high leaves so that it fell algae-colored, yolk and crystal, shimmering like a hung sheet after rain.

And as he walked something, some kind of rhythm, was gradually produced in him. Some part of him felt the rhythm and he allowed his feet to move into it, to step into a rhythm that came up from the soil, up from the shells and the stones and the cracked grassy path. It was not the hurried, awful rhythm of his youth, but a slower walk; a rhythm the earth seemed to hold in itself, like the tides.

The ground sloped downward and they passed a beehive, redolent with nectar. And here, rain had puddled in the elbow of a blossoming tree, spilling the pollen into streaks. Henry breathed in the sugary scent. He remembered the men of *Arrogante* putting their tongues to the air: *tasting the sky*, they called it, the ability to sense with the mouth something in wind and water deeper than what could be seen. A lizard, its back striped in amazing cobalt, examined him from a passing tree. Henry leaned over it as he walked by, seeing himself for an instant in the black drops of its eyes.

"Here," said Daylaylo.

Henry followed the other man through a fissure where brown sand crumbled under their feet, depositing them on a low, flat bank. There was an inlet with gradually widening edges, one end of which opened out to the sea. A crowd of pelicans occupied the middle of the cove, their necks bent into the resting position. Daylaylo shooed them and the birds scurried, foolish-footed, into the shallows a few yards off.

"They make it harder," the Spaniard said. "We need quiet water."

He searched until they found an area farther along where the inlet was clean and transparent, spilling over a momentary lip of sand so that on the near side it lay only a few inches deep.

"What are we doing?"

"I want you to listen," Daylaylo said. "Do as I do."

The Spaniard lay gently down in the pool, face skyward. Henry hesitated a moment before stepping in as well; as soon as he did there came an awful memory of drowning.

"Don't be afraid of it," Daylaylo said, speaking from behind closed lids. "If a man respects the sea, he will find what is good in her. Only if he disrespects her is she ugliness, and a danger."

Resistantly Henry crouched in the water, spreading his good fingers across the bottom. The muddy sand oozed to his wrist.

"They say that she drowns men and wrecks villages, brings suffering and lamentation. It's a lie: men drown themselves. They leap into the sea and beat at her, they hate and detest her for what she is. I am not made jealous by the sea. I accept her and let her fill me. And I listen."

For a long time Henry sat next to the floating man, unable to go farther. His silent arm was a dull weight, the fever still thick behind his eyes. The sun was strong overhead, tearing a few stray clouds.

"Lie down in it," Daylaylo repeated. "Don't think. Listen."

At first

there was only dull sound, a droning that surrounded him. Henry felt himself trying to control the sound, to fight the growing sensation of being carried somewhere by a force over which he had no power, the force that moved him wherever it willed. He hated the sound, hated what it was; hated the power that could move him where it willed and against which his own desires were as insignificant as a rag among waves. His heart began beating quickly inside him and he tried to swallow down its beat, remembering the tambourine on Arrogante *whose rhythmic striking heralded attacks on other ships. The tambourine beat was inside him: it had become his heart. Henry rose*

"Again," Daylaylo said, when the splash of Henry's sitting up had subsided. He spoke without lifting his head, his closed eyes little mounds that lapped under the waterline. "Don't talk to her, Henry. Listen to her. Listen."

Henry looked out toward the horizon. The sunlight on the water was a golden purple, anchors and rust. The pelicans had moved farther along.

This time it came more easily: there was a feeling in it now, the frightfulness of the water gone, a feeling of lying down to sleep. His heart was slower now, and the sheet of water that suspended him was a blanket in which he was wrapped. Henry listened

There was a stillness throughout the pool. The water in the shallows was a thin silver bell, not striking but already struck, its resonance sounding. The sound was touched here and there by the complaints of the pelicans. The pelicans had moved south, down to the side of the beach where the sand disappeared into grass. They were rising out of the water, one body at a time, winking out and disappearing. He could hear them move, knew where they were and how they were moving

Henry listened farther

Farther out, beyond the shallows: he was moving outward, sensing, now, the deeper waters beyond the reef. The fear started in him again but he could not stop the experience: he was passing the reef line, moving faster. The sound of his tiny heart disappeared into a thunder that was mounting, surrounding him: he heard, for an instant, the true roar of the sea

Henry rose in the pool once more, cold water streaming down his back. A shuddery feeling came over him, something dangerous and sacred.

"It came quickly to you."

The Spaniard was considering him, as if he had witnessed something he had suspected but of whose precise outlines he had been uncertain. "I have seen monks work years for something you seem to have been born with. Do you know that about yourself?"

"No." Henry wiped his face. "No."

"Everything in the water speaks," Daylaylo said, "to the right mind. Just as everything in air speaks, only we no longer listen. Men are crippled in their senses. Under water, the listening is new. Our souls can be awake."

"What do you hear? When you do this."

"Some of her voices. Not many. I can hear storms, coming closer. I can hear a ship passing."

"You can hear the sound of a ship? Underwater?"

"In fast water, no. But on a day like this, a large vessel ..." Daylaylo looked at the sky. "Men think their contraptions are graceful. The ocean is graceful. A galleon is a stupid, obvious thing."

"Tell me...tell me what it sounds like."

"When a galleon sinks, the first thing you hear is the cargo. It makes a terrible clatter. If she's driven aground, the reef cries out with her weight, and the air from the hull is like a stream opening up inside a stream. In the end ..."

He raised himself to his elbows.

"In the end it is quiet. Once a vessel is down, it's just sea over sea."

The Spaniard lay back in the pool again, stretching his lean frame. The bright sun dazzled around his head, giving him an aura.

"What do you remember about it, Henry? When your own ship went down."

"Nothing."

"Nothing?"

"I remember wind hitting our masts. I remember being on the beach. It was as if nothing came between them."

"Survivors often forget."

Henry was silent. It wasn't true, what he had said: he did have memories of being thrown in the water, only they were unreal memories, like dreams. He remembered wanting nothing, valuing nothing, as if the instant the *Arrogante* had ceased to support him he himself had become a voidal place. He remembered darkness.

And another memory, strange, perhaps untrue. He remembered struggling in bright light, the storm superseded by some irrepressible brilliance. He could see the surface of the swells as if he were above himself, see himself kicking in them. A wind was blowing fiercely and the scud made long ropy lines that leapt from peak to peak. Yet the image was silent, and the flooding light came from below, like candlelight through glass.

Sometime later—he didn't know how long—he had also seen objects. A line tangled on two leechline blocks; sheets of mapping paper, as if pasted to the waves; a bittacle trunk, made of green wood, somehow buoyed up. He had kicked until he reached the trunk and he tried to put his arms around it to ride it in. But even this memory was dreamlike, uncertain. The bittacle felt like a symbol more than a memory, the frustration of a useful object made suddenly futile.

Henry had clung to the trunk that rose now and again in the weirdly luminous breakers, the interior filling with water and depositing him once more with an exhausted sound. In the end there was a generalized sensation of objects hurrying past, of waves crowded with the detritus of wreckage, not only of his own ship but others as well; as if the storm were a wrath that churned up pieces of its previous meals from the silt. He had heard of such things, of how turtling hulls could deposit a line of objects across a high sea floor and how storms of sufficient power could bring old wreckage surfacing, like beacons out of time. The cook onboard *Arrogante* had told of how a ten-ton sloop he had served on in the South Sea had foundered across the spars of a wreck, as if even in death lost mariners retained the power to reach up and claim more like their own.

"Tell me who you were," Henry said. "Before you came here."

"Franciscan. I came to do holy work."

Henry started.

"You're a *priest*?"

"The missions in Guale," Daylaylo answered, without concern. "Many have been burned, or abandoned. We were their relief."

The Spaniard's expression was ambiguous, somewhere between condemnation and pity. Looking at the wet crown of his head Henry understood now the hair had been cut at some point in a tonsure before being allowed to grow back in.

"Man," Daylaylo said, as if summoning the thing for inspection. "We have star charts, sea charts. We think that earth has become our slave. Most of us were dead before we reached the New World."

The Spaniard watched a V-arc of white birds edge toward the horizon.

"There was fever," Daylaylo said, finally. "Perhaps *Narragonia* had it before we boarded. Perhaps we were dying men from the start. I don't know.

"It did not strike until we were almost across. Then it struck everywhere, all at once. Imagine this: men sweating so heavily it makes a paste, a whitish paste on their skins. Men who had eaten nothing—such was our vanity, Henry, that we even fasted for the Sabbath while at sea—nothing in days, still trying to vomit.

"At first we cared for the sick. I wiped heads with a cloth. I mopped chests, these chests that were turning like the chests on old men. Then the crew came down to say they needed us, holy clergy or no. There were livestock that had to be managed, bread that required soaking if anyone was to eat. They had lost some of theirs as well, and the difference between lay and religious did not seem so important. We became just men on an ocean, needing to get across.

"Later there was no time. We dropped the bodies over, wrapped in hammocks with something heavy to take them down. At first with ceremony, you understand? Ceremony. Then at least with prayers. In the end it was all the same. We picked them up and handed them over. We waited.

"I never got sick. I lived with dying men, ate off their plates. I kissed their lips. I would not allow myself disgust. I don't know if I loved them. It frightened me at the time. I didn't love them, really. My brothers in the order. People I had lived with in the monastery at Toledo, debated theology with, laughed loudly with. In my heart I knew I did not love them. But I did not know how to find that love.

"We didn't know how far off course we where, but it would have made no difference. No Spanish settlement would have us, even if we made land. A ship of diseases—we would be lucky if they did not fling torches into our sails. But some of the brothers still talked of the dignity of God's officers…still dreamed of presenting us when we arrived as *mensajeras de la iglesia.* My brothers, like nightmares now in their purple robes, their faces withered underneath the hoods. The censer, the holy censer, lit to cover the smell.

"On the last day we came into a calm sea. I was on the first deck by a young fellow, a surgeon's mate. Had we been speaking? Had we prayed together? I don't remember. I only knew when I looked at him again that he was dead. His body was leaning against a chainplate and his lips were open. Just a little opening, and that flatness of the eyes. I tried to call out for aid but there was no strength left in me. And I started, for the first time, to fear. I mean deep fear…the fear that can come into the soul that is so much worse than physical pain.

"I started to think, then…what if this surgeon's mate had been the last? What if I were alone now, the only man in a ship full of corpses?

"I tried to rise, but my limbs had lost all will. Then I saw we were drifting into a mist. I remember it smelled bitter, like sea rot, but something else as well. If empty space has a smell—just emptiness, going out forever—it was like that.

"The dead man beside me started to disappear. I watched him going into it, like something was eating him. His face, his neck, his chest with the branding mark of some worker's society. His legs were all I could see, then his little sad feet. I wanted to stop him from disappearing into that mist. I was afraid to be left that much alone."

Daylaylo paused, wiping slowly at his lips. His eyes held Henry unblinkingly.

"For a long time, everything was silent. I lay helpless in that cloud, unable even to weep. And then came the realization that I was *not* alone. There was something else with me, in the mist. Something alive.

"The pigs had come up from the hold. I remember staring amazed at them in the fog. My first thought was they had chewed through the livestock door and wandered on deck. But then I saw. They were walking on their hind legs. All of them. I could hear the sound of their hoofs scraping up the ladder, coming up from below. And they were making a noise, a kind of wet sound in their throats.

"One came close to where I lay, and through the mist I saw its face. The snout was bent so the little teeth showed. The eyes…it had sharp, thin eyes…the eyes were moving quickly one way and another. Then I understood. They were adding up the bodies of the dead.

"I crushed down my face then and prayed that I might die. I prayed as truly as I had ever prayed. I prayed to the heavens not to let me experience this. I offered anything, any penance, any contrition for my sins. And I lay in that wet mist, hearing the hogs' feet as they dragged themselves about, like children on wooden legs.

"It began to rain. When I looked again the pigs had gathered in a circle around the mast. Drops of water were running down their skin, their hairy backs. And one of them—the one whose face I had seen—raised his broken hooves to the sky. The noise they all had been making grew louder. It became obscene…a terrible shriek.

"I cried like a child when I understood, Henry. They were singing. They were singing the Holy Mass."

Henry lay voicelessly in the water. The air above him felt cold.

"Some time later I woke. The mist was gone, the sky was clear and hot. The captain had made land in some unmapped place, far south of our destination. They had abandoned ship in the longboat, probably to claim all hands lost at sea. They had not even thrown anchor. The bow was pressed into a bar, and the whole ship was just standing, like a leaf brushed up to a door.

"I put someone's dittybag on my shoulders and went over the side. About a mile inland was an empty fort. Beyond that, an abandoned town. I found some food, some old clothes. I went toward the interior. That's all."

"The devil," Henry said, after a long wait. "The Gadarene swine."

"No. No, I don't think so."

"Then what?"

"The soul very rarely witnesses itself," Daylaylo mused, after a time. "For me, shipwreck was a blessing."

The Spaniard lowered himself back into the water. Henry opened his mouth to speak and stopped: Daylaylo's features had become bright. He was making a gesture, signaling Henry to come under and listen. Henry did so. Something nearby was making a staccato tapping sound, a warbling, playful pitch.

"Dolphins," Daylaylo said. "Just listen to their joy."

6

The Caffekey stood naked in the sun-covered field. His body—she remembered it robust and young, strong as any warrior, and so handsome, so distinct—had returned now to a child's dimensions, as if he were gradually taking back the life he had led, reversing himself until he found once more the uncreated place of his origin. She wanted to tell him to stop when he came to the years in which they had been together: first as a child being raised in his house, and later as his mate, when the Caffekey's previous mate had died and the Caffekey cried out terrible, wretched cries night and day and the men, unable to work and staggering, as if themselves stricken, sat in rings outside and mourned. She had come to him, then, in the days of his ruin. She had come out of turn; she, a concubine who had yet to be taken, like a field not yet tasted. With a child's mind she had come to him in his rooms, knowing that what she did was against nature but nonetheless coming to him, bringing a child's confidence and easy conviction as she went to the beautiful wretched man and took his fingers, like ten red claws, slowly away from his face and kissed the tears that were in them.

They are not my tears, the Caffekey said, and her soul knew she had done well. His first words had not been bitter, the sharp rebuke and the call for the concubine mother. Instead he had looked at her and said *They are not my tears*, and held his hand out again for her to kiss. She had kissed the palm of his hand, understanding: these were the tears of the one who died, coming through him. From the unseeable world she, the absent one, wept for her separation, and the pain he felt was the dead woman's pain.

After she had kissed the palms and tasted the other woman's tears in them, the ghost tears, the Caffekey had sent her away, using the form of the word that meant *child*. She had gone, but she was no child. She had felt as she left the room the heavy sway of her own breasts now under her clothing, the heaviness in her hips and in her bottom that was changing everything inside her and that had told her she was needed by a man. On the way back to the rooms where the concubines lived the mother had seen her and had approached with fury in her eyes, but she looked unflinchingly back and knew that in her own face now was part of the Caffekey's face, in her eye the Caffekey's strength.

Later it was all right to bury the other woman and the Caffekey, resplendent in his feathered mourning dress, had walked with her, with *her*, to the place where the other woman was to be laid down after dark. He had held *her* hand, small in his own hand, in front of all the People. Most amazingly of all, when the burying was done he reached into his heart and then into the space between his eyes and the into the space in the air in front of him where the heart of the other woman had resided three ways and he took these things and placed them down in the ground with her body and, in front of the seeing of the whole People, he reached now into her heart instead, into *her* living heart, and took it gently in his hand and placed it where his own heart was. After that the women ceased wailing and the men were free to eat and the food tasted well again, it tasted of the World and the rich, giving sea.

That night the Caffekey had taken her outside and shown her the stars and they were for her as something she had never seen. Their points dim or light were fresh inside her, and together they drank from the double-holed cup and spoke a word of blessing to each other that would be heard by them again after one hundred moons. And a part of her spirit waited each moon and never forgot, always waiting; and on the hundredth moon, indeed, she heard the blessing still strong and clear and she answered it back, and looking into the Caffekey's face she knew he had heard it as well, strong and clear, and he took her smaller hand one hundred moons older now and placed it on his chest and together they celebrated their love.

So now she wanted him to stay there at those days, at those times, and to take her with him as well; but the Caffekey was old now and he was traveling backward to his childhood. She understood that this was a traveling he must make on his own, and that he had loved the other woman very much and that she, too, would be part of his traveling back. She knew he had loved the other woman very deeply but he had also loved her, and finally he had loved *only* her; he had no interest even in the other concubines, and when they were together the tearful ghost of the other woman was at rest and did not visit them. So that now, as he was traveling back, she wanted him to remember her in his future, and how their lives had tended toward each other in the end.

The Caffekey was speaking and, lost in her memory, she had to hurry to his side and lean closely against his mouth.

"Yes," she said.

She took his thin arm at the wrist and led him to a different part of the field, a place where his feet, once hard and resistant as a runner's feet, would not be injured by stones or rough twigs. In her other arm she carried the single yellow tunic which was all he wore now, the ending cloth, and was careful to keep any part of it from dragging on the ground. When she had led him to a new place she stopped him as a mother stops a child, placing a hand slowly in his naked chest to prevent his motion, and he asked questions about what was around him and she answered them into his ear.

She told him of the rich purple berries that were near his left hand, with three different insects feasting on them: one brown, like a funny piece of dirt, the two others honey colored like stinging insects but with no stingers on them. She told him of the waist-high grass that grew in straight thin needles to the height of his right hand, and how touching it here he was touching what stretched across all of the meadow: a level, steady sheet of green, broken only by buds of honey and red.

He said something to her ear and she went, cautious with the robe, and picked some of the little gold flowers and brought them to him and held them to his nose, the Caffekey naked with his arms still held out sideways to touch what was around him, and she crumbled the petals into a yellow fluff in her hands and held it to his nose to smell.

She told him that over them now a pink bird was flying. There, it had landed and was pecking at the ground, the pink had been in its chest and could no longer be seen. She told him that in no direction could you see the water. She told him the cliff was directly under the sun now and bright, this side brittle and white, and that some animals were running along its sides, she could not tell what kind, bringing dust.

She told him that close ahead of him now, so close she could see it, was a long fat vegetable growing on the ground, she did not know what it was but ants had already found it, so many funny ants! But the Caffekey grew sad and she told him that a wasp was circling around and around the field with something in its legs, like an old woman who can't make up her mind. She told him a thin cloud was just over the tallest trees as if it had been caught there, a foolish cloud that flew too low. And beyond that were shadows, shadows among the trees, and how odd to see shadows here in the midst of the sun, in the middle of the day. Then she herself grew sad because of the shadows and the Caffekey lowered his arms and asked for his robe again and she dressed him and smoothed back his hair, so old now his hair was becoming dry and strange, not at all the affirmative blue-black he had once possessed. But she loved his small head with his strange, fading hair, and she kissed him there and the Caffekey rebuked her for her boldness and then laughed quietly and she laughed too.

She bent to his mouth.

"Stone," he whispered, his breath warm in the cup of her ear.

She knew that every word was labor to him, and she bent quickly and picked up the first pebble she saw and placed it in his hand.

The Caffekey closed his fingers on the hot stone, bringing its surface to his lips.

"Dust."

She gave him earth and he brought it to his lips, tasting; the crumbling pieces running between his fingers. Tremblingly he passed the clump across his cheek, leaving a mark.

"Root," he whispered. "Shell." Inspecting each thing, bringing it close, smelling, adoring.

"You," he whispered.

She lowered her eyes and stepped closer. In the path of his hand she placed the still weight of her fingers. Like the others, he brought them close to his face, to his failing eyes, to his skin. He smelled her skin and tasted her and kissed the centers of her palms.

"Brought by tide, taken by tide," she said, placing her forehead gently against his cheek. "This is the rule of the World."

But he was whispering.

I would break the rule of the World.

No Caffekey would say this, she whispered back.

You are more to me than the rule.

Yes, she trembled, *and you.*

For you I would defy all things.

Yes, she said. *For you.*

You have been my World.

You have been my World, she whispered, the repetition binding, remembering him as hard and as powerfully as she could, remembering him now for the time when he would be no more. *You are my World.*

You are my World.

You are.

You are.

You.

7

There was a commotion by one of the fires. Henry looked up and, for the first time since he had come to the village, saw the native man who had led him there from the beaches. He had come without realizing it to regard that shore as a place of apparitions, that first fierce encounter as a meeting with an obscure but leading spirit.

"I've seen this one," Henry said.

"Tied Sticks. I'm not sure why ..."

The maroon face was dark with anger, staring directly at Henry now and using a word that drew attention from the others.

"*Nickaleer*," Daylaylo repeated, his eyebrows raised. "It seems this man doesn't like you."

"Me? He's the one who *found* me."

The man drew closer and Henry strained under the sharpness of his words, more menacing because of their total unreadability. Beside him Daylaylo listened, translating with that same complete frankness that was his essential characteristic.

"He says you are a...British...it's an obscenity the Carusa use. You are born from a witch, the screwed ass of a witch, some such thing. I believe...I believe he's saying you only have a left hand because you've been cursed. If not for your weakness, he would fight you."

"*Fight me*," Henry repeated, feeling the blood rise against his throat. The native man was gesturing at him now with his pectorals jumping and the sudden awareness of danger ran through Henry's nerves. "Say I don't want to fight him. I don't want to fight anyone here."

Other men began gathering around, the warriors, examining Henry as if they had not quite seen him before. Henry became terribly afraid that they were going to scream, the visceral, terrifying shriek he had heard at night, in the leafy distance, when they were doing something in the woods about which he had not wanted to know.

Daylaylo spoke loudly; abruptly the native man made a crude gesture and turned away. When he passed Henry he kicked dirt into his food.

"*Son of cunt*," he said.

Henry looked at the wrecked offering in his lap.

"I thought you said they couldn't speak English."

"Yes, well, a phrase or two," Daylaylo laughed. He was watching with interest the retreating form.

After the People had gone to sleep Henry lay in the empty hut that had been assigned him once more but the arm was strange to him, a thing of flesh that was neither his nor not his. Carefully he laid the hand on his belly, the fingers loosely curled. He saw the face of the native man, the blistering double eyes bearing down on his own like a creature of hate. He could feel the fever that was still inside him, the warm-cold feeling of his brow that grew closer or more distant each day but did not relent. In the tropical darkness the double heat came thickly, swelling like a current.

He remembered a time at the heat of summer, near the Bahama Bank, when the *Arrogante* men, their ship loaded with oils and pepper, had been bathing in a yellow cove until they realized someone was watching them from shore. Captain Whitepaul, in no way discomfited by his total nakedness, had stepped forward.

"*Pardonnez l'intrusion*," a man ambling politely down the beach said. He was one of three, slim, wearing no uniforms. "*Nous avons entendu vos hommes.*"

"*Et vous attendiez jusqu'à ce que nous étions deshabilles*," Whitepaul answered, and Henry was startled. *The man speaks languages*, he thought. *He has an education.*

"*Pas vrai, monsieur; on est venus le moment ou l'on vous a entendus ...*"

"We are not used to being surprised," Whitepaul interrupted. His crew were gathering around him slowly, preparing, Henry realized with astonishment, for a fight without weapons or clothes. The absurdity of their willingness for violence was bestial, and the image of these men, rising bare and malevolent from cove water, entered his mind like a spear of light.

"We are honest laborers like yourselves," the small leader managed, his hands open in an offering. The fingers were strangely thin and yellow, with square darkened nails. At one time, he explained, their crew had been twelve. Their crime—*péché*, he called, it, their *sin*—had been to bring to their quartermaster's attention a list of grievances, easily remedied, including the presence of brine in the pork. They had thought both their numbers and the moderation of their demands would win favor. Instead the first mate—demoniacal—had driven each man off the railing at knifepoint.

Though they were *Parisiens* indeed, and their governments sadly at odds, their British brothers could not fail to be moved at how the castaways had banded together, weeping to the fates for some just vessel to pass. Yet alas, said the yellow hands, during the interim the harshness of island life had consumed all but themselves.

"Catholics, are ye?" Whitepaul boomed.

"Huguenots, all."

"Yet ye love Mary, Mother of God and virgin forever?"

"With all our hearts." The French leader crossed piously his chest.

"I pissed down her throat last night," Whitepaul said.

For a moment there was silence. Then the French leader showed a thin smile.

"The slut enjoyed it, I am sure," he agreed.

The *Arrogante* stayed beached for several tides, the crewmen careening the hull and filling in seams where plankwood had been pulled by barnacles. It took Henry some time to understand there had been an implied significance to every line of the conversation he had witnessed, a hidden lexicon that explained the strange behavior of the crew. Frenchmen should have been enemies of *Arrogante*, many of whose number had been privateers with official letters of marque before opting for a trade less sanctioned by the crown. But being outlaw themselves, the men had a claim to community with *Arrogante* that superseded nationality.

The French leader, lifted by his silent compatriots, laughed loudly as he worked at the *Arrogante*'s sides, calling the long striations he uncovered a word Henry did not recognize but which he later discovered to mean *eel bites*. The image of the formless creatures gnawing at ships from below stayed with him, like the stories of Mary Leg, a great octopus that had lived for centuries and had grown so fat on swimmers that, at its approach, the sea underneath your keel turned moon-blue and shallow.

Toward the end of the week Henry was gathering coconuts from behind a close knot of trunks when he found the missing Frenchmen. They had been pushed down into a hollow where the island's base had fallen in, the trails left by their tumbling bodies still visible in the soil. Henry covered his lips and nose in his shirt and climbed down the drop. One man still seemed to push against the weapon that had been driven through his ribs, his stretched face upside down and his mouth slowly filling with water.

They are going to kill him, Henry thought. *They are going to murder Whitepaul and P'ter, and maybe some others, when they see their chance. They are criminals who turned on their own but were somehow left here. Now they can't sail* Arrogante *without a crew but they are already sizing up the rest, deciding who will join and who will oppose. And Whitepaul will die.*

He went back to the beach fires that were burning even before the sun was gone and laid down his offering and felt the eyes of the two silent Frenchmen on him. Their leader was down the beach.

"What about thee boy?" one of the Frenchmen said. He had a long, sparse, empty seeming face.

"The statue speaks," chuckled Hooker. He was kneeling around one of the fires, working to maintain a tent structure in the wood so the air would flow easily and hot. "What about him?"

"We doan like his face."

"*Eh*," Whitepaul muttered. He was turned away, sitting enormously on a beached log. Like the other men he was shirtless, his torso all thick flesh and hair.

"Ye liked him enoof yestiddy," the Irishman mocked.

"Today we doan like his face."

"Is that so?"

The Frenchman who had spoken was staring hard at Henry, his food forgotten in his hand. To his side was a two-handled hull scraper, sharp edged and heavy. "Mebbe he has somethin he wan to say."

"These men killed their crewmates and dropped their bodies in a hole," Henry announced. "Fifty yards from here. I saw them."

Whitepaul looked up.

The Frenchmen grabbed for weapons but Hooker hit one of them in the bicep, two other *Arrogante* men running straight through the fire and knocking them down in the sand. The second Frenchman had a blade out and made to swing but Whitepaul reached over and took the saber by the naked edge, wrenching it physically out of the man's hand. When the fighting was over the first Frenchman was no longer moving and Whitepaul was seated again, facing away.

"Bring him here," he muttered.

Three sailors dragged the still-struggling Frenchman in front of Whitepaul but the huge man did not look up from the slice across his palm that he was binding with a cloth. "Not him. The boy."

The crew turned to look and Henry rose slowly, stepping around the fire.

"Ye wish me dead, lad."

Whitepaul still did not look up, his great redblack brows concealing his eyes.

"Yes," Henry said.

Whitepaul nodded.

"Yet ye save me. Ye warn me."

Henry looked into the fire.

"I save only myself."

Whitepaul grimaced, poking at the crimson line that had seeped through his improvised binding. He rose and put the wrapped hand on Henry's shoulder.

"Roojman has the honor," he declared.

They dragged the conscious Frenchman before Henry and pushed him down kneeling in the sand. His expression was hot, animal-like. Whitepaul took a double-barreled pistol from his bandoleer where it lay in beachgrass, placed the butt in Henry's hand, cocked the hammers, and walked away.

For a moment Henry stared at the weapon; then he dropped the heavy thing like a serpent and the *Arrogante* men began beating their prisoner instead. The last image Henry had was of Captain Whitepaul sauntering down the beach. He looked like he was going toward a light conversation.

When the *Arrogante* sailed they took the French leader onboard inside a wooden crate. The crate they hung from a chain and left him swinging off a crosstree while they sailed two days, including a night in which the heat broke and it rained. On the third day they passed by a shell pile far off any routes and no more than a mile wide and dragged the crate up on the edge of it and split it open with hatchets while the man inside tried to squeeze himself into a ball. Then they left him.

"I've seen traitors to the brotherhood buried up to their necks," Hooker laughed, swiping his sideburns with a silver comb. "Facing the water so they have to watch the tide come in. I've seen men whipped with a cat-o-nine and stinging nettles spread on their wounds like molasses. Nothing is worse."

"Than what?" Henry asked.

"Than this."

From the helm they watched the thin figure of the French leader, alone, recede quietly into the horizon.

Henry woke. She was there, moving away from his hut where she had been peering, standing now outside the flap and just visible against the faint afterglow of embers. He rose and tied on his breeches and went after her, following where she had been. The night sky was clean again and somehow bright: moonless, but so illuminated he stared for a moment at what he took to be clouds before realizing the high structures were a dense wash of stars. Their light was so splendid that looking down again the dark earth shimmered before his eyes. She was there.

He went to her and she did not run. He realized he had been expecting her to run; to leap up, hesitant and afraid. But she did not run, and when he was in front of her and could see her face Henry saw that she had never been afraid.

With a small hand she touched his dead flesh. He pulled the thing away and she came to it again, not afraid as he was, and rubbed slowly and carefully the forearm down to the flat of the wrist. She looked in his eyes but Henry could not meet her there. Still her fingers, unhesitant, were lacing the unfeeling fingers. She took the hand and led him.

Out in the woods they came to a path he had not seen before and he stayed by her as she walked, reaching out with the living hand to block the twiggy darkness in front of his face. He wanted to go slowly and be sure but she moved with a faster grace, neither stumbling nor hesitating where she stepped, only pausing to listen, it seemed, somehow with her whole body: her unshod feet, her shoulders and her skin and her long neck listening, attuned to what was around them in the creepers and the fronds and the high whispering leaves. She took him across a series of hills and on the last one he reached forward to touch her, to touch anything about her with the feeling part of himself, finding only the side of her dress.

Then her legs, the calves smooth as a river of stone, stopped moving and she put a hand out to direct him. They were on the edge of a black field he did not know and when she lowered herself into the bent-knee position of the People Henry followed her down, anticipating cold earth but finding a warm resilience of grass and soil. She looked at him as if she expected something from him, something he could deliver. Henry peered closely at her for the first time, saw the straight blackness of her hair outlining her temples, the roundness of her powerful female face. Then he turned away from her and saw what she was showing him.

The meadow in front of them was dotted with lights. Miniscule lamps of blue, lamps of pale green, bobbed in the secret air: five and then ten and then, as the noise the two of them had made fell back into silence, hundreds. Quick, drifting, soundless.

Henry looked silently and she laid the arm back in his lap, keeping her hand on top of the hand and stroking the numb veins there. She did not look at him now. Instead she looked forward, into the purple darkness of a long hill at the meadow's edge. Henry examined the side of her jaw in the darkness, the curving cheek, the cheekbone, soft and yet somehow certain, somehow adult in her youthful face. But she would not turn to him now. He looked forward.

The hillside came alive with light. So faint were the patterns that after they vanished he thought they had been inside his eyes. Then, looking again, he saw that the same sparks that winked through the air were filling the tree branches by the thousands. One landed in the grass nearby. At first a credulous part of his mind took it to be some Elvin thing from a fairy book, a winged spirit carrying a lamp, or the glimmering scales of the Firedrake. Only after a moment did he understand.

Not sprites, Henry thought. *Insects. Insects that make light.*

The hillside swelled and pulsed. Henry heard himself breathing, his mouth open as if to catch an impossible word. The silent lights rippled and flowed.

He turned to her again. Only she was still waiting; she would not break her waiting. She wanted him to see still more, and he could not get her free and to himself.

Then he witnessed it, finally, what she had brought him here to see: a great sheet of amber traveled quickly up the hill, like the edge of a sail receiving the wind. For a moment Henry started, thinking he had seen fire. But darkness flowed over again, a second wave. Then the synchrony repeated, the insects following each other's flashes so that waves of light curled as they rose up the hill, spilling along the top like crest-foam.

"Beautiful," Henry said, aloud. "They're beautiful."

He turned. The girl was looking at him now, looking into him. Her expression was triumphant. On her face, that riveted question.

8

Comandante Albenix liked the taste of his own gunpowder still faintly present in the flesh of a bird. He was a bit of an epicure: especially appealing to him was the bite that included a remnant of the musket ball's track itself, the seared line burned through breastmeat with its faint acridity of ashes.

"*Tráigame al vicario*," he said. "*Ahora mismo.*"

His crew had unloaded some light material from the *Legenda Aurea*, expecting to spend the night. It was quite possible. The arrangement here was good; there had been several families living in the makeshift village and already Albenix and his men had walked down the center section where royal palms had been cut away, finding both ovens and wells. As it was early his men had gone hunting in nearby fields that were visibly rich with plover.

Two soldiers placed the old man before him, each supporting one armpit and the body weight suspended in the middle. The old man's cranium was entirely visible under the cross-hatched hair that seemed to ride on top of rather than extrude from his scalp. The few teeth he had left were chipped like carpenter's tools, giving his mouth a ragged appearance.

"*Antichrist*," the Dutchman said. Albenix reached out with two fingers and pinched his windpipe shut.

"No Carib," the *teniente* at his side reported, returning from his survey. "It's a Company station." The *teniente* was a younger man, narrow-boned and sincere, who seemed not entirely to occupy his overlarge clothes. "Sir? He hasn't been given a chance to repent."

Albenix kept the hard throat-flesh wedged between his fingers. He was studying the old man's eyes, his own lip with the trimmed wetted moustache bent a little, as if in expectation.

"*¿Comandante?*" the *teniente* said.

The old man's resistant expression became suddenly spastic, as if he had only that moment understood the conclusion to a difficult problem over which he had been laboring. Frantic-eyed, he grabbed at his own chest, beating it with one hand while the other swung pointlessly against the *comandante*'s jacket. The *teniente* stood to the side and watched as the round elderly legs bent inward at the knee and the man, his face like flour now and astonished, seemed to genuflect in front of them both before dying. Albenix continued to hold the body supported by its neck for a full minute.

"If one so fallen can still have repentance in his heart," Albenix said after a pause, "we do him a great favor by bringing him to his reward."

"... sir," the *teniente* managed.

"If not, we do also God's justice."

The *teniente* could not stop looking at the old man's body. He wanted to lean down somehow and shut the jaw.

"Of course, if you would care to discuss my authority in these, or other matters, *teniente*," the *comandante* continued slowly, "I would be most pleased to engage you."

The *teniente* stood straightly. He looked as if his skin had abruptly been drawn tight around his skull.

"No, sir."

Albenix wiped his hand and looked into the younger man's face. The *teniente* had freckles, unusual on a dark-skinned man, and his eyes were set closely, giving him an optimistic but slightly perplexed air. A mosquito landed on his flushed cheek and, gently nosing the flesh for two or three seconds below the eye, began to drink.

The *comandante* lifted his thumb and pressed the other man's face. The *teniente* remained at attention, his sharp Adam's apple hopping up and down at the touch. Albenix showed him the ends of his fingers.

"Dangerous creatures," he said quietly. "You never feel them. And then they steal from you. Your most vital substance."

The younger man looked as if he were going to be ill.

"Do not tolerate them," Albenix whispered, his gold-rimmed eyes coming close. "To tolerate them is to let them breed. To let them breed is to offer them this for the taking. *This*."

The *comandante* held up the red finger, showing it for a moment before running it lightly down the younger man's cheek.

"Do you understand me, *teniente*? Do you feel how ..."—he sought a word—"poignant...is my situation?"

"*Claro, comandante.*"

"*Claro comandante,*" Albenix repeated. "Will you *show* me that you understand? Can you make me believe that the...delicacy...of my office in this country has meaning for you?"

The *teniente* swallowed.

"Sir."

Albenix looked at the other man's mouth for a moment, as if considering. Then, smiling lightly, he walked away.

By that evening the remaining families were tied to chairs and the chairs taken into a cleared central space where they were arranged in a large circle. The young *teniente* stood over the proceedings, coming to each person's side as they were made to receive the Sacrament, whatever portion of it could be inserted. Then he stood back and the men began dousing. At one point, feeling the men were hesitant over a crying woman in an expensive powderblue dress, he pushed past several of them angrily and took the oil dispenser himself and poured it out in her lap. In a single motion he grabbed a burning fag from the central bonfire and dropped it at her feet, beginning the flame that moved in both directions until the circle was complete. Then he and the other men stood back and the eucharistic minister read loudly *tu es Domine si disputem tecum* so that his voice was heard even above the sounds coming from the circle. A land breeze started and picked up the flames, lifting smoke away from the village and raising it over the evening water. There was a smell in it, the young *teniente* thought, like the taste of cooking, and he kept his imagination rooted on the fowl that had been shot earlier out of the trees and the sight of them being plucked by his men and the sight after that of their limp fleshy bodies all laid softly together in a pile.

9

The Other One lived in the dry caves on the far western edge of the World. He had always been there, speaking to presences that only he could hear, since the two of them were children. He and the Caffekey had been born on exactly the same day at exactly the same hour, writhing out from their mother's womb in a single blooded sack. They had been children together, before the Caffekey had been holy, when the Caffekey their mother had still been waiting to see whether more children would be given her. The Other One had been five and six and seven with him, sharing in the joys of those ages, but also, and always, he had been much older; even when they were five and six and seven together the Caffekey had understood that the Other One was old even as he was young, at once child and man, and more.

The *more* he had not understood, as he did not now understand it; though he had seen it and recognized it then, as he recognized it now. The Other One was child, and man, and more, all at once; but the *more* was something he could not explain, something that swayed through the years of their lives like wind through the shaggy tops of trees. The Caffekey loved the Other One, feared him slightly, but loved him and was proud and joyous when he thought of what the Other One was and that they had (it was said) in their mother's womb shared a single breath, their lips locked to each other's lips, and had been born together, in a single hour.

Now the Caffekey seated himself before the Other One, inclining his head slightly in the bright sun that filled the cave at a slant. As he spoke the Other One did not make the small, affirmative sounds that men make to show they are listening: he simply sat.

"There is that in me which fades," the Caffekey said, beginning the traditional prayer. "My voice fails in my mouth. My moon is closing, almost gone."

The Other One listened as the Caffekey's wife repeated the Caffekey's words, louder this time so that the Other One could hear them. The Caffekey's wife was seated by the Caffekey's side, her hand holding the Caffekey's foot in a gesture of comfort and her eyes away from both men. Air stirred the inside of the dry cave, rustling the pelts that hung from wooden stakes. The Other One seemed to listen to it.

The Other One was naked from the waist up. Over his head, covering it so that his face was partway hidden, he wore the skin of a large animal. The animal's head rested on the man's head, so that his true eyes were not seen and in their place the eyes of the animal skin peered out.

Above the eyes two large and curving horns stood out into the air. The horns were painted white.

In his lap the Other One held feathers. The feathers were large, each one individually, and their colors were dark red and earth-brown and gold. The feathers were tied around each of his wrists. Sitting with his hands at rest in his lap the feathers made a brittle collection, as if he held a living thing there.

The Other One's fingers were at rest.

Around his ankles were tied roots. The roots were gray and old.

His chest was still strong. On his chest were painted butterflies.

The Other One took the skin of the animal, the skin that hung down around his bare torso like a cloak, and gripped it closer to him, like a cloak. When he used his hands the feathers tied to his wrists brushed against what he touched, making a crackling sound.

Brought by tide taken by tide, the Other One said. He said it in the sound of the shifting pelts.

Will she be with me, the Caffekey asked.

She is sea, the Other One said. He said it in the sound of cranes, stretching their necks out like dancers all in a line.

Can she not be with me.

She is sea, the Other One said. He said it in the sound of larval pods cracking open in the soil, the milky insect torsos reaching for light. In the sound of his voice the Caffekey felt their tiny longing.

You must follow the rule of the World.

I am afraid, the Caffekey said, and abruptly the anger of their childhood rose in him. For you everything is different. From the beginning. You did not grow and learn and struggle. You have known no fear. And you have loved no woman, not even she who bore us. You preceded her who bore you into the World and you could not love her. How could she love you, then? She who only wanted a daily child, an hourly child. Instead she had you. And no more after us. Her life-place was dry.

The Other One said nothing.

I am afraid of you, the Caffekey said. You killed the children who came before us. You dried up her birth-place after us. You made sure that I alone would be holy, would be chosen Caffekey. You are not a daily child, an hourly child.

The bats, the Other One said. He said it in the sound of dripping quiet, somewhere beneath the island.

The bats when they are born kick out against their mother's skin. Their faces come free and their hands, like hooks, pull them wriggling up her hot belly. The birth matter falls to the pit of the caves. Their siblings smell and come to lap. Their tongues are sharp and small. In this way is healed the opening between worlds.

In this way the new ones are given suck.

Grasshoppers scream in my ears. In time they will lie in the bellies of the bats.

You have kept your People.

The Other One was silent.

"I too am sea," the Caffekey whispered, repeating the old prayer, and the Caffekey's wife spoke his words more loudly so that the other man could hear them. "I too am taken by tide."

No man sees them. Underground they thrive. In time their mother weakens and drops. She too is devoured to spine.

"I too am sea," the Caffekey said. Inside his fearful soul dark pebbles clattered. They sounded to him like unresting bones.

When he was a young man the Caffekey had enjoyed racing because he knew he was likely to win. The canoe he used was lean as a shaft and he used it wonderfully, he could feel its power slicing through water, his strong self propelling him forward. Then he had made a mistake: he had been too bold, thinking himself incapable of being hurt. Thinking the world would step to one side if he flung himself at it, the way all the People had done for him since he had been named holy and his mother, disappointed in her desire for other children, went off to die. The stone sent him back: the chipped wood gave way, the Caffekey found himself knocked into the water and his leg was cut thinly at the knee and bled a little. Feeling too many things he made a show of swimming strongly to the shore. His companions gathered around him obsequiously and he, suddenly furious at his life, had told them to leave him and retrieve their canoes, which were drifting riderless now like stems of grass dropped into the sun.

How he remembered the mortification of that day! How it stayed with him, a feeling of terrible impotence and shame, but worse than this, deeper than this. Impotence and shame he could have ridden out. He had done athletic things and was handsome and alive: the life raced and pulsed in him and would always be there, strong as a running animal, whether he willed it or no. But something else had been revealed to him that day, and it was that the world was not tractable to his mind. That the simplest rock standing in the sun-drenched water—so simple a thing as this did not bow to him, so common a thing as this was Caffekey over *his* life. And everywhere he looked after that day he saw nothing but masters.

Then he had met her, he did not remember where, and known her and been wedded to her. Yet he had felt nothing for her even at the moment when he had expended his semen inside her, her little feminine voice crying out as she felt him not in a physical response but a soul-response, as if he had delivered her an unexpected gift. She had tiny dark hairs on her lip that had a smell of sexual enthusiasm and he examined them, bringing his nose close to her mouth and smelling her, and feeling himself loosening once more inside her now that the act was done; the act for which the whole World drummed and chanted outside his chickee, completed by him almost cavalierly, almost as bravado.

He had felt nothing and the not-feeling hurt him, the fact of his feeling nothing for her even in that moment about which the People sang songs. So he had gone to the Other One, out in the woods, and the Other One had given him Love, and the now-Caffekey carried it home to her like a small imperiled thing dropped from a nest. And he had lain with her a second time, only the Love was a borrowed thing, as the Other One had explained it would be, and the Other One had written across his forehead in ashes and told him he would feel nothing until a time when he would feel too much. And the Other One gave him Respect and Dedication, and the Caffekey gave these things to the girl, and together they kept them, but always the

Caffekey understood and the girl understood these were borrowed things.

After that many moons went by and the Caffekey, looking at the slant of the girl's face or at her arms, which were lovely and thin, wondered how all things in the world could love and he himself alone had no love in him. He felt himself dry and ungiving, he wondered that the world could be so abundant when he himself was bereft, like a dusty foot-wrapping left somewhere in the sand. He tried holding the Love the Other One had given him away from himself, to see if he would miss it; sometimes he held it away from himself for days or longer, and he felt he did not miss it, and always when it came back to him it came back devoted but a little ashamed, like the redgold bird he had kept as a pet when he was a boy. He had refused to care for the redgold bird which sang so pleasantly and refused to let anyone else care for it. He left it tied with a string around one leg on the branch of a pine tree, and it was forgotten there and died and he did not care, he told his concubines to bury it or throw it in the bushes, it meant the same to him. So now he felt this way about the borrowed Love; only he would not be cruel. But when he was walking by himself often he would dig a small hole in the ground with his hands and pretend to lower the redgold bird into it, gently, but he would never ask anyone where its actual body was or whether they had buried it.

The girl gave him children and the People sang about them, their wonderful Caffekey and his bride, and his children by the concubines and his children by the girl played together. Yet every child he had through the girl grew sad and died, and the children he had through the concubines wore the yellow clothes of concubinage and were not of him, not of his heart. Where was his heart? He placed one and then two and three and four of the girls' children in the earth mounds and felt nothing, his soul was set and unmarked by grief.

Many years had passed this way and the girl grew older, and written on her face, the Caffekey saw, was the borrowed Love and the accepting of it, the allowing it to be. And the Caffekey hated what he saw there, he went back to the Other One in the woods and he told him to take back his borrowings, all of them, he wanted none of them any longer. Better to know I am bound, he had said, to feel nothing for another person in this life. The Other One had taken back the Love and the Respect and the Dedication but said they could not be removed without hurt. I have felt no effects up to now, the Caffekey laughed dryly. That night when he felt himself approaching the moment when he would drive lifeless promises into the girl's womb he hated himself more than he ever had.

More moons passed and when the girl began to grow sad in exactly the same way as the redgold bird had the Caffekey cried out as if he had been struck. He felt in that instant the shame and humiliation of toppling from his canoe, the physical blow coupled by a deeper, spiritual humiliation. He took the girl by the shoulders and he shouted at her, he shook her in her ornamental dress and shouted at her, his anger becoming confused now with something deeper: fear, fresh and vivid. He shouted at her to come back, to be young again and unmarked by him so he could set her free; he did not want the face of the redgold bird to look at him through her eyes. But the girl only wept and allowed him to shake her, his concubines and her own ministering women standing elsewhere in the room and looking away.

All during the last moon before she was gone he crouched by the mat where she lay and stroked at her fine small head, and the girl looked away from him and would not see him, only enduring his presence as her owner and her God. The Caffekey listened to her breathing and expected his own breath to diminish, as hers did. But there was a terrible life still in him, and he touched at her straight hair and felt her enduring his presence. When she stopped breathing she was only as an animal that had died; he was not present at the time, and everything inside him was lost.

That had been the first one. After that there was nothing inside him, and a great fear, profounder than the first: fear of what he himself might do: and he wondered what the People would say if a Caffekey were to do *that*. And then there was the other girl, younger than the first girl had been but a woman already, womanly in her eyes, and seeing her take away his hands and kiss them he remembered the stone in the water that had opposed his wish to be master of all things. He saw in her the intractability of the stone against which he had fallen and in her he saw his mistake—that he had desired to be master of all things, and in his desire he had kept even the smallest thing from coming to him without ceremony, without disguise, coming to him only as it was and as it needed to be.

For a long time the Caffekey rested. He was happy, his life had come in its meandering way to the correct course, the one it had been fated for him to take. His memories flowed through him and his soul was too weak to catch them or prevent them.

"There is that in me which fades," he whispered. The Caffekey's wife repeated the words.

The Other One reached out a hand and laid it on the Caffekey's heart. The feathers tied around his wrists pushed against the Caffekey's breast, dimpling the skin.

Carry me with you. Carry me now. I have kept my People.

"One more task I give you," the Other One said.

10

Henry woke to firelight. Shafts of yellow were dancing through the leafwork all around him, and even from inside his sick-hut he could tell the three communal fires had been stoked to their full. The sound of the drumming was there, powerful and fast. Startled moths wheeled and staggered through the air, the branches that formed the structure in which he lay shimmering with brightly lit cracks. Just beyond their thin walls, the World was burning.

Then the doorflap was swept aside and a congress of beings revealed behind it: shagged men, humped men, men whose heads were nightmarishly large. The sweat ran across him in little streams as the creature who had thrown back the door grabbed him with a laugh and he was lifted, now by two and three others, carried the same way he had been carried off his uncle's merchantman and out of his life. Henry made a choking cry.

Something was tied across his back. He saw the ground swing over his head and feared he might vomit and then he was being stretched over a low, hard surface, not stone but hard solid wood with rope knots that pulled terribly against his spine. His hands and ankles were bound. His breath came fast inside him but was growing smaller as well, panic breath, like a small insistent fire. And still the dreams would not leave him. The rolling flames, belching up unreal shadows over lizard men, serpent men, men made of coral parts, men made of bone. His sweat came in a delirious pour.

A creature walked forward whose head was a bear, the upper teeth grinning and black. Henry felt a powerful hand press against his shoulder, forcing the muscle away from the neck.

With terrible clarity his eyes perceived the hatchet as it rose, saw the heaviness of the sharp iron head. He watched the blade rise higher and the shell-string tied to it swing like a tail. Almost at a leisurely pace he watched the handle tip in the creature's grasp as it reached its apex and the fingers took their final hold.

Then Henry looked away. A small track of water, not sweat water, moved down his jaw. How hard, he thought quietly, how hard he had labored never to let them see that! He had labored against terrible forces; he had done all he knew how to do.

Head resting, he saw them now—the animal men, their own eyes turned not to him but to the place above him where the blade hung, waiting, hungry to descend. He had time to examine their faces, the foolishness of their masks, time to see their mouths open slightly in anticipation. Time to see her among them, behind them but coming forward, dressed not in dream costume like the rest of the People but a single piece of fabric draping over one shoulder and knotted at her waist. Time to see her eyes that, alone now, looked not at the blade but at him, at his person, his unconcealed face.

There was a sound. At once the drumming stopped; the string of blue shells swung in the air, its motion arrested. The man whose head was a bear, looking now at the source of that sound, stood amazed and then turned the blade sideways as if to relieve it of its striking power.

The sound came again, sharp and rising. It was the warrior cry, fierce and powerful as a young man's cry, coming from the mouth of the Caffekey. The Caffekey's wife, astonished, stepped back and averted her eyes.

But Henry was not watching as the Caffekey came forward and, having taken down the blade, cast it aside. He was not watching them, the crowd, as they removed their carved heads in mute astonishment and knelt. He was watching her, the girl who had seen him on the beach, who had been with him as he slept, who had summoned him out from himself when everything inside him was expiring. Each time she had come he had known nothing about who she was or what she insisted, except that she insisted it; except that it would be hard, killingly hard; except that he said yes to her, yes, from the very beginning.

The girl came closer and stood by him, mouthing something. For a moment Henry did not understand. Then he followed the gaze of the crowd, found where they were looking: found what the old man had seen and what had caused him to speak once more with the cry of power.

They were looking at his arm. Henry blinked. His own hand—his dead hand—was reaching for her, his fingers reaching for her fingers. The girl, knowing now that he had seen it, knelt down and took his palm into her own.

The Caffekey spoke, quietly this time, his voice that had found its youthful power gone once more now into whispers. The Caffekey's wife, understanding, repeated his words so that everyone could hear.

"The arm lives," Daylaylo translated.

Henry squinted into the light and found the Spaniard. He was among the natives, halfway in shadow. His own sinewy arms were folded across his chest. On his face was an expression that resembled pride, but was not; an expression that came closer, finally, to awe.

Part Three: The Sea Was Full of Bones

Red rose the clouds from the Atlantic in vast wheels of blood
And in the red clouds rose a Wonder o'er the Atlantic sea …

—William Blake, *America: A Vision*

11

When Henry saw her the first time by daylight she was with a group of three other women, making a kind of dye in a wooden bowl into which they were crushing fruit. The bowl was several feet wide and low, so that all four women could work its contents at once. And there seemed to be an understanding of what they were aspiring towards: the colored water, berry-thick and sap-thick, would grow purple under one woman's ministrations, pale and bright under another's, with the addition of seeds or roots or sharp-smelling honeycombs that were warmed by a small fire. Then at once, as if at some sign, all four would drown great stretches of fabric in the mash, their hands working hard now to insinuate dye quickly into the fibers like a massage at a living body.

She did not look at him as he came near and somehow this prevented him from sitting, as if she had drawn an alchemical circle around herself beyond which his foot could not pass. He felt foolish coming near her, all his wit left him and he rubbed at his nose bone with a quick angry motion and looked at the treeline instead, as if considering something. He wanted to be seen doing something other than what he was doing, which was simply being near her. But she would not see him. Her eyes, lively brown for a moment, fell once more to her task and when she lifted one stained slender hand to take hair from her face she did it as a person does who is being watched but will not return the gesture. He knew in that quick motion that she was aware of him but would not make contact with him.

As Henry came closer the other women looked up and began chattering, their strange faces interested, sizing him up with knowledgeable smiles. Henry felt shame and moved away, the women laughing a little after him and making a noise with their teeth. He felt shame in front of these strange people and as he walked away he cleared his throat and spat, wanting to feel nothing and be seen feeling nothing.

"Speaking Owl," Daylaylo said. "*She-Speaks-Owls*. That's as close as I can come. She isn't one of the People."

"She isn't one of them?"

"She's *Ais*, and has an Ais name. When she first appeared, apparently, she kept saying her name over and over, trying to make herself understood. The People thought it sounded like an owl making its call. They say she speaks the language of owls, and is perhaps a child of an owl. I believe it's partly humor." The Spaniard shrugged, smilingly.

"How long has she been here?"

"Years, now. She is more or less as a member of the group. The People are very welcoming, which isn't true of all the tribes. In the end, though, she will always be a guest in the World. As will I."

Henry could move the arm. Gradually as the motions became more and more definite it began whispering to his heart a story he could hear but not interpret, full of pains and the labor of beginning. Sometimes he sat for an hour or two hours in the warm sun rubbing his muscle, making it tingle like the swarm of lights in the field, or simply leaving it stretched alongside him and listening to it, listening to the energy working through tendon and fiber as if it were an oration of which he was the sole audience. Sharp, quick points thrilled about his fingertips. Often he lifted his hand and viewed it, and closed and opened his fingers, slowly, and felt a kind of fatness in the wrist and real pain in the fingers, but the pain was good, it was a living pain, and when he had moved it as much as he could for the hour he lowered his arm again and listened to the new life in it speaking and speaking.

Once when he was ten he had been sent for a time to the estate of a relative on his mother's side in a suburb of London. He had been walking hand-in-hand with his cousin to a street market where she was supposed to buy a wrapper of sheep's brains when they had gone past an Anglican church. The building was made out of hewn stone, rough and orderly at once, and rounded and squat like a castle. Inside people were singing metrical psalms and his cousin, excited as by something she knew, led him to a hidden alcove away from the street. For minutes they had listened to the chant, his cousin holding her money in a bag in her lap and her yellow-lashed eyes closed with pleasure. Then the sound had been interrupted, covered over a by a different, intervening sound, and when they went around to the other end of the church to see what the matter was they found the small courtyard there filled with orphans who lived in a workhouse nearby. His cousin was angered at the interruption but the sound of the children playing had seemed to Henry far better than the sound of the psalm. It was abler, more…but how could he say what the sound was? It seemed worthy of worshipping, far truer than the dull math of the melodies. After that his cousin had turned happy again and before they went home that day she had told him they had a secret: they knew where the Church of the Laughing Children was. That night, his mind full of the blue smoke of overfull streets and the wheels of carriages, Henry felt the other place too—feeling somehow that even when the Anglican church was dark and empty with no one singing and no one listening, the laughter was still there.

Now the new arm spoke and sang like the laughing children, he woke from the communal afternoon naps to its voice and he slept beside it, and if it did not laugh, exactly, there was something in it that was of the same stuff as that laughter.

Henry watched the girl from a distance. She was with the same crowd of women often, baskets heavy with dirt-crusted vegetables all balanced on their heads, colorful beads wrapped tightly on their necks like a row of tropical birds. He saw the way her hips moved in order to balance her basket's weight, the gradual appearance and disappearance of her thigh as it pushed against the fabric. It seemed the most natural of motions, the fabric pushed out by healthy flesh, like the rhythm he had felt walking down to the pool. The motion of her walking seemed to be the same motion he had felt then, something close to the growth of the trees and not far, even, from the motion of the sun. Henry looked without looking, making certain his head was turned away, but his heart was absorbed, fascinated by the discovery.

She walked barefoot wherever she went, small brown feet aware of the earth. Often she helped with the amassing of shells into piles that the People built for some reason, saving every empty cup and collecting them all in one spot. At these times she worked with a large, shovel-like instrument and he saw her bend her back muscles into the task, raking shells, and as far as he could tell this was not thought to be anything unusual for a woman. Afterward she would smooth back her hair which was black and straight like a creek down her spine and bind it and walk away from the labor, the easy motion still in her step, as if once having found that rhythm the work and the relaxing afterward were not separate things.

On the third day he went to her. She did not look up from the pots of dye where she once more stooped and he endured the high sweet noises of the other women, noticing him with interest.

"Tell her I thank her," he said. Unlike her the other women all had tattoo markings on their faces and up their left arms, complicated woven lines that reached across their breastbones and sloped down to make circles around their breasts. She alone had skin that was unmarked, and nothing on her showed the mark of piercing. "I want to thank her for what she did."

Speaking Owl was not looking at him, the other women chattering now over their work. Something caused a problem with the process and they argued about it for several minutes so that Henry, feeling the blood in his cheeks, thought he was being ignored. Then the other women stood and, as if in general consent, took their smaller bowls carefully away. Alone with her suddenly Henry's heart fled him: he felt only confusion, some terrible inadequacy. But he would not turn around, he would not walk away from her again. Forcing himself he stooped to the ground.

"I want…I'd like to …"

But Speaking Owl would not look up at him. She stayed at her work, her dark arms darker from the dyed water, from the woven fibers she was working. Slowly she removed three small twigs, bark-peeled, from the concoction and arranged them along its edge.

Henry sat. When she did not look up he slid his right hand into the colored bowl.

"See? I want you to see that it works again. My hand."

He showed her the slow-moving fingers, stained purply blue. Her own fingers kept twisting, kneading.

"You see?" he said. "I can feel this. I can …"

His words failed him. The girl did not respond and Henry cursed a little and rearranged himself so that his legs were comfortable. Impulsively he put both hands in the bowl and began massaging the wooly mass. The material was thick and slow to contract, forcing the muscles of the hands to squeeze, to pinch stiffly and prolongedly before releasing. The wakened hand flashed pain and joy. With each motion he felt the hot thick water spreading between his fingers.

"Like this?" he asked. "Like this."

Speaking Owl stayed at her work and Henry imitated the motion of her arms. He watched the lean forearms that controlled her hands, adding weight to them, the weight of her torso; then the release, the expansion, the visible swelling and relaxing of her chest as she leaned back slightly, letting the fluids resolve.

He put his hands close to hers and for an instant her body stiffened and rejected him. Then her fingers, sliding out of the cloth, moved a little to his side of the bowl. He felt the skin of her upper hand pass lingeringly over his own.

Then she gathered up the fabric and made her way quickly off toward the others. Henry stayed sitting, his heart jumping inside him and looking at his hands, the living hands before him, dripping fire-blue spots on the dust now like pieces of the sky.

In time Henry came to think of his hosts as the Moon's People, or People of the Moon. There were no days here any more than there were particular hours, but he tried in his mind to maintain an imitation sense of time, to feel that whether or not he could name them, blocks of twelve and blocks of seven were making orderly progression somewhere in the cosmos. The People, however, kept time by the moon, and many evenings there were dances—celebrations, he had at first believed, until he saw the serious meditative faces, careful and intent, as they witnessed the enormous beach fire around which the dancers circled.

At twilight the wood would be gathered, pieces of drift that had been elevated to remove the salt-soak and deadwood taken from the forest in great sloppy bundles. Out of this the fire was lit on the eastward beach and the dancing began. At first it was a kind of flatfooted stamping into the sands, from the hour the lunar disk was visible over the water; then rising in pitch and ecstasy as the orb itself rose; to the time, hours later, when over their voluble chant it stood silent and high and like a presiding figure.

The dancers traded places when exhaustion took them. A stake was set in the beach, painted white and black, which they touched always before resting, and somehow Henry felt certain that the stake represented totemically the moon, though there was no clear resemblance between the wood and their high object of veneration. Now and again a breakaway group would leave the rough circle and orbit the stake itself, singing to it, sometimes shouting or gesturing at it in voices that sounded strangely like accusation. When enough people had left the fire a second circle was drawn around the stake and the men stamped around its perimeter instead, leaning toward but never touching it, as if drawn and repelled by its unseen force.

Then, in the most surprising moment of all, the same stake would be pulled up and flung aside irrelevantly, the dancers leaving it and rejoining those around the fire. Henry wondered whether the dance filled the stake with energy or drained it; he wondered whether the moon was the stake, or the circle around the stake, or whether the circle was the moon's path in the sky. He wondered whether the wood flung aside was the body at death, or a sacrificial dying, or some other thing of which he had no clear conception. Alien to it all, cut off from what bonded their community, his mind could only invent stories to go with the action before him. The moon was the lover of earth, romanced by the priests; the flames were the sun, which danced around men. The costumed man with both false breasts and a goofy gourd-penis was the Caffekey's spirit, or possibly the earth's, giving birth to itself. A complete cosmology played out in his imagination, with a beginning fire from which life sprang and an ending fire in which it was consumed. But the stories were purely his own.

All that was certain was the moon's centrality. Always the dancers looked up toward it, fat and white, while the chanters chanted to it, and the drummers drummed to it striking instruments hardly larger than their hands.

Men who were not dancing drew sweet smoke out of the same pipes he had earlier seen. The pipes were passed communally but, Henry noticed, could also stay in the hand of a given smoker for twenty or thirty minutes without concern. The dancers did not smoke but drank a dark brown liquid kept in buckets, tipping it to their lips from a wide, flat shell. Henry was not driven from the ceremonies, as he had first expected to be, but neither did he belong. He merely sat, sometimes far off, sometimes near enough to be warmed by the great fire on nights when the sea wind came in cold and spoke of rainstorms out across the dim waves.

One night Henry turned his head without knowing what had caught his attention and saw Daylaylo among the dancers. His European skin had been painted in zigzag patterns and as he danced he leaned far over to strike at the ground with his hands. The others rose and Daylaylo too reached for the moon, making a motion that Henry could not understand unless it were to somehow cast the orb into the fire and raise it back out again. The Spaniard circled the flames and was gone, back into the general praise.

"I saw you at the ceremony," Henry said, the next day when he found the Spaniard working in his garden. His tone sounded faintly accusatory in his own ear, though he himself was unsure why.

"*Sí,*" Daylaylo stretched, drinking from a gourd. The sound of calling birds was loud around them. "*Si, me viste.*"

"Do you believe it?"

Henry sat down. The hand was well now: hot, too hot, burning as if stung and strangely red, but alive now, the undeniable life rushing through it like a stream. "You act as though you believe them. The People."

"Believe them how? I belong with them now."

"Didn't you bring the gospel to them?"

"No."

The Spaniard laughed a little at his expression.

"When Tied Sticks saw me, he asked if I was Jesus," Henry said. "Or, maybe, if I was one of the Jesus people. You must have told them that name."

"I explained to them what I was. What I *had been.* That was all."

It was a clear morning and Daylaylo was separating out tiny seeds by their color, laying them on a cloth in careful rows. He went back to work, three different bands emerging before him from a general pile.

"But then …" Henry began, and felt his words fall short. "It can't…it must be a sacrilege. You have your own God."

Daylaylo thought. "Let me tell you a story." He tied the cloth to a wooden rack and sat back, cleaning the dirt carefully from his hands. "I grew up in Toledo, just outside the shipyards. It's a busy city, an envious city, full of gossips…always a good tale to be heard about someone else's misfortunes, someone else's merchandise on the sea. When I was a child, younger than you even, I saw a man begging outside the cathedral there. He was wrapped in rags—not clothes, not even ruined clothes. Rags, everywhere, like a man of rags. He smelled of sweat, of urine. He had a small stick to help him around, because his legs were bent inward at the knee, like this. He sat on a kind of…*carrito* …"

The Spaniard made a shape with his hands.

"A small box with wheels, and pushed himself from place to place. Beggars next to shrines were common in that city, but this man...*allí es.* I remember it was the feast day of St. Colun, the women and men were all well dressed for the Saint. Perfume, hand-carved rosaries. And here was this man...everyone coming out of the cathedral was offended by him. *Offended* by him because, I think, when we see the poor we see ourselves, as we might become. If one man can fall to such a place...if that can happen, then not even the rich are safe. You understand? They are only rich.

"This beggar...I realized someone was speaking loudly to him. I don't know who it was. He was a grown man with a white beard, nicely cut, with a notary's badge on his cap. I can still see his face. I can see the thick collar he wore, and the expression. This man hated the beggar with something deep in himself. You could see by the way he was speaking, louder and louder, that he wanted the man punished. His cheeks began to turn pink over the line of the beard. The people around him, they could have calmed him down, a woman perhaps. Instead he *moved* them, somehow. They started shouting too. It was as if one man's hatred had opened the way. Everyone was shouting now and throwing things at the beggar. Dirt, little handfuls. Not enough to hurt, but some began adding stones.

"The beggar tried to get away. Pushing himself on his cart, he looked like a man rowing. It was comical, you see? His helplessness was amusing. People threw garbage, anything. People who a minute before would not have stooped to the ground or soiled their gloves lifting up a clump of waste. I remember I could feel my mother's hands go tight on my shoulders. And I knew that she was angry, not because the beggar was being chased, but because he was *escaping.* Those fingers on me, my mother's fingers—if she had been alone, she would have been throwing stones as well.

"That was all that happened. Perhaps he was unhurt, even. But all the rest of the day...I saw young men coming from the fort, soldiers laughing with their sleeves rolled high, holding each others' necks. I watched servants spread their linens along the banks, singing a song that was popular that year...the food markets, a painter, two dogs in a fountain I remember, someone rolling a long flag onto a holder...the rest of the day, all I could see was the beggar. I could feel his fear, I could hear his breathing, the mucous in his throat, the way he struggled terribly for breath when he tried to get away. He had been written into my mind.

"My father had many lovers and brought them home with him, which my mother pretended not to understand. She called them his *primas*. If she ever had to talk about these women she said my father was with his *primas*. One night I rose from my bed. My nurse was asleep. I remember there were two *primas* standing in the hearthroom, looking into the fire with the grate moved aside. They were reading their fortunes in the ashes there, whom they would marry. They both, I think, wanted to marry my father, who was a rich enough man. When they saw me they smiled and let me by. My father was asleep on the bench. It was summer, and warm. I went outside and walked all the way to the shipyards, to the place where the beggar had been."

Daylaylo faced the sun, eyes closed. He seemed to be marveling at the images before him.

"I remember everything so well from that night. The faces of the *primas*. Their necks, their hair in the firelight. Their beautiful skin, so different from the skin on my mother's neck. It was the first time I understood that sorrow appears in the skin, the first time I understood age. I remember the feeling of my mother's sorrow, alone in her bedroom. My father, having everything a man in his kind of life, a man with his kind of soul, could have. And the night, so peaceful, so calm."

"Did you find the beggar?"

"No. I don't know. How can that be? He was at the middle of that world. He seemed to be everywhere. But my next memory is later, more than a year." He paused. "Hearing the gospel the first time, Henry, I knew it had something to do with that night. Something to do with that beggar. For me, there was never any question of faith. I saw him once and I wanted to find him again."

Alongside the nearest huts a native man began blowing on the end of a conch. The sound was incomplete, tentative. Another man was explaining the technique.

"*Un traidor a la cruz*," Daylaylo offered, as if he had been thinking about the sound. "Maybe when you look at me dancing, you see a traitor. Christians love the cross. To them the cross is a God in itself.

"But Christians don't love the Resurrection. We think that by nailing Him down, we can keep Him for ourselves. We can seal Him in a tomb, we can finally hold on to Him. But, with the dawn, we find He has escaped us. Again and again."

Henry lay himself flatly along the hard, swept ground next to the seeds. He saw the green shoots pressing their way through the Taverner Bible. The first thing he had done on the island—before anything else, before even finding water—was to remember the secret book.

"When I came here," Henry said. "Almost as soon as I knew I was alive…I thought I should pray. I wanted to pray. But I couldn't."

"No?"

"To be alive, on that beach…to be anything…" He struggled. "The Rector would have called it a miracle, clear evidence of grace. But how could my life be a miracle after everything that had happened?" Henry stared at the thin trails of clouds overhead. "I tried …I wanted to pray. To thank God. But my hand wouldn't rise. There were sand fleas on it…it was like praying with a dead man's hand. That was when I knew. If there was a God for me, he died on *Arrogante.*"

"Listen," Daylaylo answered, unperturbed. "Here is a better story. One day a young man was sailing to an island when thieves captured his ship. They made him a prisoner, but the young man was not afraid. Instead, he walked around the deck and said to each one, because you have stolen me, some day, I will crucify you.

"The thieves kept him for forty days. Then they gave him back for some gold. A year later, the thieves were captured. As they hung on their crosses, the young Julius Caesar walked in front of each man and said: You wanted to have me but not to pay for me. Now you will pay for me."

"What does that mean?"

Daylaylo laughed, that breathtaking sound.

"Just that the gospel is a story I should think you would understand."

In the long solid afternoons the People slept, staving off the hottest hours, when the sun was a glass cauldron. Speaking Owl, though, seemed to feel no heat. She moved easily along the white shorelines, her toes finding holds among sharp coral and shallows, her fingers flashing down and pulling forth tiny creatures. Edible plants and shelled and unshelled animals she dropped, newly washed, into her basket. Until the little bodies came purple and wriggling into the light, pried from their stones, Henry could neither see nor feel them; the tidal spill to him was one undifferentiated wash. Watching her go easily from spot to spot was a mystical display, in which the empty shoreline yielded up life again and again out of nothing.

She showed him air-blue snails that populated certain trees like an impossibly slow wave spilling against the bark. The creatures evidently lived out their existences entirely in one place, for littered around the root systems where they knuckled out of the soil were thousands of opalescent wings, the record of entire generations past. A quick shower came and went and in the changed light afterward Henry picked his way almost reverently among the shells.

She showed him tiny corn-like plants that grew yellower on their southern sides, as if colored differently by the rise than the fall of the sun. Henry felt their vegetable love of the light, the warm growth and response to that simple giving. She showed him plants that resembled lettuce heads, only greener, and soft as velvet. She showed him a salty fruit like an olive in shape, only fatter. She showed him whole tumid rivers of ladybugs crawling between branches; myriad tiny lives, unthinking, unsouled.

"This *wa-ee*," Speaking Owl said.

It had surprised him at first to have her speak phrases in English, her proud face working hard, so that he understood she had been watching him too and listening to his speech. To each attempt of hers he said *yes, yes, I understand*, feeling an almost ridiculous happiness. Being with her became like hearing a gentle parody of himself. He had heard her say *Come, come now; to me; give this;* something that sounded like *here give*. Each word that appeared unexpectedly from her lips seemed miraculous to him, as if the flowers that erupted everywhere on the island had pursed their soft lips and spoken. He too had learned a dozen or so words of the People's tongue, but the meanings, other than brute names of things, he could not grasp. When he tried for full sentences she was so amused that he retreated in shame.

She showed him a sea turtle hiding in a grassy retreat. The creature was too large to lift without both hands, its toughened skin reminding him of tooled leather. The face was mask-like yet dignified, a hawkish beak set under motionless eyes. Speaking Owl followed the animal's trail down the edge of the water until she came to a clutch of eggs, taking a large, yellow one but leaving, for some reason, several others, even covering them again with loamy sand.

Each time she took something she prayed. To Henry it seemed a kind of apology taking place, to the turtle for taking its children, to the egret and the wading birds, to the long-legged frogs she had trapped in a hanging net near the edge of a stream. It was also, perhaps, a kind of thanksgiving, not to a God separate from the world but to the actual world from which she took and ate and lived. But was he even close to understanding her actions? He felt the improvised character of his mind at such moments, the sentimentalizing of those things over which he had no grasp. It could all be wrong. Like the stories he invented to go with the dancers, he had the irresistible impulse to assume.

Yet he did assume; she was *person*, she was not other than he was, not separate from him. What she felt, what she seemed, must be in some way connected to what he himself felt—perhaps, even, through a connection that ran deeper than their different cultures. They were separate trees whose roots drank one source. He forced himself again and again to this conclusion, that through all the incredible difference of their circumstance, they were bonded at the center.

Smaller beaches dotted the edges of the island, some no more than twenty or thirty feet wide, and she went to these and passed her hands along the water lip carefully. Henry watched as she reached into different part of the sand, dimpling it first with her fingers as she searched and then parting the amber-white skin, the strong first finger inserted and prying the sand into a mouth, working two and then three fingers into the wet darker regions underneath, out of which she would withdraw a glossy prize, blue and gleaming. She was firm in her insertion, knowing her right; insisting with her hands sunk even to their wrists on what she would have. And the island resisting, coy with her and secretive, even a little abashed; then wooed by her and yielding, water spilling up over her palms and gift after gift coming free.

The skin up to her calves shone wetly as she took the basket to a pool in the woods and rinsed its contents, and when she took them from the water again the tiny hairs on her wrists dried quickly and stood up. Her dark legs dried also as she walked more and more out of the pool and Henry watched them drying as they came, that same motion that had fascinated him rinsed now in clean water, her basket both dripping and filled.

At the edge of the pool water Speaking Owl stooped to examine her goods and Henry saw the base of her spine, bending in a smooth turn. The muscles of her spine showed themselves to him: lean and strong, rising on either side like gradual hills, like breeze-blown sand carrying the impress of the wind. He wanted to touch her there, to run his hands along her spine, to feel the unimaginably fortunate rise and fall of her small healthy muscles. For the instant he felt he was seeing something privileged, some rare precious sight.

Speaking Owl said something and Henry looked: three tiny deer were standing on the other side of the pool, their spotted backs no higher than his knees. She said something to them and they listened, their ears turning slightly to regard her; then she left the ring of sunlight where she had been crouching with the basket and came to him, her face bright as if she herself had produced this vision. Her hair was untied and the fall of it behind her ears was like a fall of black water. She came to him and Henry reached out with both hands and felt for the first time that cascade, the softness and utter straightness of her hair, let his hand touch it and feel the day-heat in it and follow its course up to the little bulge behind her ear. He touched her skull and felt its small solidity, felt her scalp warm and alive as she stood curiously and let him touch her.

The fascination of his hands took him from himself for a moment and when he looked down at her again she was moving closer still, like a ripple, her mouth small and questioning. Henry let himself be tasted by her mouth, felt the presence of her small dark body touching his own, his fingers still against her scalp and knowing her only there, another person, a person whom he too tasted in his own mouth like food.

She backed away looking at him easily and her eyes were soft, the color of them so dark that it merged with the pupils, and she said something to his eyes and slung up her basket and walked past him, smiling.

At the World that afternoon several people were gathered around a man who held something in his lap. When Henry passed by he saw the man was holding a viola against his belly.

The people all stopped laughing. They had been raking the strings in a choppy way and the feeling of laughter was still there, but seeing him now, seeing Henry, there was a different feeling.

"The bow," Henry said, looking around. "Where is the bow."

He asked each man in turn.

"The bow," he said, gesturing. "Where is the bow."

The owner of the viola watched the motion he was making and, saying something, stood up and left the circle. In a minute he came back with the case in which the viola had been preserved, floating evidently when they found it, brought in with no mark upon it of the course of events that had taken it, perhaps, from some Austrian parlor somewhere and flung it voicelessly into the Atlantic. Henry looked in the case and the bow was still there, clipped into place with a small velvet band.

He removed the piece and examined it. The horsehair was ruined but unbroken, the wood itself only slightly warped. Someone began making assertions; fingers pointed at him and at the instrument, at him and at the bow. They touched his chest in the breastbone, a casual gesture he had seen often, a gentler version of the one that men onboard *Arrogante* used when they mimicked grabbing and offering their hearts. The instrument was put in his hands.

Henry lifted it. The sounding board was ruinous: sand had caked and filled in one of two sound holes, becoming like a plaster. The second string was not broken but missing, apparently not strung on when the whole had been lost. He played the bow across what remained and the men recoiled.

My name is Henry Cote, he thought, the assertion coming from nowhere and seeming to him strangely necessary.

He laid the wood under his chin and drew over it. The string, brittle as straw, resisted a moment longer before giving out a single note. The men were caught between speaking and silence, watching with uncanny eyes. Henry arranged himself on the stump, stared for a moment at the dirty grass in front of him.

My name is Henry Cote. What strange ways my life has taken!

Men were speaking to him, making comments, making accusations. But the words were unimportant. The feeling of the language he had already learned.

"Strange ways," Henry said to the men. They pointed and pushed at the bow hand. They seemed to agree.

He lifted the viola and played. The music that came out of him was Italian, a melody line he had memorized under his mother's hand. He played it on one string in a box warped by sea water and grizzled with sand, his left hand moving slowly to the vibrato of the notes, his renewed right burning with the simple motion of the bow. The melody hesitated and then announced itself, leaping momentarily clear. For an instant the viola sang.

But it was all he could do. The instrument was too far gone; he laid it back down.

The men were looking at him with mute wonder. Some boys had come around too, drawn by the sound. One of them showed him a face so indignant and blackeyed Henry was confused, feeling he had done an unforgivable thing. The boy looked like he hated the European for showing him this, yet demanded it go on.

Henry lifted the bow again and repeated what he had played. This time he strained for the high E, achieved it, and completed a slow series of runs before ending on an easy trill. When he set the instrument down in the grass several of the men looked at it there as if something else might be forthcoming.

And the boy, the one with the outraged love, shouted curses at Henry and ran.

That night he did not need to see her to know. Henry rose in the darkness and made his way into the forest. His feet were determined; he found the glowing path. At the end of it, backed by a blanket of stars, she stood waiting.

He went to her but she was gone, running down hills in a silence of footfalls. Henry gave chase, the sudden leap of a fish telling him on which side the ocean lay. He found her again at the edge of a thicker wood. When he came to her she pulled his body in by the sides and he kissed her, her dark interior taste filling the night. Then she blocked his mouth with her fingers and led him instead, and he walked through areas he had not yet seen, his body nevertheless understanding the island so that walking by starlight was done easily. Together they passed through secretive trees, their sound less than the rustle of branches. She turned and clutched him.

They were in front of a glade now, only large enough for two people. The round level patch shone in the starlight, circled on all sides by overhanging leaves. They had climbed a little as they went, approaching the hills that led to the island's promontory. Above the trees that encircled them was only the crystalline ice of the sky, a flawless visible arch.

As before, Speaking Owl wanted to show him. He tried to go to her but she resisted; she wanted him to see. Henry looked where she was looking and saw only darkness, the trees with their absolute shade. Then, straining, he recognized what she was pointing toward: two parrots, soft and heavy, perched together on a high twist of branch. They were grooming. As Henry watched one animal, its nighttime face two wide rounded eyes, gnawed lightly at the feathers of the other. The receiving bird squinted and accepted the care, turning its head as the grooming bird moved, stroking its plumage until it lay even. The bird who gave the attention was moving its white toes in and out on the branch.

Henry turned around and she was naked before him, her body slight as a warm gust of air. Her hair was hung forward over her breasts but did not come down to the nipples, dark centers he knew she wanted him to see. She took his good hands and put them there.

He felt the hardnesses in the centers of her breasts growing until they forced their way demandingly into his palms. He was astonished, his entire being fixed on that sensation. She laid her head against his chest and as he felt the soft excitedness of her nude body pressing him a deeper awareness opened in him, as he knew it had opened in her. Her eyes closed slightly, as if she were sleeping, as if relieved already of the burden of the thing that was coming to them; as if wrapped in the extraordinary release of being finally understood.

12

A man was standing by the water.

The water was only partly visible, its presence made known mostly by the luminous flashes it added to the border of trees. Their thin white trunks mixed with the rippling light, creating a hybrid screen.

A woman came and stood at the man's side. They stood with just enough space between them that, reaching out, it would not have been possible to touch. The man stared at the water through the intervening trees.

"I do not need you," the man said, not looking at the woman. She was not the person to whom he addressed his words; rather she was the representative of that person, the interlocutor. "But I *expected* you. I *expected* you."

"I too have changed," the woman said. She did not look at the man when she spoke. She was the go-between, and was not important in herself.

"I have been watching you," the man said. "Even before you found the *nickaleer* on the beach." The tone in the word hurt the woman to hear. "I follow you in the woods. To see you. Just to see you."

"I know this," the woman said, not speaking for herself. "I know you are following me because at times, when I am walking alone, I hear nothing. The woods grow silent. Then I know you are near."

"I do not want to follow you. But I do. I hunt you. I want to kill you. You and your *nickaleer*."

"I know you want this," the woman said. Her face was sad; but not for herself.

"I have a dream," the man said. His expression, which had for a moment been approaching sorrow, contracted again and was furious. "In my dream I hunt you and I catch you in a trap, and I tear your body apart, into small red pieces, and eat you. Then I am well again."

"You are well again now," the woman said, speaking suddenly

for herself. She turned and looked at the man with terrible pity. The man turned his thorn-marked face.

"No," the man frowned. "I am sick. I know what they call me."

"You make them afraid."

"The witch was strong. He remains."

"You let him remain."

"Speak for *that one*," the man barked. He stared back into the trees.

Then:

"I expected you."

"Your expectation has only been inside you," the woman said, defying his outrage and still speaking for herself. She came to him and placed a hand on the muscles of his arm. "As the rest has been inside you."

The interlocutor walked away. When her form was no longer visible Tied Sticks opened his mouth; with his face alone he made the gestures of an extended howl. But he made no sound. The pressure of making no sound thrust his veins out against his skin, making his neck and his cropped head grotesque. His eyes, forced down to slits, were damp and wild.

Tied Sticks made himself *werowance* this way: when he was called Ema'o he was favored under Achtu. He had been favored because he had shown talent as a hunter and because of his physique. He had the ability to run without stopping and with a sharktooth club he could be sudden and very swift. He was possessed since childhood by a constant low anger like a smoldering in his spirit, and conversations with him turned often to dispute and even hostility, even among friends. Even when he began by trying to offer help or advice to friends, the smoldering in him showed and the listener would be turned against him; as if helpless he would hear his own words turning bitter and bringing about argument. It hurt him to listen to himself growing impatient and to see the faces of people to whom he was trying to speak and know that in a moment he would be challenging them, insulting them, but his anger was like a horse between his legs and he could not prevent it. One day when Ajapeu, older than he and stronger, had laughed mildly at something he said Ema'o pulled out his sharktooth club and struck the older man down so quickly, and so without fear of the consequences, that though he was beaten badly afterward by

Ajapeu's friends Achtu, in watching it, had been impressed.

In the summer Achtu led his warriors against the Calusa in the war of the Three Sticks. They were not fighting the Calusa as a whole, but three smaller tribes who were part of the Calusa and who fought for each other as if they were one. Their willingness to fight for each other made them more formidable than three scattered tribes would have been, but aside from the pact they had made they did not know each other well and their strategies were still three different strategies; and together they were uncoordinated and slow. The three-Calusa felt strong because of their pact, and because they were associated with the Calusa in general. But this, Achtu said, could also be taken as their weakness.

The fighting went evenly, the warriors of the People fighting with dignity throughout the hottest days and neither losing nor gaining ground. Then in the third moon Achtu died in his sleep of nothing at all and the responsibility of *werowance*, according to his wishes as he had expressed them to his closest, fell to Ema'o. Achtu had always preferred quick small skirmishes when three-Calusa were seen going into narrow passes or places that could be blocked, or when their horses could be stolen or driven away, or when they had their backs to water. Ema'o, however, broke with this approach and rode out alone to the heart of the closest encampment and spoke directly to the face of the Carlos.

The Carlos had tiny black eyes like a fish and wrinkles all about his nose and mouth so that he seemed to be perpetually laughing from some hidden place inside himself. Though a small man and wrinkled, he could eat a cactus pod without removing the quills; he could make his urine turn to burning rain that would fall on an enemy camp; he had lived for seven lifetimes already, and was not yet winded. As Ema'o spoke to him of Achtu's death in his sleep and the dignity of the People the Carlos made a grumbling sound deep in his chest and, working something up from his throat, spat it into the grass. Ema'o took his warriors back to camp and had counsel, listening to none of it, and the next morning he had counsel again, hearing none of it, and then he led his warriors over the walls of the encampment and they killed every one of the three-Calusa warriors over their morning meals, sustaining bad losses on their side, but on the three-Calusa side ending the life of every one there, until Ema'o had reached the Carlos and forced a wooden shaft through the tongue that had spat at him and tied it to his horse and dragged the Carlos around the perimeter of his own encampment until the tongue came free.

After that there were many battles with the two-Calusa, which depleted the People's numbers but which Ema'o won again and again, always attacking, without discussion, rapidly and completely. Then one night before sleep Ema'o smelled his hands and smelled blood there. It was no dream, no metaphor: he smelled the strange bodily smell of other men's blood on his fingers, beneath his nails, in the grit of his skin. The smell made it impossible for him to eat with his hands, and he refused his food for several nights until Tom Kit suggested teasingly that Ema'o had a bowel illness. The warriors laughed at this and Ema'o challenged Tom Kit to a wrestling fight, a foolish thing in the middle of all their losses; but the ring was drawn and their wrists bound, left to right, and the fight was had and Ema'o won it. After that he ate with his hands, taking food enormously and swallowing it down in everyone's sight, even though the hands stank more and more of the black insides of other men's bodies.

At the end of the year the Carlos for one-Calusa gave peace offerings and Ema'o, having untied the three-Calusa union and become Tied Sticks and *werowance*, went home. Only Tied Sticks left behind him something in the fields where the bodies of Calusa men and bodies of warrior People lay. For several days of traveling he was silent and reserved and behaved like a man struggling to remember something he has lost. And indeed, he had lost it; on the third day he realized his soul was gone; he looked inside himself and he saw a bloody emptiness like a rotten fruit, like a coconut that has been hollowed out by birds. He tried in horror to hide the emptiness but the warriors saw it. They had seen such curses before, and Tom Kit, no longer mocking, began to snap his fingers around him, signifying the dry snapping sound a drummer could make flicking his fingers against an empty gourd.

Tied Sticks bundled himself under extra clothing, saying that he was cold but doing it for fear that his hollowness was becoming more and more visible. He began to fear that men could see right into him, that his ribcage and his spine were showing, that when he swallowed now the food fell from his midsection and when he breathed the influx of his breath stank out again from his open stomach. And he smelled the odor of himself and knew it was the black smell of dead men's bodies. The smell of his hands had permeated all of him, it had eaten his body out from within.

The hollowness was seen by all upon his returning to the World and was attributed to the Carlos having been baptized, which was true, and his having reached out as Tied Sticks dragged him around the perimeter of his camp and touched the back of the horse's hoof on which Tied Sticks rode, his poison touch creeping up the horse's leg and along its flank until it reached Tied Sticks himself and slowly made him hollow. Such things had been known before. Once a pile of blankets had been found that had been abandoned by a passing group of people from no tribe in particular and the blankets should never have been used, because they had been shat on by witches and now whoever slept in them fell silent for half a moon though they seemed to be trying to say something and then grew terribly sorrowful and died. Tied Sticks' hollowness seemed to be a similar case.

Because of his hollowness the People had kept away from him, using his new name as if honoring him but keeping their eyes blank, inviting him to meals and dances but keeping themselves from feeling his touch. After three moons he had decided to place a knife under the bulge in his throat and fall forward with his chin lifted. Several times he approached the water with a knife pressed to the bulge, feeling the sharp tip poking there, and standing and standing and feeling just that tiny sharp tooth where it rested. But never had he been able to slam the handle back.

Then there was she, the Ais girl. She was not half his age, but she had been the only one who was not afraid of him, who for some reason he could not understand was unashamed to be seen walking with him. To his warriors he had become a kind of a tragic god, the sense being that a hollow man feels nothing and is thus undefeatable in battle. He can run arrows directly into his flesh and pull them out the other side and feel nothing; he can step on a flaming brand and feel nothing. He was not so much a man to them as an unstoppable ally, a vessel in which a battle spirit resided, but a thing, not a companion. He had told the Ais girl his thoughts about the future and what they had been before the war and what they might have been otherwise, and she wept quietly and held him, unafraid of touching him truly so that he could feel himself in her hands, a way he had not felt since the curse. He realized then that since the hollowness he had lost all sense of himself. When he stumbled and stuck a root with his foot he felt nothing, even when the toe turned an ugly purple color the next morning he felt nothing, and he knew that his warriors were right and he could do anything now. In a strange moment of pride he told her that before the Calusa war he had been angry, yes, but also bright and powerful; he had been beautiful, too, and abruptly he saw himself again, beautiful as he had been. She tried to show him how to see himself again, and he tried, leaning over pools after rain. But when he looked at himself he saw the black smell of blood. He saw the fields at two-Calusa and one-Calusa where men lay putrid and ruined now and were pulled at by birds. That was what he saw when he tried to see himself.

But it was enough that he was seen by her, and touched, and she did not see him the way he saw himself. He lied to the girl and told her that sometimes leaning over a pool he could see himself again and she saw through his lie and he felt shame, shame in front of this girl who was not half his age and had none of his status.

But he was back among the People. They spoke to him now, seeing that the Ais girl was not afraid. More and more they were able to look at him, and when they spoke of him sometimes he heard them using his original name as if they had forgotten and an impossible flame of joy leapt up in him, he tried to pretend he had heard nothing unusual but his hard warrior's face was illuminated by an impossible joy. Could the terrible godhead be removed, were such changes given to men? She stayed with him, not as his lover perhaps but something more important, until he was able to be touched by old men and children and then finally by grown women. He became able to lie down with concubines again, even though he felt nothing, nothing but a kind of red mist around his eyes; but he was able to lie with them, and touch and be touched by them, and the change was amazing to him. He avoided anything that reflected and did not want to look in still pools, not for fear, now, of seeing the smell of dead men's bodies and the fields at one-Calusa, but for fear that the thing he so longed to see might truly be there again. He longed for it so greatly that he was afraid to know.

For a long time then it had been that way. He was on the verge of wellness, the trembling verge, not wanting to question too much for fear of forcing the issue. But it was enough. Men spoke with him and looked in his eyes and children did not flee him and at the dances he was given a position of honor with his remaining warriors around him, and he began to feel something, perhaps *home*, and he began to think that soon he would know for certain. Then one night lying on top of a concubine with his penis stiff inside her, happy and flushed after the dancing and sliding himself quickly in and out of her like a playful child, he lifted himself up on the palms of his hands to look at her naked skin underneath him, and as he held himself up he saw that underneath him her body was greasy with blood: his own body, he saw, was open from just underneath the ribs down to his genital and his intestines were hanging out in blue loops and dragging back and forth over her breasts. The concubine had her eyes closed and moved slowly beneath him, trying to regain his attention, but he withdrew in horror. For suddenly he had been in her mind instead of his; he was the woman being entered by a corpse man, a man whose rotted insides draped and painted her freely with every sway. In nausea he pulled away from the concubine who simply remained lying on the ground looking into the shadows, so that he wondered if she too had experienced a sudden moment of horror and revelation, or whether all along she had seen him as he truly was.

13

As the life came slowly back into him Henry began to explore the island on which he now lived. He went out by day, leaving the People but not traveling beyond the point where he could hear their commotion, then moving gradually in wider and wider circles until he was ready, almost without knowing he had come to that time, to step away on his own.

Inland he found a dried stream bed in which almost every section that had been flowing water was filled in with dark blue stones. Whatever process had gradually culled out this single color had smoothed the pieces as well and the remnant were bright veins, like a sewn blue thread.

There were slash pine gardens and cypress gardens. There were fields of pure brilliant gold, seen momentarily through parting trees as if he were approaching a blessed land and which, upon entering, he found to be filled with straw-like grass, its tops turning to powder under the bright shell of sky. And everywhere, the flowers: flowers whose heads emerged pink and lavender from honey colored knots; flowers that lolled and swayed from stalks taller than a man; flowers that put seed into the air until the afternoons swarmed with it, as dense as the spawning water around corals. Daylaylo told him the Spanish name that had been given to this part of the world, the string of islands on which he had washed up. These were *Los Mártires*, the Martyrs; but the region as a whole was *Pascua de Florida*, the feast of flowers. Wandering through their heavy sweet scents the idea of flower feasts filled and danced in his consciousness.

There was a creature like a moth that emerged only at twilight and whose wings, no larger than Henry's smallest fingernail, were rainbowed like the wings of cherubim. There were standing birds, walking birds with stem-like legs, *ibis* and *egrets* and others he had never seen, even in paintings. At darkness came shapes that vaulted to and fro through the flower-sweet air, and when he snuck closer to examine them he saw they were no birds at all but something like a squirrel with skin spread between its limbs.

Inside the island he found a series of sandy strips, fronted on three sides by angular rock. There Henry had seen an even stranger species of animal. It was small, small enough to lift in one's hands, and walked on four stumpy legs with a comical sense of entitlement. The hair was bristly hard, exchanged only at the brow for a thin coating of delicate fur, as if it were wearing a kind of jacket. Henry followed the creature for several hundred yards and it proceeded on its way, snuffing once or twice at a mass of old fruit before disappearing into the underbrush.

Other creatures were more common to his experience. He saw cockroaches, rabbits, a brown, snouted mouse. He recognized mourning doves and plovers. The tiny deer he had seen with Speaking Owl emerged almost every evening, the mother or father standing watch while the younger ones danced in the honey-colored light. Daylaylo told him about these animals: the deer were sacred to the People, untouchable. He said he believed it was their extreme vulnerability, somehow, that made them holy, as if their existence were evidence of the final goodness of the world.

One afternoon Henry ran across a small clutch of eggs, lopsided and brown, and knelt and watched them with no thought in his head until a fat, spotty toad came and took them one by one carefully into its mouth. As Henry watched the brood mother hobbled back into a mucky space and submerged itself down to its eyes, watching him with implacable mistrust.

He felt the impulse to catalogue, the drive—a drive that, even as he felt it, he recognized was somehow essentially European—to draw lists and descriptions for all of these novelties. But the impulse was checked by an absence of words. He had no terminology with which to comprehend the life of the island, he could attach to it no ordering series. Merely *colored hopping bug* or *like-a-tiny-dog* did nothing; the terms were immediately vacant. For a while he tried anyway, to see if repeated use would lend authenticity. The gray-headed fox was *graybob*, the snake that propelled itself rapidly sideways was a *scurry*. In an improvisatory mood he tried gibberish words like *meeblebox* and *splee*, but the gibberish had no other mind to reflect it, to laugh it down; and after each try there came the terrifying absoluteness of the word, its utter willingness to be real. The actual item—the green shoot, rising into a knot of whorled amber leaves—caviled not at all to be *spindleleaf* or *cuts-my-foot* or *spikyplant.* In a sudden vortex of feeling he realized that nothing had ever been named, not truly *named.* The world was not ordered, only play-ordered, and in a dizzying moment the things around him seemed to blend and discompose themselves until the very walls between objects shimmered and deliquesced.

In Whitepaul's cabin Henry had spied once a small shelf of books. The captain's room was tightly packed, flanked on one side by the leaded windows and on the other a suspending device that could hold out a vertical chart. There was a framed painting of the Queen with a slash mark across it; a series of stout paper boxes; an enormous flag, coal-black, in the center of which a corpse drank skulls from an hourglass. In the contents of the boxes Henry had never been able to discover a pattern. Hemp shoes rested by brass speaking trumpets, ends for spare lines, a Chinese letter opener, a jagging wheel. In one foot-long crate with crumpled cloth lining lay a dozen clay soldiers, children's toys, painted like dragoons. There was a packrat feeling to the whole, a sense of the complexities of a man's life not having been worked through but simply held on to, even hammered into place.

Facing this hodgepodge the books formed an uninteresting shelf, but when Henry discovered them it was as if he had struck treasure. The captain was not present one evening and, creeping fast, Henry dared to slide out a volume and crack its leathery spine. It was either by, or about, a twelfth-century friar named Bacon and his design for a floating copper sphere. Henry scanned quickly the pages where illustrations of liquid fire had been colored by brush. The corners were glossy where the thumb rests, as if by the captain's repeated and meditative stroking.

He returned the volume and his crime had gone unnoticed, but the mystery of the books had stayed in him. Their presence on a ship where space of any kind was at a premium suggested that words had once been important to Whitepaul, while at the same time their present neglect told him that whatever relation there had been between him and the intellect had long since foundered on unknown shoals.

Perhaps the man only kept the few titles as a bluff to have present in negotiation. Not every assault the *Arrogante* made was marked by violence; sometimes the opposing vessel would quickly drop colors and her captain come across to negotiate terms, speaking almost casually over his scented kerchief of bills of lading and underwriters at Lloyd's of London. In this way Henry had seen that even so radical a thing as privateering was part of some larger economic coherence, Whitepaul's violence not so much spilling lifeblood as channeling it through a dozen locations, seen and unseen. On the next chance he got, Henry stole one of the books.

He kept the small object hidden under his shirt and had lived in a steady pulse of anxiety until the first night watch was rung. Then he rose midway into the rigging and, when he was certain he was unobserved, unearthed it.

It was *A Catalogue of all the Playes Printed for Henry Herringman. By the Duke of Neweaskle.* After this initial information a water stain marred the text and Henry found, to his sadness, that beyond the discoloration was merely a list. And yet the presence of any words, after so long an absence, thrilled him. His heart quickened, he felt an almost erotic fixation as he moved a wax lump candle slowly down the oversize page and the ship listed monotonously into twilight:

Henry the fifth, by the Earl of Orrey.

Mustapha, Black Prince.

By Sir William D'avenant. Albovine K. of Lombardy. The cruwl brother. News from Plimouth. The Distresses.

By Mr. Wicherly. The Dancing Master. Mock-Astrologer. Tymon of Athens, altered by him. The Humorists.

By madame Phillips. Pompey.

By Mr. Killegrew. Tomasso, or the Wanderer. *Two parts. Bellamira's dream. The Prisoners.*

In the back end, part of a mini-volume had been affixed to the same spine with string. Cautiously Henry tipped the pages of this smaller text, revealing *The History of Lentulus:*

When I received the Emperor's Orders to march a second time against the Getes, *and reduce them to their Obedience, he considered this Expedition, as a Work of only some few Months; and I assure you, I myself thought it was not of that importance, as the sequel declared it. I was acquainted with the manner of fighting, the military Laws and Stratagems of that People: This experience gave me great advantage over them. Their Revolt was yet so young, and so newly crept out of the shell of Sedition, that it wanted growth and age to establish it with firmity: and the Troops, which were committed to my conduct, were all of choice and select men.*

Henry was bowed, awed. The words had little sense for him, but he felt their torrent, like a swift-carrying music. He loved them for reaching out to him, here, in the extremity of his imprisonment; loved the rich ornamented feel and sound of them in his head. He could feel the words moving in his mouth and across his tongue, he could hear them as if falling through the silent air.

in the meanwhile the almost inexpugnable obstinacy of this Nation, gave me more trouble and laborious exercise, than I could have imagined: and prolonged a War for two whole years, which I hop'd to have concluded in less than one Campagne. This repugnance provoked me to those acts of severity, of which you have been informed, to which my ordinary temper is naturally loath.

The second book he stole was *The Unfortunate Heroes; or, The Illustrious Exiles*, of which only a page remained. After that was *The Loves of Great Men: Socrates* and *A Journal of the Travels of Several Persons*. Each time he was driven back with greater passion, feeling cheated when the object of his thieving was written in Church Latin, or was moth eaten, or was, once, a series of wordless illustrations of hands stopping frets on a lute. When finally he was able to abscond with the largest book, *recto-verso* with Italian and English, he tasted copper, his mind numbed under the danger. But a wildness for reading was in him.

But to return now to Sarsi, *it is his claim that I supply him with arguments to prove the rough concavity of the Sky, because I myself claim the moon and the other planets (understand that they be also bodies, albeit heaven'y) have surfaces that are mountainous, irregular passing rough; And if this be true, why then may not one say that such rude Irregularity may not be found in the body, that is, the dome, of the Heavens? Here* Sarsi *himself may indeed take as reply what he would say to one who sought to prove to him that the sea was full of bones …*

"You steal from the captain's library," came a voice. Henry was drawing up seawater in canvas buckets; the holystone they were using to scrape the decks was attached to long ropes fore and aft and needed to be constantly wetted. "Do I find that you have the gift of letters as well?"

Hooker eyed Henry with a grin, sliding up a deck stool. He had been a learned man in his life before *Arrogante*, a paid tutor who had fled Oxford for having made pregnant a magistrate's twin daughters while "teaching them both the French tongue."

"I am sure, sir, that I don't …"

"Do you know what we are, lad?" Hooker sparkled, waving aside the lie. With a quick finger he grabbed at the manuscript pressed between Henry's belly and shirt but his bearing showed he would not reveal the transgression—that he had, in fact, become more interested in Henry because of it. "We are *Pyratae*. Say it."

The snow-headed man pronounced the word *pee-rah-tie*, plucking the last syllable with a theatrical lilt. "We are followers of an old Greek Queen. Hers were the first bands to take fire to sea, and use it, lobbing torches into other men's sails. Our trade is twice a thousand years long.

"But Whitepaul is older still. Whitepaul is *Viking*. You have some history, too, in that blond brain of yours? Go spy on the captain's Articles, next time you are about your thieving. *Quirinius Nicolai Whitepaul*." Hooker wrote it on his leg. "*Nicolai*. That's Russian. You know about the Russian?"

Henry did not.

"The Russian's what's survived of the Norseman, lad. The Rover made his way past our own little island, crossed the North Sea, the Baltic, and on into rivers.

"Into Asia he went, scouring the land. The people there lived in stone huts, and the Norseman tumbled their huts. The people there spoke a language he didn't reckon, and he cut it out of their throats. The Viking was your Alexander reborn. He never had his bellyful of loot or of killing. Now who does that bring to mind?"

The scholar splashed his goodnatured face from the bucket.

Henry watched both their reflections reform in its trembling disk.

"*Nicolai.* When the Rover had sailed far as he could, he left the women full of his sons and daughters. He gave them their evil red hair. That's Viking hair Whitepaul has—he's a red man, a blood man, tip to end. You've seen the scar?" He grinned. "They say his own mother tried to cut out his heart in the crib. But he was born that way; it's the marking of a warrior. On the day the man first drew breath, the ancestors reached down and claimed him their own. Now when our Whitepaul sweats at a fight, Eric Red sweats for him. Thor, Odin, they cry him on. No centuries can change what he is."

Hooker took from his breast pocket a dry end of cigar and, pausing to move aside his wet lip hair, sucked it with genuine amusement.

"Who are the great men of our day, Roojman? Not William Orange and this fellow *Le Roi Soleil* and your Peter the Great. Bah! The *pyratae*. Captain Searles. Captain Ranson. Whitepaul himself. These are the modern Vikings. These are the makers of the New World."

Henry had returned the text safely and nothing had come of it. Yet for weeks afterward always in the background of his mind the *sea was full of bones*: lame but lingering wreckage. He sought to clean his thoughts of the unfinished sentence, yet the attempt led only to more fascination. Hooker's diversion had solidified the random line inside him into something elliptical, harrying. He saw in the very markings of the typeface on the paper an image of a tumbled sea floor, the lowest portion of an abyss, with along it the scattered bodies of men and animals. He saw fragments and piles: the ribcages of horses that were driven from downing ships; the bodies of livestock, flung to lighten the ballast; the bones of men, their final grips empty of sheets and their skulls of ambition. He saw the collection as a whole sinking into the dark, into the blocky tumbled bottom where the typeface lay, changing slowly to whitened coral. But the coral contained within itself the power of the horses and the leviathans and the men, the power of the words, to reanimate them, their lives metamorphosed once again by the great oceanic will.

Now, on the island, that same mystery of words haunted him fresh, in this region where the meaning of things blew hopelessly about like loosed spirits. For all the terrors with which it had whelmed him, for all the radical instability of his course there, *Arrogante* had given him grounding. His place on its bows was the place of one who suffers, but in the suffering he knew himself, knew the undeviating lines of his existence. To be *Roojman* had been something. The experience had been an injustice, but it had not been the threat of immateriality that now filled his view.

The island, like most he had seen all along the Spanish Main, was generally flat. A sharp hill rose over one end of the World, though, the first in a series of increasing rises. It emerged unexpectedly from the foliage and terminated in a white rock face, exposed baskingly to the sun. Henry hiked up the nearest rise and found a resting place there, clear of scrub. From here he could see the ocean glittering on two sides, and the island itself took shape as a distinct mass with specific, contoured edges.

The experience of rising above the land was reassuring and he rested there, muscles twitching, with a sense of command. The hillside replicated in a small way the feeling of riding aloft on *Arrogante*, of a world perceived to the offing. He felt the energy of height, an expansion of awareness, as if his soul too were filling with air. Crouched on *Arrogante*'s masthead he had witnessed once or twice strange phenomena of the sea, flashes of green at sunset or luminous ovals that flickered and danced above the clouds. Such things had come to be associated in his mind with height, so that the superstitious part of him felt being raised up allowed transcendent powers of sight, as if proximity to the heavens changed one's ability to perceive their devices.

Henry stretched, taking the cooler air. The sailors too had spoken of "tricks": of figures made of lightning that walked across decks, waving long, inhuman hands; of whole ships that appeared in the sky, birds passing under their keels; of watches in the dead of night where the shadows of men who had been drowned in buckets, or beheaded, or sent to the gibbet, were seen to pass along cabin walls where they stayed. Hooker himself spoke of an entire island that had sunk under the waves in Plato's time, and how philosophers believed it possible that the people on it had become fish-men and still went about living their lives as before, carrying baskets to market and marrying each other and mending a cart wheel, all concealed in the black salt of the sea.

During such times Captain Whitepaul was mentioned as well, in a lower tone, as if the speaker were in danger of invoking a devil. The man was a privateer in the Queen's wars who had gone rogue; a descendant of the family of *Whitchapel* or *Witchchapel* who had once been a hero, and an artist, but whose patroness had betrayed him, turning his mind. In other tales he was no man at all. It was said how the infant that would be Whitepaul had been found on the Isle of Man harbors on the morning after a storm of such ferocity that it toppled boarding houses all along the quays and had driven a lighthouse keeper who witnessed it mad. That the unclaimed babe had been taken to an outpost of Catholic nuns who practiced their weird rites of chastisement when the cratered moon rose orange among the waves. In still another he had been discovered in his crib, cooing and sucking the end of a crab leg, down in the stateroom of a gunship that had grounded on a sandbar in perfect calm and when the pilot men reached it they found the decks everywhere splashed with blood. Not a soul onboard but had taken his life, with yard-long butcher's knives, with ropes slung around cabin beams, with smashed bits of crockery turned to killing edges. In the room where the child captain lay peacefully dawdling was a woman who had opened her throat with gardening shears so that the wedding dress she still wore was half an explosion of crimson. Her dead eyes were fixed on the babe, frozen into stones, and could never be closed.

Now from this high stand of rocks Henry felt those magical possibilities again, *tricks* and tales, horrors and wonder—as if he were riding the thin blowy air, not imprisoned in his life but riding above it, away with it. The wind was a light wind from the east, unsteady and changeable. The island stretched green and brown on all sides. And the oracular possibilities of ocean were around him again, ocean that could produce anything, give rise to anything.

He was with her often now. The outer landscape of the island was of a part with his gradually dawning inner landscape and he went to it alone, sensing the need to discover. Then her image would come to him, not a picture so much as a feeling of her, and he would sit fascinated at the memory of everything they had done—repeating moments as he took them from the collection in his mind like trinkets from a special trove. When they were in the World together Henry was embarrassed at the intensity of his own fascination. He wanted to be near her always, yet he did not dare. She was Ais but she was People, and he was white, foreign, his presence in their lives accidental. Still the People knew he was with her; they knew and they did not know. Publicly they did not know, but privately he could sense the shift in speech and intonation when he was around, when Speaking Owl and he were in the same place, the same room, engaged in similar tasks. And he understood that the change had been witnessed.

Then, breaking away from the World, he kissed her freely. There, in the woods, he could stand where his soul wanted to stand, next to her soul; he could give free reign to the energy in his blood and not labor to look away or to seem as if he were not feeling and hearing and sensing her there, nearby his soul. She kissed him and he felt the smooth foreignness of her body, the skin hot and smooth under his fingers and the dress fabric brittle and dry. He tasted her fingers and her jaw and the salt-tasting muscle of her neck.

She took him farther to the island's interior, far enough that he began to worry, wishing he had a weapon of some kind. But the thought was hateful to him. He wanted nothing when he was with her that could cut, that could wound. She spoke to him more rapidly in her own language, as if the intimacy of their bodies had brought with it a presumed linguistic intimacy as well. Henry struggled to follow her gesturing hands, to find the meaning inside her sounds. But he failed; he was a fool and he did not understand.

"I don't know what you want," Henry said, grabbing at her wrists. "Owl, stop. What are you trying to say? What do you want me to do?"

But she would not answer him when he spoke with anger, and when she left him he was sorry, he felt a terrible pain. Somehow when she looked at him he had the right to be angry, but when he drove her away with his anger he immediately had no anger any more but only a dull kind of grief. When she left he was a key worn down on all its edges.

Other times he allowed her to speak, not understanding but simply allowing himself to be in the presence of her mouth-sounds, and being comforted by them merely for what they were. He began to speak to her in the same way, making no effort to be literal, word for word, and he saw in her comfort and in how she drew more closely to his side that this was what she had wanted. She did not want exact speech, exact meanings; she wanted the company of his human voice, the envelopment in each other that only sound could achieve. Then they spent entire afternoons like this, climbing and hiking the island and lost in their personal talk.

The People, for reasons Henry did not understand, did not bring their stream-catch back to the communal area, leaving it instead at prearranged locations. Others went out and retrieved the prizes while the stream fishers themselves returned later, visibly empty-handed, as if avoiding the guilt of a necessary crime. The stream fish were white and long, different from sea fish, and were held while they waited their reaping in a partially submerged basket. Smaller kinds turned slowly in the trapped recesses between boulders but the People did not disturb these. Only those captured by the fishers and deposited in the holding places were taken.

The process seemed so unnecessarily complicated that Henry laughed. And stopped: it was the first time that sound had emerged from him, the first time since his abduction he had laughed in response to the senseless. Speaking Owl spun toward him, bright. She put her fingers to his grin and made a drawing motion.

"You want me to laugh again? *Ha ha*," Henry said, into the small scented palm. "Ha ha. Ha ha."

Then he laughed truly and he could see her evenly set teeth; she was laughing as well. He put his hand to her lips and she laughed into his hand. The laugh in his fingers felt like his own laugh.

"I don't know, Owl," Henry sighed, kissing the skin, kissing the inside of her elbow and her arm. "I just don't know why this life is mine."

He searched his mind for something to say to her that was sound, to tell her of his life without telling stories of his life. He sought out a memory that was only noise-memory.

He remembered his mother's voice, how she hummed while he was seated in the tea room like a little academic with his reader. On Friday mornings and Sundays she sang to him psalmody. More lovely, though, was how she hummed as she worked wholemeal with her fingers, or arranged napkins into tents, readying the house for guests. Her voice was an affirming presence, the sound of wellness.

He remembered the sound of an empty red oak by the local river, in winter; how he had stood in front of it with a crowd of other boys after ice skating, its frozen edges clicking and speaking. He remembered the clapping sound of rain just beginning to fall on the neighbors' cut gardens. He remembered the music his cousins in London had played with him, he unsteady on the viol and his aunt so accustomed to clavier that without stopping she could tell her children who were working their instruments to highlight this passage, highlight that one, *now forte, now withdraw*. Her hands strayed over and found little bits of melody even when she was conversing, as if instrument and speech were one. He imagined her voice now singing, now speaking, her fingers now playing, now lilting in the air.

"*The water waxeth clear*," Henry said. "The water…*the fishes draw her near.*"

Speaking Owl was watching. Henry closed his ears to the meaning and listened to the syllables the way she would listen, listened only to their roundness, their coolness or warmth, only to the tenor of his own voice.

The water waxeth clear
The fishes draw her near.
The sirens sing her praise
Sweet flowers perfume her ways.
And Neptune, glad and fain,
Yields up to her his reign.

When the hot sun had descended among the trees they came out of the woods once more and stood at the gate to the World. Henry stopped and held Speaking Owl's sides and leaned back a little against the weight of her. He wanted to see her well, to include her once more in the catalogue of his mind, so that stepping back into the little village and the awkwardness there he would not be separate from her.

Tied Sticks was coming through the gate with a bundle underneath one arm. When the native man saw Henry he made a kind of cry and, flinging the wood in Henry's direction, charged forward and punched him in the mouth.

There was noise of shouting. Henry found himself in the man's grip, trying to turn his face away. His breath was blocked; the air he could get in was immediately hot and whistling. The older man was not striking him but trying to straddle him like a horse, holding fiercely to Henry's hair and pushing his face into the ground. Henry flailed but his fingers only scratched bare scalp; when the man let him breathe he opened his mouth wide and Tied Sticks forced a fistful of sand into it. Henry twisted free and fell and the native man leaped away, kicking him once quickly in the stomach.

Henry coughed and spat on his knees; some of the dry stuff had actually gone down his throat. Tied Sticks began shouting for others. He did an absurd little dance among the men who gathered, slapping his hands together and laughing. The others did not seem to know how they wanted to respond. They were not laughing but as Tied Sticks shouted close to their faces they nodded a little and smiled until he moved on to the next one. Henry straightened.

Kill him, a voice said. It was quiet, personal. *The point goes under the breastbone. Up to find the heart.*

Very slowly Henry looked at the dancing man's ribcage. He could see the soft tissue in front, the place of entry.

A thin dirk. Your dagger.

The voice, whispering now.

I showed you how.

Tied Sticks stopped dancing and, angered at the lack of response, stood glaring at Henry. His cheeks burned with live blood.

Henry examined the ground carefully in front of him. A small stick was there, its end broken into an edge.

Suitable. Oiyay.

Instead he looked for Speaking Owl, saw her watching. She was looking not at his shame, not at the physical hurt, but at the change, at the slow voice that had emerged in his head. Henry pulled his legs up and sat in the dust.

"All right," he said, not looking. "He wins."

The others stood by, neither condemning nor accepting. Henry's teeth bit terrible grit.

"He wins."

Tied Sticks spat on Henry's shoulder. He hollered something at full bellow, the laughter that had been in him revealed now as nothing like laughter, as an overwhelming fury that rocked his lean, solid frame. The veins stood large across his skull.

Henry looked up at the man's face. Twice Tied Sticks made a motion to kick at him and when Henry flinched but did not oppose he shouted something almost insanely at Speaking Owl and went off. Henry stayed seated where he was, not cleaning away the ridiculous spittle until the other men had left. Speaking Owl crouched down next to him and began stroking his face, looking above his eyes. For a moment Henry thought she was peering directly into his spirit and then she reached out and touched a forehead cut and showed him her fingers. Henry looked at the terrible red and even after she wiped her fingers off in the dust he remained looking at it, like something inescapable, like a marker on the earth.

Part Four: Moon Dancer

Whoever possesses God in their being, has him in a divine manner, and he shines out to them in all things; for them all things taste of God and in all things it is God's image that they see.

—Meister Eckhart

14

Though from land the impression given by the ocean is one of unlimited excess, the reality is far more humble. Scientifically understood, the distance a man of average height can make out standing at the water's edge measures fewer than five nautical miles. At the five-mile radius, the bending sea has already vanished—ships that recede on it dropping away so that the last thing seen of them is the long flags lapping from their spires. From European ports, every vessel bound west is eternally sinking, as if dragged down to a Protean hold to be released again only upon its return.

Five miles out, by the same measure, no land mass is discernable from deck. Any craft there exist in a world in no way differentiated from that same trackless water that will have greeted their course from the time they last heard the cannon at Lisbon or Cadiz. To the eye located onboard such a vessel, the five-mile-mark signals not the moment at which they descended, but when the stone wharfworks and dock fires of Cadiz or Aarhus or Gothenburg did. Each sees the other performing absurdities: hulls dropping and returning, entire port towns emerging, land masses once swept under waves now rising, refleshed, made whole.

At the smaller beach King George Skanondo raised the swim bladder that he had taken from a yellow fish and breathed gently into it, striving to form a pocket of air. The open end was sticky against his mouth, like an unpleasant kiss. Such little fleshy ovals, when dried, made excellent ornaments; he wore three already bound to his left ear, and though the attachment of a new object in general was meant to suggest some achievement or change in life, there was a vanity in him as well that loved simple decoration.

The creature he had caught with a thin long spear, standing still in ten inches of water until his feet were no longer threatening and then, when the wide yellow fish came ambling by, slipping the point down into the spine just behind the gills. When he killed fish and used them this way, for ornament, he thought of the story his father had told them when King George himself was a child. His oldest brother had been almost a man and the youngest one almost a baby. What he, King George, had looked like at that time he did not know, as he was not able to see himself. It was a story of a fish that squirmed on the end of the pointed staff, and when the man in the story lifted the fish out (King George had always imagined the man was his father, though the man in the story had a name which he had now forgotten) the fish spoke to him, saying *spare my life and I will foretell you of the future.* And the man, thinking he would make himself powerful by knowing the future, slid the point backward out of the gills, but the fish looked serious and added *but do you want to know the future* and the man said yes, you promised, and the fish said *but do you want to know the future*, and the man said yes, and the third time the fish said *but do you* the man held it up to his ear impatiently and shook it and it whispered to him that even then an oyster it knew was growing the pearl that the man's newborn son would one day swallow and choke on: that his wife would die of grief when she found the boy: and that the line of his progeny would end there.

Do you understand this story? their father had asked. King George Skanondo's older brother had nodded gravely and when the old man turned to him King George said indeed he did. And now, how many years later? for this reason he never looked to see if any fish he struck at were trying to speak. Who needed them when all they had was bad news?

In their chickee Ten-point and his wife had been arguing. She was like that: clouds, sun, clouds. She promised him she would not talk to the Spaniard at the mealtimes any more, or at least not laugh, at least not when he was speaking, and above all no more ribald stories. Only she smiled when she promised these things, remembering one especially delicious tale about him and the embarrassing thing he said in his sleep or sometimes during sex when his guard was down and he…and he…but it was too rich, she had started to giggle already. Ten-point's anger rose up inside him and then somehow it was replaced with hilarity and they both laughed, the kind of laughter that had attracted them as children and which had been the path of their love all their lives. Ten-point knew that his chance for playing the disciplinarian was passed, to try it now would be ridiculous. And inside he was even relieved. Let her tell, let her tell them all. Let him be the point of every joke: why did he care? She tutted, now that he had forgiven her: he was such a dignified man, she said, he had a deep dignity in him that her always-joking could never touch. And the surface he put on, that was all pride and look-at-me and it was just her nature to poke fun at it. But she was sorry. She wouldn't tell anyone about the jellyfish that his brothers had one day hidden in his…or the time he was trying to pee quickly in the water when a sudden wind came up…or the secret, special name he asked her to call him whenever they… but it was too much. She was giggling again.

What am I to do with such a wife? Ten-point shook his head.

In between her happy tears Wife of Ten-point began arranging the leafwork walls, which could be closed off for some privacy. Why was she closing the two of them up inside their home in the middle of this hot day? Ten-point laughingly asked, as if he did not know. Wife of Ten-Point tied the last wall in place, turning around with her shining face and beginning to unwrap her dress. Whispering that name.

On the opposite end of the village from the gate was an open flat pen that had once been a prospective garden, but which the gardener, a man with no talent for the thing whose name no one remembered, had, after clearing and flattening three times as much earth as he needed and proudly claiming that he would grow delicious melons for everyone, failed utterly to do that and moved in instead with his sister's family, almost as if to get away physically from the shame of the thing. Now the blank level space was untenanted and a perfect location for crab races. A small cadre of children was engaged in this task, having come in from swimming in which there had been a debate as to who could hold his breath the longest, that competition being won not by the dark-eyed boy with heavy brows but by another, younger child who came up with a nosebleed, hollering and dramatic. The crabs they had were witless, hostile things, and could only be gotten to move with repeated prodding from sticks. Once in motion, however, they leaped up like startled lizards and covered ten or twenty paces at a dash, the big claw arm held defensively high. This afternoon's race had been slow in beginning. One crab, missing an eye and poked almost to the point of tipping over, refused to oblige its harassers; and when its white shell did indeed tip entirely the startled legs began flailing in all directions and the dark-eyed boy received such a pinch that he ran to where his mother was, presenting her with the enormous suspiration of his woes.

There, she said, there. Hurts me, he bellowed, all sadness (the skin was unbroken). There, she said, touching his arm and his hair. Here play with me. What shall we? But that was no good: who wanted to play with his mother when there were races? But realizing now that he hadn't even a bruise to show from the pinch embarrassment came to him and he found he could never return to the abandoned garden where all joy that might be known to exist was now concentrated in his absence. The boy stood in the chickee door and his mother looked at his little round head from behind, the strong natural neck, and love kicked at her. She heard the sounds of the other boys racing crabs, having forgotten her son the moment he left them. She felt his new pain eclipsing the small insult of the pinch. How sensitive he was to everything around him! How he fought against himself, wanting everything, then allowing himself nothing!

She said other soothing tones but the boy heard none. His sadness had spent itself in the quick way of children and he began walking around the chickee in the manner he had taken to of late, whistling mysterious sounds between his teeth and imitating with his hands the drawing of a bow across strings.

At his hut on the western edge of the World Fray Juan de Daylaylo was weaving. The bowls he used for food he had been ruined by mold and now something would have to be constructed to hold his bread. It was a small matter: he had no compunction with learning a new skill, and in his adopted environment any craft was of value. Yet though he feigned attention to the woven bowl, his mind was on the color *azure.* Now he had three colors, which the women had showed him how to make, and the brightness of the hues he was able to produce was increasing with every batch. The bowl, when he had woven it tightly, he intended to dye a deep, royal shade.

A year after coming to the World he had built his own hut, not following the pattern of the People's huts. It came down in a wind storm. The second one he built not high enough and the floor washed out, though the walls remained standing. The third he built following exactly, step for step and moment by moment, the methods of the People, and it stayed. In joy he had wetted with simple egg-dye a series of cloths which he then hung on the walls, trying to imitate the draping effect of the archways at the Toledo cathedral with its wondrous *Spoliation*. It was not a success aesthetically but his heart had been proud. Looking at the colorful hangings of his brownish green house he had loved his life and everything he had made of it.

At first when he had come to the interior he had been deeply afraid of meeting Indians, those same people whom he had vowed spiritually to aid. He realized then he had only imagined them in the context of a friary—as souls to be shriven, grateful bodies he could touch and cure. Afterward, missionless and outside any context, true Indians were a terror. Every story of cannibalism and blood rites came darkly from his memory, as if they had lurked there always, waiting for an unprotected hour to begin their recitation. Indians squaws mated with dark things of the forest, their holy men presiding over the unions. White skin drove them to a frenzy; they filed their teeth, which they used to grab hold of objects and carry them. Clearings near Indian villages had been found in which human intestines, bloody and blue, had been carefully laid out yard after yard in the shape of a Masonic star.

Yet in the coastal forests he met only Europeans. The people he came to stay with in time were wanderers: refugees from ships, from trade, from militaries. Pockets of unlikely Danes and Welsh and Portuguese were living in the backwoods everywhere, little enclaves of people, new members coming and going without introduction or interrogation. Sometimes a whole community he had been with would disperse, as if at an unspoken signal. He would wake to a still-smoking fire, companions gone, the trees around him wet with rain. Once the general nature of these groups was understood he knew where to look for others, what markers to follow, and gradually he made his way down the coastline, an itinerant member of societies that didn't even exist.

Like his hunger, his fear did not last. He found ways of assuaging both. However temporary their bonds, the people he found worked together almost always, feeling the instinct of solid community in conditions as transient as words written on a beach. There was a life *in general* that was found among them, life that asserted itself once society was removed. They wanted food, company, the smells and the sounds of other human beings. They weren't interested in creed or nation. No one knew him to be well-born, a linguist and a scholar, a Franciscan who had outraged expectation by leaving the family guild. There were times when he wondered whether anyone would have cared. And then, after some months of southward travel, he stopped *being* these things.

It had taken him a while to understand the change. He was no longer a Daylaylo. He was not of Toledo. He was not accomplished, nor saintly for what he had given up, nor even a man...finally, not any thing at all. He was just living, breathing the air, heating stew over a fire, wiping the pot afterward with a cloth.

His facility with languages allowed him to listen, and he began to hear stories of the Indians, different from the stories he had heard in Ávila and Madrid. The Alabama, when they found their local group numbering over a certain limit, broke off to live in separate areas, regarding each new band after one year as strangers. They could ride horses standing. Their name meant *broken trails*, and glass beads would persuade them. Right or wrong, the *irrelevance* of this kind of information fascinated him. Never had he heard tribes depicted in wholly neutral terms, even tedious ones—how they slept, how they bartered, how they managed their days.

Yet Indians were never a part of the communities he joined. He had seen Dutch men eating with Swedes, eating from the same flat pilot's bread and touching hands even as they passed the bread. He saw a young English woman binding the leg of a racially nondescript Mexico City man, the Mexico City man pantless and the woman salving his sweaty leg with an ointment and her husband sitting nearby smoking and not even watching her touch another man like that. Yet for all this, the Indians were excluded. They remained different, their lives circumscribed and avoided by these mendicant people, people surviving on the same land, people arranging themselves around the same problems.

One morning Daylaylo awoke and found he was free, overwhelmingly free. He rose from the thinly buried coals over which he had slept and made his way through the impromptu tents and walked out into the woods, he did not know toward what; only that he was going in the direction of his novelty. By afternoon he remembered the people he had spent three weeks living among, the woman nursing a child through a torn slit in an Acadian trappers' coat, the blacksmith who stared at the evening fire the way carpenters stare at unused wood. He had forgotten them in his freedom, as the nine lepers forgot Christ, and he understood then why the groups through which he was traveling were capable of vanishing entirely in an hour. And he knew something too about where they had gone.

In Madrid he had discussed with the oldest brethren, the ones who had been in Ocone and Ibihica, the idea of faith. They spoke of trusting in the divinity behind all waste, all disorder. He had known before they sailed that riders on Catholic ships were hanged if they touched ground in wrong parts of Nova Spain, that religious conflict in Europe had not been escaped but merely exported. He had thought himself brave, thought he understood danger and was offering himself to it. But the greater concern among almost all the superiors, even among the retired, had been the danger of failing their *trust*—of failing in their belief, during starvation or satiety, that ultimate meaninglessness was not the nature of man's existence.

Along the expanding coastline where he now walked he stopped noticing the desire for that trust. When he was hungry, he was simply hungry. Building his own campfire that evening, the flames stirred by a salt-filled wind, he understood. God wasn't hungry in him. When he cut wedges from seabiscuit and chewed it that was him eating biscuit: God didn't eat biscuit in him. The next morning when the sun erupted cloudless above the level horizon he rose and cracked his sore spine and pissed in the leaves, and it was his piss and his leaves. He rubbed clean his eyes, almost laughing.

The first Indians he saw were on the southern tip of the continent. He ran across some kind of hunting party by accident and stayed with it for several days, on a nearby hill, within view. When they went out in the mornings he hiked down to the place where they had camped and, making a little mound, stuck his crucifix in it. At first they left the symbol untouched, the band of People moving on, Daylaylo following. The second time he made the same gesture someone left a trinket in the dirt, whose meaning he did not know, but which he had felt served to make contact. The third time they left him food. After that he had joined them, ridden in their canoes down to the island where they lived and become *Man-in-tree*, the name given for the little symbol with which he announced himself. The name which the People, he later came to understand, had taken as a kind of self portrait: and which, later still, he found they had taken to represent a wizard bound inside a trunk, stretching his arms and bursting from imprisonment.

15

Five miles over the Straits, and thus beyond the curve of the world, the air was growing cold. In the pillared space between clouds small jewels of snow coalesced, wafting toward the blowing waves. Following the sun-driven course of things, the frigid air masses dropped down to replace their warmer neighbors, lifting tables of rapidly condensing vapor over and again like Diana hoisting a sooty Vulcan. Darkness spread on the face of the sea.

On his promontory the boy felt the change. Around him white grasses, bleached and thin, were beginning to sway. His eye observed the distant sky; he opened his mouth, tasting at the changing air. When the first cool gust blew against his exposed chest he began running.

His legs were fit and strong. The breeches he wore had torn repeatedly until he had cut the shredded cloths away just under the knees on both sides. Under the exposed length now the musculature showed, leaping; he made the lowest level of the island and continued east, diving into a wooded area. For a little while there was silence, the slow brooding greenery resettling itself like a startled bird. Then the far edge broke open once more and flung him out, moving quickly, making his way toward the beaches.

Henry stopped where he was and looked again out to sea. He knew the unseen storm was still there, crouched over the rim of the horizon, the way escort ships did when they went hunting.

He had come to the cove where Daylaylo had lain down. Stepping gingerly over a long spill of shells he splashed out to a shallow place and knelt.

The water was cool here and higher here than it had been when the Spaniard showed him the trick of water-listening. Some shifting of balances, tides flowing into tides, had added more in the interim to this particular reach of sand. Sea water, Henry thought, was like perfect justice: not the smallest alteration could be made in one place without instant redress elsewhere, the tables precisely and democratically balanced, whether on this bit of land or some other, a thousand leagues away. He pushed himself slowly around like a raft until he found a spot where the pool was thin. He let his ears fill.

The sound this time was like struck iron, swinging heavily. For a moment he remembered the field near his father's house where he had sat at twilight listening to the gleaner's bell and the way the sound made the grass shimmer before him until his ears questioned his eyes, that they did not see.

The memory faded and Henry sought to quiet his mind, emptying it of expectation. After a time—his last mental image, for some reason, was of a clock left rusting in the sun—he no longer heard himself trying to understand.

The water-sound was clear and thin. It touched the thinness of hot sand along the edge of the pool. The water was aware of his presence: his presence had altered it, only faintly, but altered the voice of it. It sang of him now as well, his immersed body part of the singing. He could feel the strange presence of himself in the song

Henry listened beyond himself. Fish were swimming in the shallows just under this side of the reef: they made a thin sprinkle of needles, tiny perturbations. Their ripples slid under the harder mass of coral; they were searching the coral, gnawing it for food. He could hear the tiny mechanisms of their teeth, the *tip*, *tip*, *tip* of their hunger.

A wave swelled over the coral and did not crest, down-swelling again and relieving the pressure, altering by one half step the monody of sea. With its rising and passing the coral inspired, exhaled. Its tiniest recesses were breathing.

Henry listened farther. The slow pulse of waves rising and falling became his breathing. He began breathing to the slow up-pulse of waves, the down-pulse of waves. He let his breath and his heart begin to move in the breath and the heart of the waves.

He could see them, feel them now: out beyond the reefs were laughable clusters of fish, flashing bright, round and skittery. His still-Henry consciousness laughed at their number. Never when sailing above or beside one had he known how replete was a reef, how overfull with life. The waves up-swelled, down-swelled; he felt barrages of fish life rise and fall in them, as effortlessly as motes in air. His spirit drifted.

Thin limbed plants moved swayingly toward him, pink and green, beckoning him deeper. Taking him away from the shore, away from the reef, into the depths, out toward that place he had almost reached before but had pulled back from in fear. The still-Henry part of his mind felt the roar approaching and his heart was afraid. But he allowed himself to move toward it this time. He would not listen to the fear, not to the fear. He would listen to the true voice of the sea

And in a sudden rush he saw of what the roar was made: the whole black ocean was a reef, its sound a thunder of living beings. Its center was nowhere, every direction crying out with life. The deep ocean was a symphony of millions

Henry lifted his head, his fingers gripping the sand.

Something else.

He had heard something else out there. Some jarring note, breaking the symphony.

Henry lowered himself again. He could sense the storm now, clearly, feel its presence like the touch of cold glass. Miles out, he felt its crazed whip break the surface of the waves. He saw the storm, as if from below: its wind-ripples passing over the water, cold hands seeping into hot green salt. But the panicked voice he had heard was not there, not out in the deep turbulence. It was closer, much closer. It was on the island.

Henry raised himself from the pool. Raindrops large as pebbles were smacking around him now, making the surface quiver. The sky had gone the color of soot.

A human voice, Henry thought. *I heard a child.*

He rose out of the pool and stood in the downfall, peering inland. Nothing could be seen beyond the darkness of trees. Everywhere falling rain rebounded, forming a silvery haze.

Ignoring the pummel he picked his way closer to the shore line but still could make out nothing. The sound of the drops breaking leafwork was quickly becoming deafening.

Go back. Go under.

Henry stumbled back into the pool. The echoes of his intrusion bounced and fluttered.

Listen now. Let her speak.

The rain sounded like high pitched notes, confusing the great tympanum. But the rain was not sea; he willed its confusion away, separating it out.

Listen. Don't speak. Listen.

His spirit sank, sank.

There. Across the spit of trees. Not far. Not far.

He vaulted out of the water and ran, his woven sandals leaving foot marks. The tangle was too dense to push through here and to get around the tree-covered spit he had to swim, out deeply once and beyond where his feet could find ground, his heart jumping inside him. Then he was around on the other side and coming back into shallow water, rising when he found sand once more and running up onto land, up toward the child who was thrashing in the windblown surf.

The child was dark-skinned, unclothed save for a band of plaited grass that was tangled about its neck. Its kicking form stood out strangely against the milky spume that whipped off the water and up along the rooty beach. Each time the child found footing the wind threw wavewater across it again, dragging it backward in a powerful undertow. It struggled pointlessly, choked, unable even to scream.

Henry lifted the body in his arms and for a moment the child fought against him as if he himself were the force trying to drown it, an aquatic god seeking sacrifice. Almost immediately, then, the small limbs went slack; not dead, but exhausted past fighting. Henry carried the half-conscious body up into the trees and, turning the little head to clear water from the mouth and make sure it was breathing, began making his way back toward the World.

That night Henry sat with the crowd of men around the central fires. The mother—he had heard her name spoken several times but could not remember it—stalked animatedly among the group, repeating in apparently ever-growing terms what Henry understood to be the story of himself. She carried her child with her in a sack that was strung tightly around her shoulders so that her hands were free to gesticulate. The boy, on being returned to its mother, had wept furiously for twenty minutes before falling asleep.

Knowing nothing of what she said, recognizing only a handful of words—*rain, beach,* something that he had thought was *morning* but now was unsure—but understanding the tenor of her speeches Henry felt an almost ridiculous pride.

The mother came crowing toward him one and then two times and the third time she pulled up on his shoulders Henry stood automatically like a man at a formal roast. Embarrassed, he remained standing while she spoke praises to his face; and when he began to sit down again after a minute the mother took his cheeks in her warm brown hands and lifted him into a standing position once more and kissed him.

A cheer went around the fires. The mother threw her arms wide, as if extending the kiss into a banner that hung in the air.

The storm, although brief, had been windy and parts of the central roof were damaged. Several of the long lines of inner leafwork had come free and lay uselessly on the ground, the gaps they had left behind letting in burning light. When the pools from the rain had dried Henry joined the men who were lifting each other up on ropes, imitating the motion of their feet as they walked animal-like up the tall carved poles until he hung half-suspended, grasping at beams up where the damage had been done.

"This wood is rotted," Henry said to the man who swung next to him, the two of them dangling midair like angels in a stage production. "It was bad even before the storm. See here?" he pointed. "Rotten. And here."

The man answered him in word-sounds.

"Okay," Henry said. "Okay. But look here. And here."

He dug his thumbnail into the old construction, revealing its softness. "This is going to fall. Maybe not this year. But soon. It needs ..."

The native man answered back, disagreeing. He waved the demonstration away, was interested only in seeing how many rows of leaf-fill would be needed.

"Fine," Henry said. "We can do that. But even if we refill it, this wood is no good."

The holding team complained and Henry came down again to the ground, his body reorienting itself just before he landed. He wondered whether this technique had been learned somehow from European sailors running safety lines from their belts to stays when putting tar on standing rigging, or whether differing groups of men arrived eventually at the same mechanical solutions, the same compromises of likelihood and dignity that resulted in culture. For a moment Henry saw the other man, still overhead, sticking his thumb in the beam where Henry had pointed and examining what came out.

The structure he had in mind he drew out for them with a stick.

"Like a boat," Henry said to the small gathering. "Like a boat? Beams don't have to be straight up and down, the way these are now." He drew the roof as it was, imitating the half-models he had seen shipwrights draw out in sand. "This pulls here, and here, every time there's a blow. It gets weak. You see? If we make these curved…like a keel, with graving pieces…you see?"

There were discussions after dinner for several nights and then they built the thing upside down, also the way Henry had seen it being done in shipyards both in England as a boy and from the anchored stern of *Arrogante*; and then tied its keel piece with rope and hoisted it up into place where it hung like the inverted skeleton of a hull. The twins were often at his side during the work, talking to him in an undifferentiated way, evidently with no concern over whether he understood. Henry liked them both. They were thin, unassuming persons, one all smiles and his hair held out of his face with a band, the other more defensive but good hearted and wanting company. Lifted up on lines, the crew of native men crawled carefully along the ribs—the extent of the damage was clear once they had gotten the failing beams down—and tied the new keel into place. Henry thought ironically that the years away from schooling had left him with at least some material knowledge, something he could turn to positive use.

The men in return had shown him how to produce a kind of sweet-smelling tar from the insides of nuts, resembling coconuts but green and each small enough to fit in the closed hand. The nuts were easily severed with a rock to reveal gummy interiors that could be pried out in little wads. These gums were collected in a pot and boiled. With this paste they covered the wood when it had been carved, making a resistant exterior that also slid easily into place and could be bound tightly without gaps. From the ground again Henry stood among the men, watching the magic ship fill itself in against the face of the sun. The men spoke without any explanation of what they were saying but he could feel the difference in their speech, he knew he was no longer being mocked by their words; and feeling himself nodding his head, nodding sagely and taking the water gourd as it was handed him equally with the others, or looking up into the now-one-quarter completed, now-half completed shape, he felt the satisfaction of working among peers.

He and Speaking Owl were able to be together. He did not know whether the roof, the missing child, the scene of violence at the gate or some other thing had been the initiation. But the World seemed to have accepted their relationship.

Still she was different than the other women, but that difference was contained in her assertive personality and had nothing to do with him. She worked energetically on the shell piles, seated herself boldly at mealtimes and rose without comment when she was finished, a gesture that made Henry grin. When she was with him, the men with whom he had been working all day spoke a little more quietly but no longer looked askance, and eventually they did not even lower their voices.

One evening she said a word to him, over and again, and laughed teasingly as she closed his eyes with her hands. Her flashes of sudden enthusiasm were among the most appealing aspects of her person. Speaking Owl could be spontaneously amused, with him or with others, and laugh easily and unselfconsciously. Other times she was impatient with him, even rude. But he did not really mind. In her rudeness too he saw the boon of a truth teller, of a woman who spoke her mind and who, if the general tide were against her, was in no way bothered by it. Several times now he had seen her keep her own in debates with women and even men. Always she was strong, driving home her claim—whatever it might have been—well beyond the point where the others, evidently defeated, had begun making deferential gestures and drawing away. At these times on her face alone, Henry thought, was no sign of discomfort, but only the unflagging knowledge of her rightness.

She placed something around his neck; she opened back up his eyes. It was a necklace made of small amber shells linked together and culminating in a dried starfish. Henry saw her smile at him, pleased with her own gift, and then rise to go about her business and he was honest enough with himself to understand that he was happy.

The boy had brought him something. It was papers, thin with water stain. A cadre of followers came with him, one girl giggling and touching at Henry's knee, evidently on a dare.

Henry looked at what they had put in his hands. The first thing was an unattached cover which he laid aside. The second was a manuscript on which had once been an owner's name. Henry opened carefully the flaps: three pages of sheet, taken from the middle of something larger. He looked at the markings, running his fingers over the bars.

"This is lute music," Henry said, remembering then who this boy was. "It's not written for this."

The boy made an expression, fiercely sawing the air with one arm. Some of the other children followed suit. There was laughter, open eyes, the curiosity and the wanting. Someone gave him the viola, little hands tapping at its sound hole as it passed from child to child as if to grab its incantatory power.

"All right," Henry said. "All right."

He lifted the body to his chin and bowed the E, recoiling before the grating cry. The children watched him amazedly, the insistent one holding open the pages now like an altar server. Looking at them Henry understood: there were little violins drawn in the corners, some filigreed vanity. Henry found a clear space on one of the strings and played something, a line from Purcell, emerging in its basic form from a deep pocket of his memory. When his mind reached the end of the phrase he improvised, stopping again on a long foolish trill.

There was excitement and the boy stared at the viola and made a gesture. Henry raised it once more and repeated the trill, understanding for the first what it was he had done that gave such joy, that brought this native child who had never seen a quartet or danced a *gigue* or chanted psalmody of a Sunday that look of total, unfeigned wonder.

"Yes," Henry laughed. "It sounds like a bird doing that. Yes."

The boy's smile stayed with him that night, emerging from the dimness of his mind hours later, sitting in the hut they had now cleaned out for him with the lutenist's pages open in his hands. He listened in silence to the score, not in the mystical way of listening to the sea, but only in the human way: the run of the octave, the mark reminding the finger to release. The smile stayed with him and eventually he could hear it inside himself as well; could hear it where the music played, where the music had always been playing.

16

In the hot afternoons Henry began running on the island. He kept a stone in his right hand, the sharp end digging into the fat of his thumb. He did not intend to use it for anything, oftentimes throwing one away and picking up another. Only the feeling of the stone seemed right to him, seemed to free his feet to move and his mind to let go of what held it. Discarding any sense of compass directions he followed the course of a red-tailed hawk, its body solid and enormous when it collided with the earth once not twenty feet from where he stood, grabbing something writhing out of the grass: then small again, a dreamlike object in the sky.

After a while he removed his shirt and then after that he ran only with the grass belt and codpiece, finding the material to be light and dry on his skin so that the old English cotton seemed now a labor to wear. His hair was in his face and he stopped to knot it back.

In the first hour the bird led him to a place in which the land swooped down into a bubbling inlet. He tasted the water and spat it out: though streams and pools crisscrossed the island, he had found none of them fresh enough to drink except in the hours immediately following rain.

The pool trembled before him and suddenly a sleek body appeared inside it, causing Henry to start. It was man-sized but had the shape of a fish, and when the head broke the surface and the great round nostrils fumed air he recognized the animal: a sea cow, brown and docile, its face like a whiskered bear. The creature's back was peppered with moss and it turned gradually under the surface again, eyeing him with bland curiosity. Henry smiled broadly, then felt a sudden guilt for the number of this species they had killed and eaten onboard *Arrogante*. So simply did the huge creatures give their lives up, the sailors had only to wade into lagoons where they were basking and beat them silent. The hardest part had always been dragging the enormous bodies to a fire and skinning the tough leather and flab. As a result some men did this labor in the shallows where the carcasses bobbed and rolled, an oval of grease moving out from each one until it lapped quietly at the edges.

Stooping to the water Henry reached his hand out but the sea cow passed underneath it, unwilling to be touched. Henry felt the string of rejection. Abruptly it seemed to him that the hand he had dipped in this pool was dark with blood, staining the pure water with his human corruption. His was the hand of Cain, and the peaceful island recoiled from it.

An hour later he found the red-tailed hawk again and followed it onto higher ground. He was approaching the promontory from the far side, and the landscape here became vast, pouring walls of pebbles, mounds and shelves of polished stone. Walking through them his feet made a liquid clicking, the sensation like stepping on water and land at once.

The hawk settled in the high shag. Nearby Henry found some finger-length fruits and sat down to eat them, grinning at the absurd profusion of seeds they deposited in his mouth. The taste was surprisingly sweet, the meat thick and runny. He felt very alive.

When the bird moved once more he came to an area full of ashes and burnt stumps where lightning had done its work. There were blast marks running down the sides of mahogany trees and he put his cheek close to them, feeling the scar, feeling the hard work of regrowth. In the underbrush a white heron, thin-legged and stalky, was waiting with its eye on something, the whole body concentrated on a point.

By mid-afternoon he had made his way around in a great circle and was surprised when he came across the sea cow's pool from its opposite end. Seen from this better vantage the pool was only half of a two-part indentation, like the impress of a cloven foot. It must have underground passages, Henry reasoned, connecting it to the sea; and his mind played joyfully on images of root-filled tunnels where golden fish darted and turned, where the light shivered down between mangrove roots. Henry halted.

On the other side of the pool a figure was standing. Its head was the head of a bird, as if some creature of enormous wingspan had draped itself over a man's shoulders. As Henry watched it disappeared into the sun.

Henry crossed the far end of the rise and, finding nothing, doubled back. The figure was there again: higher up now, along the golden slope. The wings of the creature were tied around its wrists, he realized, and when it turned he could see the long tail of the bird draping down its back like a cape.

Halfway up the next hill he lost it again, and found it again, higher still: the figure always distant, turning to go, but never seen climbing. Henry was winded but exhilarated. He felt the former toughness in his torso and knees, the powerful, shimmering sensation that came with physical exertion. There was no thought in his head. He lifted himself over a low sharp bush and went up the rocks.

At the height of the cliffs Henry stopped. He was standing on a smooth, grassy shelf that hung against the white edges. He was well above the highest ridge to which he had previously climbed; without his realizing it the figure had led him in a clockwise path that mounted the peak. From here he could see the western portion of the island entirely. The World, with its rising smoke lines; the semicircle of bougainvillea-covered rock that protected it; the empty beachfront wherein he had almost starved and the second, smaller beach where the People danced, marked at one end with black smudges of fire. Henry rested.

And turned his head. The figure was there, visible once more with sunlight behind it. A man, old but thinly muscled, the body still firm. On his exposed chest were painted two butterflies.

Henry stood. The figure wore the body of the raptor across its shoulders and head, hiding the human eyes. The wings, golden brown, hung down past the elbows.

As Henry watched the man began to dance. First the motions were slow, dipping and returning. A question. The bird head watched Henry fixatedly, riding the human one as if on an updraft of wind. The dancer's arms reached out once, elevating the wings. The two of them, bird and man, began to move.

Hnnnnn, the dancer intoned, low in his hidden throat. *Nnnnn-nnnn.*

Henry felt the pulse of the sound. He gave back a single motion, a step.

Hnna-a-a-a-a-a-a, the dancer moaned, soft, introspective. The sound was nothing, in any language; simply the feel of his physical movements put into a noise. He let his hips begin to sway.

Hnnnn-aaa-aaa, the dancer sang. *Water-boy. Water-man. Spit out of the sea.*

Henry heard the words forming inside the steps, inside the motions the other man made.

Water-boy, water-man. Birthed from the sea. Horse dream freedom. Terror and tranquility.

A third presence, unannounced, had joined their clandestine union. In the still air behind the dancer a daylight moon had appeared, whisper-thin.

Water-boy, water-man. Brought by tide, taken by tide.

Yes, Henry said. *Yes I am he.*

Henry danced.

17

Legenda Aurea lay at anchor for the duration of the storm which, though the best instruments onboard had predicted a severe blow, turned out to be little more than a casual rain. The captain had not ordered the single, heavy fluke anchor be dropped but a combination of smaller bow and stern anchors instead, an arrangement which limited the swing of the vessel in a highly effective way. The *teniente*, who had assisted in loading the new bow-and-stern-anchor combination at Ribadeo, was impressed with such accomplishments as this. He was proud of Spain, and what Spain was doing. He believed in the future of mechanical devices, how they were going to advance, improving on previous knowledge in the way the compound anchorage system had improved on the traditional fluke, though the improvements he imagined would occur in every field, from agriculture and medicine to the mercantile arts to painting, until some future time when—he hardly knew how to envision it—Spain herself would become new.

The *teniente* smiled lightly as he often did at this point in his reflections. He was seated at a mess table on the second deck, where those in rank underneath the commanders but still with officer status took their meals. Outside the windows men were circling in the longboats, and the inlet sparkled brightly, as if it too had been washed by the rain.

These were pleasant thoughts, and he stirred them in with the creamy garlic soup he was enjoying. He was a man with a kind of vision, he could not name it—a picture of the future. Was it not likely that improvement would follow improvement? He had already seen, at Oviedo once, mechanical statues that moved their arms and were able to pour *café con leche* from pots. You held your cup under the statue's pot and the operator would make it work and it poured your tea, just like a living servant. He had seen a harpsichord that stayed in tune from the lowest key to the highest and a small metal hand into which you could place an egg so that when you struck the shell it broke in a convenient line. Would not the future improve on such devices? And who could say the general happiness that might attend the generations to come?

The *teniente* sipped easily his garlic from the warm bowl thinking on the future of Spain and did not think of the events at the Dutch West India Company settlements they had visited or elsewhere, or of what he had done in these places. These were of course not pleasant things to think on but then, they were engaged in a necessary task here and so there was no benefit to thinking on such actions after they had been completed; one simply went on. In general, it was best not to think of such things, which in truth was not difficult to do. Not, really, difficult at all; there were other matters to think on.

Two shiphands passed through the room and touched the badges of their hats and the *teniente* raised three fingers in mild blessing. There were pleasant men on this trip. Even the shiphands were not bad men, though one (poor fellow!) had become quite ill during the long crossing and had as a result used language unfit for his position while racked with vomiting. The *teniente* had looked the other way at this lapse in decorum. He had no time for truly bad persons, for the immoral; when one of the dockworkers under his watch had been found stealing meats from the loading area at Ribadeo he had not hesitated to reprimand the ingrate, cutting his pay immediately. But at small transgressions he could wink.

Albenix could be heard speaking to the pilot on the deck overhead and then moving away, his feet making their steady, untroubled thump, like the ticking of a clock. Always, the *teniente* thought, the *comandante* moved in that same unhurried way, measuring his steps the way a mathematician would, regardless of the task in which he was engaged. Their regularity under any circumstance was the very seal of his authority, his appropriateness in wielding the scepter, and the *teniente* bowed inwardly to this. On the floor underneath the *teniente* now the Carib made some commotion in the hold, but some keeper struck the wall and they fell quiet once more.

In the same festival in Oviedo he had seen a tall clock, the pendulum on it as long as his arm, that would keep proper time (it was said) even when carried onboard a ship. By the use of such devices it would becomes possible one day to reckon the time in Barcelona even when one was rounding the Bermooths, or indeed midway across the Atlantic; the empire would with such improvements become universal. And he was involved in such changes, which were a pleasure to think on. He was here, among the important men of his generation. He could be proud of what he did. He sipped at his meal and his fingers shook a little, causing the bowl to tremble.

He would write a letter to his sister in Gijón soon. She had always laughed at him, at his freckly face, asking if he was their father's son where he got all those dog-spots? Because their father was a smooth-skinned man. He would tell her all about the work they were doing and what he had seen on his travels, the exotic animals, the birds, and ask her whether she remembered the wonderful devices they had seen together at Oviedo. Albenix, he would say, was a good man. He had passed the *comandante*'s quarters once quite by accident and seen him at prayer, and on his cabin wall a painting of blessed Ignatius as well as the dried head of a marlin, so that for an amusing moment the *comandante* seemed to be praying to the fish and not the saint. But he was a prayerful man, the *teniente* knew, and the others were good men as well and now the rain had stopped they would be continuing their southward trek, taking advantage of the wind. How this garlic was like fire on his tongue!

There was, of course, no way to deliver the letter unless they refitted at another outpost of Friars or passed a common trader heading back eventually toward Europe, but in his mind at least he would begin the letter. He would tell his sister of the wonderful things he imagined for tomorrow, the clocks and the musical instruments and the statues that moved, and how things were going to be better; and really it was better to think of the wonderful things that might come, the statues that moved (so lifelike!) and the harpsichord in perfect tune from its lowest key to its highest, and the funny fat gentleman in silks who had sat at it and tried to play that theme from Palestrina. But sometimes the work here was hard, very hard and it was difficult to think about the things he had done, which was why he did not care to think about those things; he did not care to remember them; no, nor to discuss them any longer, no matter how she nagged him; no matter how she pushed at him to know what they were, in all their terrible details; and in a sudden anger he tore the letter he had been writing to his sister in his mind, tore it and destroyed it, spat on it, for why should he try to explain himself to this ridiculous witch who did not understand the world, who knew nothing, and who in the end was only a stupid, stupid girl.

"*Mi teniente*," the shiphand said. "You have spilled your soup."

Obsequiously the little man came forward with a cloth. The *teniente* rose to go. He examined himself in the cabin mirror, straightening his long jacket. For a moment he stood at the companionway door.

"Some day a statue will replace you," he said quietly.

"*Si, si*," the shiphand answered, his eye averted. He had never cared for the *teniente*. He wondered if perhaps the man were going mad.

18

The game was played with fat sticks of pinewood that had been knife-peeled so they were tacky to the grip. The ball itself was black and leathery, stuffed up with dry grass until it had a lopsided appearance. When found, it was rolled along quickly in a beating motion, accompanied by shouts.

The game began at sunup and lasted for days. Older men stayed behind at the village but were filled with vicarious energy; a communal excitement ran through the routine of events, from the repair of a crushed shell wall to the digging of a low cooking pit to replace the one that had been improperly sided and had fallen in with the storm. Henry was given a stick by a great hairy man and jogged along with the players when the ball was in view but did not understand the rules or purposes enough to do more than holler. When he dropped away from the action he found small clusters of players, their sticks in hand, standing and talking or stretching their backs, though apparently still in the game. Many of them were so far from the actual contest that Henry wondered what their function was.

Then the sound of whooping came across the canopy of trees and they pursued the action and Henry went with them. A cry, the signal shout, marked the location of the ball, though often the whoop came across great distance. Losing his group he ran to the edge of the trees to search the open fields for runners and when he saw them, their cheeks painted with the bright colors that symbolized the game, it was like seeing magnificent forces moving across the land.

That night he did not return to the village and slept instead in a small grotto, round and concealed, under a profusion of pinched flowers. In the late darkness he could still hear the occasional yelps of the players, stealing the ball and moving it south, stealing and moving it north. A beetle walked fumblingly across his shoulder and he did not even bother to scratch it away. Sleep was a beatitude.

In the morning Henry opened his eyes. The flower buds were

open all around the little enclosed space now and the air was rich with their scent, a wonderful tang like rum and honey. Henry blinked. A deer was standing in front of him.

It was one of the tiny species, no larger than a dog. Its fur was marked gracefully by specks of white along one flank. Not smelling him yet among the density of flowers, the animal had come so close that Henry could make out the sparkling of it nostrils, the soft breathing ribs.

For a moment the deer seemed to examine him sidelong, its body immobile and only the tail hopping from time to time. Then it made a faint rotating gesture with its mouth, and Henry saw that a long stem of chewed plant hung there. Without finishing its first meal the deer lifted its wet chin and began snuffing a clump of berries.

There was a crackling sound and as the deer perked its ears an arrow hit it clean in the flank, punching between leg bones and stopping somewhere near the heart. Henry stared in mute astonishment as the animal stumbled forward and, seeing him for the first time, looked into his eyes as if for confirmation of its experience. It lifted one hoof, set it down again, tangling itself momentarily in the vines. There was a terrible grace in its motion, as if so pure a spirit were incapable of ugliness, even *in extremis.*

When the body fell sidelong it pressed on the shaft of the arrow, driving the tip in, and the deer raised its small black mouth in an inaudible cry.

"Why do you kill them?" Henry shouted as Tied Sticks emerged stealthily from the brush. The native man dropped his bow and for a moment his whole body trembled with guilt, paralyzing and extreme. Then, seeing who it was that had witnessed his crime, his expression went baneful.

"Why do you kill them?" Henry spat out again, thrashing his way out of the gloom. "Murdering these animals…it's the worst crime… the worst your people can commit. Is that why you do it?"

The man was immobile in his exposure and Henry went and stood on one side of the fallen deer, where the white underbelly had gone tacky with sweat. The animal was still breathing, its sloped face examining pointlessly the grass a few inches from where it lay. A green fly, sensing the all-important odor of blood, began to give it attention.

"Why?"

Tied Sticks looked down at the animal's form and, for a moment, an expression of absolute terror began in his eyes.

"The others would *despise* you if they knew what you do. Even your soldiers. Your warriors. They would drive you out."

The native man stared fiercely at Henry's mouth as he spoke, as if all of Henry's person were concentrated there. All at once his face twisted into a rictus: he shouted something, a stream of hurtled words.

"I know what you think of me," Henry screamed back. "And I know you are a *liar*. Whatever you are saying to me right now, you are *lying*."

Unable to make himself understood Tied Sticks reached out and shoved Henry's panting chest.

"Lying!" Henry shouted into the other man's face, coming back. Tied Sticks' cheeks were bent upward now in a lunatic smile, as if he had been madly laughing; as if the depth of his feeling were such that it had taken on in his mind a wildly amusing cast.

"It isn't because of her. It isn't *her*," Henry hissed, terrible with his own emotion. He lifted the starfish necklace and shook it at the tattooed man, who batted it away. "You aren't jealous of me. You hate me because you're just *like* me. A castaway. Isn't that it? Isn't that it?"

Tied Sticks continued to grimace fiercely, his whole torso quivering. In a mad gesture Henry bent down and bloodied his hand on the deer's hot side, wiping the mark onto Tied Sticks' cheek before the other man could slap him away.

"Murderer!" Henry shouted. "*Murderer!*"

"Ma-*dah-dah!*"

"*Murderer!*"

"Maa-*aaa*—*daaa …!*"

From the grass Tied Sticks grabbed up the bow again and drove its point into Henry's gut. Henry let out an involuntary sound full of shame and astonishment and grabbed at the wood, Tied Sticks pulling it away once more and coming around the body of the deer.

"Murd …"

Tied Sticks jumped and Henry felt the second blow come into his chin, shoving him back into a tangle of leaves. He got one arm around the wood and twisted; Tied Sticks tried to knee him in the stomach and the knee collided with Henry's pelvic bone, causing a terrible stabbing sensation in his bladder. Kicking out Henry managed to push the man down in the dew-slicked grass but Tied Sticks rose again and swung the bow like a whip, missing his forehead but catching Henry's nose and ear. Henry thrashed backward in terror of actual violence and then they were rolling, simply hanging onto each other and rolling in the cascade of blossom pieces as if laboring to make a uniform motion out of their mutual hate.

There was a shout from outside the hollow and Henry felt the older man's body go rigid. Tied Sticks had the wood against Henry's throat and Henry slapped ridiculously a few times at him before Tied Sticks even felt the blows, thrusting Henry down and scrambling backward. He threw away the snapped instrument as if it were the mark of his guilt and looked all around the indentation, seeking an exit that would not involve crashing noisily through flower and branch. Two young players peered into the grotto.

"There's no way out except through them," Henry choked out, sitting up now and coughing helplessly. He wanted to destroy the other man, to annihilate him utterly, as if condensed in his grotesque person were the sum of all wrongs cast over Henry's existence. Tied Sticks looked back at him like a caged thing. He wiped at his cheek and saw with amazement the guilt-mark that was on him.

The two players, flushed with the energy of the game, were blinking into the shade. They spoke again and Tied Sticks went slowly to them, his expression blank. When they saw who he was the two chattered rapidly, laughing and holding up their sticks. A few steps from the opening one noticed his cheek. They were repeating a question and Tied Sticks was looking at the two of them as if he were not certain where he was.

Henry went and stood in the light. The other players reacted again when they saw the English boy, beginning to laugh but uncertain as to whether they understood. Henry inspected his teeth and, finding the rich sting of blood in them, spat on the ground. He grinned at the two men.

"*Nickaleer*," he said, gesturing at Tied Sticks.

After a moment's hesitation they grinned back, slapping Tied Sticks on the shoulder. Tied Sticks looked at Henry as if he were experiencing a dream. Then, wiping the blood away from his cheek with a wrist he laughed as well. Henry punched him hard in the breastbone and Tied Sticks made a faint gesture. He was staring at the sandy ground.

"Son of…son of *bitch*," he managed.

Henry walked back toward the grotto and looked at the deer lying hidden in the tangle, its legs spread out evenly as if it had been laid there. The green fly was walking over its pupil.

"Son of bitch!"

When Henry looked back the other players were already moving off, their sweat-marked bodies brightening again with the return to the chase. Tied Sticks turned once but Henry would not answer his gaze. Squinting into the incredible first light by the grotto's edge he wondered what the native man saw: a young foreigner, his skin absurdly white, sitting by the opening like the opening of a tomb.

19

The Caffekey died in the dark middle of the night, after kissing his nine sons and eleven daughters each in the spot over their eyes, where the spirit resided, arranging himself in his burial raiments, and lying head westward on his reed mat with moss beneath his head. The Caffekey's wife lay next to him not demonstrating sorrow of any kind, while outside the Caffekey's hut the sons and daughters of the Caffekey in a first ring and the sons and daughter by concubinage in a second and the rest of the community in a third made wails and beat on drums tied to their chests so that the playing of them was the same gesture as the striking of one's self. While he was dying the Caffekey's wife lay still and composed, saying nothing and moving not even to eat, for almost three days. At the center of the third night the Caffekey had died and his spirit gone up to the moon, which was shining strongly overhead; a fortunate circumstance, as no cloud would be present to make difficult the passage and cause him to become a wanderer of the earth or the upper air.

When he was gone the Caffekey's wife emerged from the shadowy interior of the hut, holding aside the fabric, and the crowd fell silent and dropped to the ground gripping their knees closely in what seemed to be an imitation of a fetal position.

"It may be," Daylaylo agreed. "They are imitating him, the present state of his soul. Death is not a conclusion here, triumphant or otherwise. The pulling free from this life takes him to another, where he must again grow, and learn, and become."

Many of the symbolic gestures, Daylaylo said, were not literally explicable. Some of the oldest member of the People themselves had told him that they did not know, for example, why the Caffekey's wife was required to let her breasts show during the time of the Caffekey's dying, or why she carried stems of headless flowers. The robe itself was heavy and several times, seeing her in the intensity of midday, Henry had thought it must have been almost unwearably hot. Like the weaving over the doorway, the robe had been soaked in deep melancholy purple until it was the color not of blood but blood gone over into dryness, a cavern of ochre.

The Caffekey's wife made a gesture and the crouching men unfolded themselves from the ground. The sounds of the drum were not repeated, and now she alone was heard to weep, quietly but with reality, the sound immediately different in Henry's ear. And for all the distance between their lives, he believed he understood. The dying of the Caffekey had passed from being one of communal proportions, a public event, to being simply a loss of her own.

Three sons entered the hut and brought out with them the body of the Caffekey, wrapped in the cloth that had been the doorway so that the central hut was left socketed and hollow, and now Daylaylo and Henry joined in the long somber walk through the midnight forest toward the burying place.

"It's called *The Rest of the Old One*," Daylaylo said. He had his hiking staff with him and stuck it to the ground before each step, wedging aside branches. "The *Old One*, not the *Old Ones*. They are specific about the word. There are over a hundred graves here, each marked for a family. But all of them—the community of the deceased—are known as *The Old One*, as if together they compose a single person."

When they reached the gravemounds Daylaylo took him aside. The digging began only now and, Henry thought, would surely take until sunrise to complete. Instead of watching they walked the length of burial hills.

The People illuminated their work with conch shells filled with an oily fluid that burned without a wick so that the entire thing could be carried like a lamp. The flame, once lit, emerged from the shell's narrower opening in a clear blade, eventually leaking backward in a slow retrograde motion that illuminated the interior chambers in faintly-visible spirals. There were dozens of such shells carried among the procession, their number stretching back though the nighttime forest.

"Look here," Daylaylo said. They had come far enough away from the ceremony to be able to speak again with comfort, and the older man placed his own shell-light by a stake that had been driven into the ground. At first he thought it might be the striped one around which they danced but coming closer Henry realized the stake was cut out of stone, different markings visible on each of its four sides.

"These images tell of the family of the dead. This one here," —the Spaniard pointed to a curve with, underneath it, three carved circles—"This is *Mother*. It's an image, I believe, of a pelican feeding her young. This one is *Brother*. Two, three brothers, possibly, are all buried here. Here is *Sister*. And here."

Henry peered carefully at the drawings, simple and yet humanly expressive. He touched the feminine ovals, the pride in sharp angles, the union of the whole that signified *Family*. His spirit marveled at the condensation. The bonds between persons were shown by lines, plain and direct, as if to assert in the maw of an unknowable cosmos that this tiny thing—the feeling of contact between people—was significant, had occurred here and was worth recording.

He lifted the shell carefully and light crept over other images—pets? infants?—the jagged line—a falling out between lovers?—as he crouched around each side. The Church of the Laughing Children sounded in his mind and abruptly these strange markings on an unnamed island in the West Indies seemed truer to him than the elaborately scripted stones of a Highgate graveyard. Suddenly the vanity and arrogance of baroque tombs seemed to him shameful: the insistence against death, the claim that worldly power or material acquisition would stand even over the final futility. How much softer, how much more hearted, these anonymous markings! In one piece of stone seemed captured an entire narrative of two sisters—the connection between them—here, they find mates—one couple has children, one loses a child, perhaps their only child—and in the end, the last figure, two sisters again, reunited as they had been, after the complications of two lifetimes.

"They themselves don't know how old these last few are," Daylaylo said. They had come to a farther field of stones, cool feeling, where burial mounds had once been but had fallen to nothing. Tiny lizards scattered away from the light, running into the underbrush. "These are the originals. They aren't recognized by any of the People today. It's possible they were begun by a separate tribe altogether. When I ask them they just tell me the Old One once spoke with a different voice."

These markers were reddish and glossy to the touch, their inscriptions visible but buried as if under a waxy film.

"That's wood. It's become stone-like in some way, I believe

across centuries. Look here."

Together they paused over the lost messages: three radiant suns in a gradually-tipping series; something that looked like a prickly leaf; an eye, almost certainly; curving lines that might have been a river. In a sad moment Henry felt the loss of these voices, the idea that out here, in the night and across the great waters, yet another loss was possible, another alienation. These mute distinguished markers, standing for no one, their words and their intention ciphered by age.

"Do you think of death?" Henry asked.

Daylaylo considered the question. The ongoing burial made a constellation of lights in the distance.

"Not my own. I think often of death, but not death as it will come to me."

"But ours is the only dying we know."

"Perhaps. In another way, it's the only one we cannot know. Others pass before us...my father and mother, both I saw die when I was still a boy. My father of *una enfermedad venérea*, my mother of what, we didn't know. For my father it was painful. My mother, no. She was asleep in the bath. Two serving women were pouring salts out of paper bags into her water. I remember the sound of the grains sliding out of the paper. I was outside but the portico doors were open to get a breeze, and I could see her clearly. She looked at ease. She was not disgusted with life, though she had reason. I believe she was...what is the word, *sated*? She had lived."

"They make it seem less alone." Henry gazed off at the twinkling community by the graves. "With all of them...with the People all following him here."

"Their fear is that the Caffekey's body will become lonely without his spirit. The spirit has gone on, but they hope to keep the body unafraid until it is buried. Otherwise it would have to walk out here by itself."

Henry felt the poignancy of the image: the triumphant soul vaulting free and leaving the lonely corpse to wander to its burial, uncomforted.

They left the ceremony and hiked back toward the village. There had been no dances tonight and at the edge of the beach Daylaylo built a bonfire in a pile of cold ash. As the flames began spreading Henry felt the breath of the ocean, still there, whispering.

"Three persons," Daylaylo said. "In communion. Trinity is an image—an image not literal, but one fit for the human mind. It is in relations…human relations, yes, but all relations, all witness…that God is with us.

"One person, alone, is simply himself. Two can be lovers, or villains. Three who come together and do not kill each other, even with love…three together…three begin community. Three is the seed where humanity is born."

Daylaylo was grabbing bits of wet wood and flicking them aside, pulling the ash away to make space for a new flow of air. Abruptly he sank his hand into the pile. It came up white, bleached past the wrist, the lean fingers gripping a fistful of powder.

"*I see Him in this*," he said fiercely, pulling harder as if to wring from the grit its concealed nature. "I see His body here, His true body. In destruction I see Him, as much as in glory. He is here, in this lifeless heap.

"When I see a corpse I see Him. He is in ruin, in salvation. To be alpha, omega, is not to have history. It is to *be* history—to be that which begins at the moment it ends.

"He is not metaphor, not symbol. In my hand I have Him, the manna, that for which men have fasted and prayed. I have Him, here, more than Moses had his own fire; more than the paschal meal; I have Him; I do; here, on this tiny piece of land. Here on this beach where *el Vatican* itself would pass with a blind eye. Here, unseen by the world, I have the firmest grip of all."

Slowly Daylaylo scraped his hands clean. The sandy pulp fell, tracing white arcs in the air.

"You seem to have made your peace," he said. "With Tied Sticks."

"You can see that?"

"I can see what isn't there. Tonight at the burial. The hate wasn't underneath his eyes."

"I never did anything to him."

"Perhaps not," Daylaylo agreed. "But peace is precious. Accept it however it comes."

Henry brooded.

"Look there," Daylaylo instructed, after a time. "That brightest one is Jupiter. They say it has moons."

Henry turned upward. He realized then that he felt no fear of darkness, none of the deep-rooted animal dread he had experienced his first terrible nights on the island. This environment, shorn of light, was no longer alien. It seemed only undressed of all its dazzling colors, like a woman asleep.

"Mars is rust," Henry said, pointing. "Gemini. Pisces. The lyre."

"Your captors taught you well."

It was true: the men of *Arrogante* had always been aware of the stars. Often they set courses by them, correcting small errors made during the sun-blanked whiteness of day. A sense of wonder had been there also, even for such lost men as they. It was as if on a star-tossed night all the paths of the heaven were open to the right navigator.

He remembered coming on deck once in the midst of some astral phenomenon, when the numbers of visible lights had somehow been doubled or tripled, filling the sky like an overstuffed basket. Sheets of silent color had been waving overhead, like the breath of firedrakes. And the night watchmen—men whose lives were robbery, the gibbet and the gallows—had been silent before it, grinning broadly, like children.

Daylaylo gestured.

"You see this line in the south? To the People that is a fox head. The three stars beyond it is a mother bird pretending to have a broken wing, trying to lead him away."

Henry tried, but the recognizable shapes were too familiar to him, refusing to be reconfigured. The labor of even dismissing them caused a kind of mental anguish.

"Look at the three followed by two. The cross is the center of her nest."

"Southern Cross."

"Is it? The People say the fox climbs up toward the nest half the year; the mother bird always fails. In winter he eats the chicks, and their blood falls on the earth as rain."

But it was *Crux*: the lodestone, the guiding lights. Henry could not will it into being something other. His mind fought against him, he almost felt a grinding in his soul, like the sensation of weight. Then, without expecting it, the change came. He could see the large open bowl, the teeth of the consumer, the martyr's pain. The sensation was like being flung suddenly from his skin and returned without motion.

Henry's father had kept a constellation wheel in his study, a one-room structure separated from the main house by a root cellar. Round like a table, the thickly coated surface of the wheel had been impressed with dozens of points to mirror the shape of the heavens. Characters were then painted over the dots, making their way around its dial: Ursa, Leo, *Camelopardalis* speaking his own name. Under each was the affixed symbol of an Apostle, a second illustration on the wheel's other half showing his relation to the Christ in a curving recreation of the Last Supper. Henry had known always that the images on one side of this sky were unreal; that constellations were constructed in human minds, not written across the shell of heaven. Their fluid continuity with the other half troubled him, though, hinting at the Bible itself as a dream.

His father had told him the constellations spoke God's forgotten truth to those who had eyes to see. With all in the world that could not be trusted—kings, burghers, priests—the sky alone, the old man insisted, was eternally so. Now the experience of seeing even the stars fall into new shapes was harrowing to his soul.

"I was so much like you, Henry," Daylaylo mused. "When I was young. I think all missionaries must have weak faith, smaller than the mustard seed. We want others, all over the world, to take up our ideas, because we are afraid they can't live on their own. We want an absolute, a single story, for all men. But what can I say about the shapes in the sky? Perhaps there is no Southern Cross."

Henry suddenly hated.

"You never loved God."

"I loved Him too much," Daylaylo answered calmly. There was a surprising lamentation in his voice. "Too much. To believe in Him was to do Him an injustice."

Henry shielded his eyes so as not to let the firelight close them. He leaned back, willing the stars back to their appropriate courses.

"Something new?"

"Something of mine." Henry slid the ornament back inside his open shirt.

"Now I understand," the Spaniard laughed, with genuine warmth. "They call you *Starfish*. She does. Speaking Owl does."

"Starfish?"

"Apparently you came up with all the starfish, after the storm. It's a good name."

But Henry's spirit contracted. "I've lost my name once already."

Still he could not trace the source of his own anger. He thought of her, of Speaking Owl, and did not want this man, this fallen priest with his visions, to know anything of that. She was the only thing real on the island; Daylaylo had nothing to do with her. Her body, her scent, mixing with his scent when they sat pressed close together and breathed hot into each other's mouths. The feel of her strong legs moving under her clothing, under the dress she wore that he had colored with his own hands. Nothing of her was unreal, she was the first and the only true thing he had encountered, perhaps in the whole of his existence.

"The things we carry have life in our minds," Daylaylo said. "She gave you a starfish."

Henry did not see.

"A *starfish*," Daylaylo repeated. "If a starfish loses a limb, it grows a new one in its place. She isn't being clever, Henry. She is saying that your hand, your arm, has become new. That the old arm is gone.

"What you do with your new hand is your own decision. Think about the chance you have. You can go on blindly, like most men. Or you can stop now, while your life is fresh. You can create yourself again. You can make yourself right."

"Sometimes ..." Henry whispered, after a pause. "Sometimes I want another life. Sometimes another... everything."

"Then bury the dead."

Henry rose. The bitterness was through him completely, carrying him. He saw the munitions lockers at the stern of *Arrogante*: the deadly cutlasses, Whitepaul's own with a scallop-shell bowl, kept like an umbrella in a corner stand. He saw the cabin, the gyrocompass, the pantry for his books and his wines. And above all, the skull. Always the skull.

"It was his mother's," Daylaylo said, as if reading Henry's thought.

Henry turned.

"Whose else could it have been?" Daylaylo held open his hands. "For him to have treated it with such devotion as you have told me. A covering of gold. What did they call that place he could never escape? That he sailed to again and again?"

"Blind Island. It was a hump...a nothing. The crew just called it that because they weren't allowed to see it. They had to wait in the schooner. Even when he made me come with him, I had to wear a blindfold. No one but P'ter could see his treasure...could see where it was buried."

"Was that really why he plucked out everyone's eyes? To conceal some romantic box?"

"They said ..." Henry struggled; the idea was new to him. "They told me he had treasure there."

"And you thought it was gold dust from Guinea he was digging up, two or three times a year, just to pore over it like a miser. I think it was her corpse."

His hatred of the Virgin. His portrait of the Queen.

"You're wrong."

"*Quizá*," Daylaylo admitted. "But I've been a Ghostly Confessor. I've seen the faces of women who strangled their own children to hurt the fathers. I've seen men, rich men, who robbed graves simply because it was obscene. I know what hell looks like."

"Whitepaul didn't believe in hell. None of them did. They had a chant, back-and-forth, one would say *where are we riding* and the others *to hell, to hell.* It was like a celebration."

"Hell is never far. Perhaps your captain didn't believe in it. But that wouldn't stop him from sailing its waters."

Daylaylo paused, his face shadowed in the flapping light. It was clear he had more.

"The People have asked me to say something to you, Henry," he began. "Something that amazes me. They want you...they invite you to join in the hunt."

The Spaniard looked up at him carefully, holding his knees for balance. In the unquiet light he had the appearance of an ancient man.

"It is the most scared act in their religion. The People want you to come with them."

"Me? Why?"

"That was my question. You, a European. A white. Almost a child. Have you wondered why they have warriors at all, for a community this size? The People were once much greater, spreading across these islands. They have lost their best men in tribal wars—stupid, pointless wars. They need someone fresh. And in ways you are already more like them than I have ever been.

"But I do not believe that is why you are chosen. I think there is more. I think they believe...they feel having you there will help them find what they hunt. What they seek."

"And what are they seeking?"

Daylaylo said the word. At the sound of it the darkness crowded close.

"If you go," the Spaniard continued, "with the others...a small group of men, not warriors, but chosen hunters...do you understand what it will mean?"

"I'm strong again. I run. In the hills. I'm as strong as I ever was."

"I don't mean that only. The People think you are different, marked perhaps. The way you found the child; the way you saw the corruption in the central roof. I have a similar suspicion. Since I met you I have thought you were a kind of...what shall we call it. They think you are a seer, a good omen. I think your soul is loved by the God you will not accept. But everything is required of the men who go on the hunt. Body and spirit. Everything."

Daylaylo waited until the wood shifted and fell, trickling down orange cubes.

"*El pantera*," he repeated, and for a second time his intonation made wild shapes dart in the shadows. "That is what they hunt. *Pantera* is an enormous animal. And dangerous."

"You've seen it?"

"Once. Coming south, just before I met the People. They were on their yearly hunt when they found me. What I saw was a cat the size of a man, longer than a man even, with a tail that looped out behind it. It was walking through the grass with no sound, no whisper. When it stopped, I saw it had a deer by the neck and was holding it there—just holding while it looked at me and decided, was I...how can I express this?...was I *worthy*."

Henry listened to the fire.

"Were you?"

"No. I was not. As I watched, it broke the deer's neck and jumped up the trunk of a tree. It hung the body on a branch, the way a man hangs a rug to beat it. I remember its muzzle was marked with blood, and it eyed me as it licked the blood clean. Not with blood lust, but with a feeling...with a kind of *dominion*. Then it looked away. I was released."

Daylaylo paused, then said a phrase in the People's language.

"That's what everyone was shouting," Henry said, "when they played the stick game."

"Yes," answered Daylaylo. "The game is an imitation of the hunt, in which everyone can take place. And that is their name for the great cat. It means something like The One Who Kills The Deer. But something more than that. I am still learning. The words are closer, I think, to He Kills The Deer, They Weep. The cat will hunt *bebés*, infants that have been chased from their mothers. When the deer becomes lost it makes a sound, trying to be found again. The cat follows that sound.

"But understand this, Henry. The People say when it cries, the deer and the cat are the same. They have a picture ..." he drew it in the dust.

"I've seen that."

"Cat and deer, deer and cat. It calls to *pantera* to come and take it. And the cat cries out as well. I heard the sound, that night. It makes a wail, a kind of ..."

Daylaylo fell silent.

"It hates what it is," Henry scowled. His soul had become dark.

"No," the Spaniard said. "It isn't sin, or remorse. It's nothing so small...it isn't anything we can speak of well."

Henry walked out to the edge of the night. For a long time he listened to the whispering.

"Listen to me, Henry," the Spaniard said, coming up alongside him. "Whatever you think of God, that is not important. He has given your arm back. The right arm, the symbol of power. It's like the heart of a man, a new heart, a new power. God has not given you your power back in order to dig up corpses."

"I don't understand that."

"You came here carrying that dead captain on your shoulders like a rotten weight you could not put down. I saw it the moment I met you. But then I did not understand why."

Henry looked at the other man.

"Is it because you enjoyed being one of them?" Daylaylo asked. "Is that why you punish yourself?"

"I'm not one of them. I never was one of *them*."

"They showed you things, and not just sails and lines. How to fight a man. How to throw a hatchet. I saw you building supports for the new roof, working with the People. You cut a small piece and when you were finished you pitched the hatchet into the thick part of a tree without even looking. Your aim was perfect. No one taught you how to do that in Bristol."

You're what we are, lad.

"*I'm not one of them*," Henry said, louder. Then, under his breathing: "Antichrist."

Daylaylo slapped him in the face.

Henry took a step back. He put his hand to his lips.

"Why do you *really* hate, Henry?" the Spaniard hissed. "Where is the evil that is in you?"

Henry pushed furiously at the other man's chest, driving him back but not toppling him.

"He took away my father, you *bastard*," he shouted.

"Ah," Daylaylo grimaced. "Is that it. Your father *sent* you away, Henry. Because he didn't love you."

Henry started to strike and the Spaniard grabbed his wrist.

"Not this," he said. Henry spit on his shirt.

"What do *you* know?" Henry shouted, pulling away with violence. "What do *you* know? *Your* god let my mother die when she believed in him her whole life. *Your* god made her children into murderers. And *you worship that*. You ..." He stopped. But the rage was not done; it simply had lost words.

"Love is not made out of lies," Daylaylo said. "Your father sent you away. He didn't come looking for you when you disappeared. He isn't looking for you now. All Captain Whitepaul did was follow his orders."

Henry swung stupidly, missed, and went off into the darkness of the beach. When he was swallowed and unseeable he sat down in the cold black sand. All he could see was the firelit drops falling down off his lips, falling out of nothing and disappearing into nothing.

Wind came out of the forest like an animal, reversing direction at the water and bringing in deceptive scents. It was as if beyond the night's curtain vast armadas of spice-laden ships were moored. After a while Henry walked along the beach, breathing the mixed air, letting his feet sing in the water's cold edge. Eventually he returned.

"I'm sorry," he said.

"Yes," Daylaylo answered, with truth. "And I."

Henry sat.

"Do you still have a bible?"

"No." Daylaylo poked at the flames. "I had a sailor's testament once. I let it go."

"How?" His soul was blank against the fire. "How did you let it go?"

"Into the water."

Henry saw the image: the tiny leather square, slipping down.

"Do you know any of it? By heart?"

There was a long silence.

"Yes," Daylaylo said.

"In English?"

"Yes. I know it also in English."

"I want you to say some of it. To hear it."

There was a second period of emptiness, colored only by the click of the tiring embers. The wood was spent, its inner wealth gutted, brooding in smoke now more than flame. Henry looked at the Spaniard's silhouette. The chin was raised, the brow lifted up.

"Something is coming," Daylaylo said. "Something is falling between our lives. Yours and mine. We will not be friends much longer."

Henry gripped himself, aware of the cool damp ground. He closed his eyes, still flutter-filled with light, listening to the other man's voice.

Daylaylo said:

And I saw a new heaven and a new earth:
For the first heaven and the first earth were passed away;
And there was no more sea.

And I saw there the holy city,
The new Jerusalem,
Coming down from God out of heaven,
Prepared as a bride for her husband.

And I heard a great voice out of heaven saying,
Behold, the tabernacle of God is with men,
And he will dwell with them,
And they shall be his people;
And God himself shall be with them.

And God shall wipe away all the tears from their eyes;
And there shall be no more death,
Neither sorrow, nor crying,
Neither shall there be any more pain:
For the former things are passed away.

And there shall be no night there;
And they need no candle, neither light of the sun,
For the Lord will giveth them light,
And the Lord shall reign forever …

"And forever," Henry whispered.

"*Así es*," the friar said. His face was in darkness.

Part Five: Child of the Panther

… the movement of his powerful soft strides
is like a ritual dance …

—Rilke, "Der Panther"

20

The great animal lived past the World. Its region was in the long stretch of nullity that was left after creation, the loneliness, the unformed place.

The hunters told tales. They sat alone, away from the People, ringing a collection of objects. The objects were small and disparate: the skull of a woodpecker, strung through with beads; a flat stone with, painted on it, a fish; brain coral; a charm of wine-colored shells.

To travel toward such wastes, Isi said, was to cross water past where it was no longer water; nor was it land; nor air; where there was no sea and no sky. To go towards such places was sacrilege and holy.

Taca. He drew a marking in the dirt.

For a man to go into the wastes, Shot-Caw said, was to become un-man, un-self. Shot-Caw used sand as his metaphor, lifting it in the sieve of his hands and showing its insubstantiality. Under the cool flow the men melted away, their differentiation melting.

Taca. Shot-Caw drew his symbol.

To be in the wastes was to reverse sky and sea, King George Skanondo said. It was to put the reflection of the man on the land while the man himself went into the water.

Taca. King George drew his marking.

To return from the wastes was to be *become* man, Achtu-brother-boy said. It was to cause the first creation. Achtu-brother-boy used as his symbol the sea-rising sun, emerging hot and effulgent, the source of itself.

Acuera. We go to make men.

Henry squatted with the others, his brow down over his thoughts like their downward-pulled brows. They were waiting for him to complete the circle of images that ringed the central drawing of the cat. Henry reached out and drew the I H S in the dirt.

Taca. We go to make men.

None of the People spoke to them, or of them; not the warriors; not the women; not the teams minding the fires. They had become non-citizens of the island, not even dead. They slept away from the settlement, on raw earth, under sky.

All things beginning depended on the success of their returning; all things ending depended on the bravery of their going. Isi, the leader, used as his metaphor the sea-grape seed, which leads to the sea-grape, which leads to the sea-grape seed. One by one the hunters swallowed the small sharp objects, took possibility into their bowels.

Henry cried aloud. Something had burned his arm: he looked and saw King George Skanondo had singed a mark on his upper bicep with a flaming Dutch rapier taken from the fire. Then the men drew on his body with thorny twigs and leaf ink, their fingers quick and adept, adding the second eyes under his eyes and leaving on his arms and his chest markings like their own, boxes and lines that flowed and swam and knotted into one.

On the third evening they ate ferociously and laughed and wrestled.

On the fourth morning they ran for the sea.

Henry had seen the wastes before. *Everglade*, the sea captains called it, investing in the word a sullen kind of deference. *El laguno del Espiritu Santo*, or simply *the grass*. *Everglade* was wide and far: a man walking in it could walk months and find nothing more than marshes and deep mud dotted with sudden pools of quicksand. All traders avoided it, as did those who fed on traders. It was not an area where villages or forts could be stationed, nor where ships could be caulked, nor where ships could be hidden; but one that merchant caravans had to pass on their way north toward the great ocean stream, like a chastening vision.

The hunters paddled unspeaking, several to a canoe, Henry seated in the middle so that his pulling strength added to the motion of the whole. He leaned his torso down into the stroke, watching the tight bag of stones that was the flexing spine of the rower ahead of him. His mind was solid and clean. His muscles, well-worked, jumped and plowed at the water like the working of a field. The men paddled unspeakingly, each timing the downstroke by a single iterant grunt: a command, no word, not even in the People's tongue: it was the out-sending only of breath, the vocal expression of the act of rowing. The island drew off into the distance, was filled and surrounded by water, sank down so that only the high cliff showed; was gone.

For a time then there was nothing but the paddle. Henry's universe narrowed to the working of the wood, to shaft in hands, the sound of the water slipping by, the feel of his arms' twinned thrust. He sent himself into the paddle he held, opposing the blueblack water and laboring and his muscles beginning to speak and then to cry, and finding his mistake, finding the aches beginning already in him, shoulder and chest, he cast his mind through the paddle and down into the water; he did not oppose the water but moved into it; he did not thrust his way forcefully or oppositionally, but listened to it moving, its uninterrupted flow. The lean boat flew.

Sunlight began changing across the surface and Henry, startled, realized the afternoon was already high. He had paddled unceasingly since dawn, and now it was past noon. He had felt nothing but the unending voice of the hunters, that profound exhalation. He felt no fatigue. In the distance a narrow blueness was emerging from the horizon, marked by clouds. Isi leaned toward it and when the sun was moved another notch across the cloudless sky they pulled onto the first island.

This was the experience of it: all the men simply ceased, their bodies on the land once more but retaining the fetal position of rowers. Henry followed the pattern. Only gradually did the hunters begin to move: first an arm, a hand limp on the grass. Imitating their motions Henry understood the intelligence of it, knew that if he were to have jumped from his seat as he had wanted to after hours of rowing he would have been incapacitated, immobilized by cramps. This gradual emergence was the only way.

After that they passed several smaller islands, some just upcroppings of scattered rock. Shot-Caw and Achtu-brother-boy guided their motions unerringly, though they used no crossbar and Henry never saw them take directions of any kind. Their knowledge of the route was more felt than known, the knowledge of a path taken in dreams.

As they covered more distance Henry began to understand how amazingly unlikely had been his survival, how rare to have wrecked just off on an island anywhere in this region with a true length of beach. None of the others they passed had sand to speak of, sheltered as they were by wave-breaking reefs. And he understood now that the long, sloping question mark he had seen in deep water from his promontory was a line of pulverized stone, broken into fine sand and forming the twin beaches where it came in through a fissure in the reefwork. On any other isle he would have washed into mangrove clutches, watery and without foundation.

At evening they approached an island whose dirty edge seemed to be made of small round upcroppings, as if some natural grinding action had worn smooth a collection of stones to the same unlikely width. The entire shore—brown soil laced with dry white plants—was peppered with these bloated eggs, and only when they tied up and climbed it did Henry realize what they were. The ground here was littered with human skulls, jawless and pressed into the soft earth, as if in enforced observation of the tides. His mind shrank inside him as he stood among the things, their congress marked here and there with the odd finger or thigh bone. Shot-Caw spoke and the hunters took careful directions now, some of them gesturing toward the low sun, but this time they did not eat or rest. They rowed until full dark, and in the black waters Henry saw the skulls still rising before him, dull and monotonous and horrid.

In the morning the hunters cut sharply away from the direction they had been heading and moved through a collection of low trees. It was not an island but simply a water-bound garden of stalks, their trunks evidently rooted no more than ten feet beneath the point over which the canoes passed. Henry had no idea that the water they were traveling in contained such variations in depth; abruptly he realized it might in some places have been possible to stand. The plants created a cathedral through which they navigated, shadows thrown across glimmering wavelets and its leafy roof sighing overhead.

Under the intense sunlight Henry let go of thought. He did not know how long they had been paddling, how many hours. The question became one with no purchase. His body was narrow and thin and strong, the air moved freshly into his nose and down into the pit of his happy body and emerged again in the grunt, the *hah-hah-hah* which all shared. Once they came to the tilted mast of a British sloop that lay on the bottom, the visible wood above the waterline sun-bleached and buckling. Another time the canoes slid through upcroppings that were nothing but sea grass, as far as he could see but hardly troubling the surface, slow silver waves drifting their lengths.

Then they passed another, true island on which women were evidently living, five or more coming down to the edges and calling to the men in their chattery language, which was not the People's language; lifting their hands and beckoning; and the men intensely, almost violently avoiding them with their eyes. The women had extremely long hair and it hung, black and unbraided, about their bodies like animal fur. They had flat, dullish faces, rather expressionless, Henry thought; but there was something meaty about their bodies, something soft-boned and too large. Just as his canoe lost sight of the women Henry looked back. One of them had climbed a high stone and was showing him two fat brownish breasts, as if in final suggestion.

On the second night of rowing they neither ate nor spoke. It had the feel of approaching an enemy camp; or of recognition of that spiritual obliqueness into which they were traveling. The air around them was not dark, for the final island on which they rested was volcanic-seeming ash, black and lifeless, revealing scattered flames in the distance as if these had been dropped by a passing laborer whose task it was to carry fire.

When they reached the continent the hunters tied down their canoes, dragging them against tree boles and lashing them in place. Henry knew he was in *Everglade* now because the earth spoke differently under his feet. It spoke of dirt, true soil, rather than the stone-root of the islands; rock, rather than the tangle of shells and silt. But something else, something richer than this. The continent behind this land had a pressure to it, it resisted his step with a bearing both enormous and proud.

The last rowing had been brief and now the hunters started running almost immediately, silently and in line, and Henry fell in with them, his legs challenged by the sudden motion. They ran directly into the grassland where green spears stood higher than their heads, Etcho and faster-footed Isi calculating direction and finding it, a man whose name he did not know checking the hazy sun and choosing without discussion a new turn, a new alleyway through the grass.

On the island of the World he had felt the pulse of sea, the pulse of land; here, running, the land was all a single beat, a great *in medias* flow. A tremendous white bird was startled and rose like a banner in the sky, its wings spread for a moment wider than a man's body. Henry stopped amazed at the thing but the hunters did not stop and so he lost his place in line and had to hurry, crashing through sharp cutting grass and thick mud, until he could re-enter the correct formation.

The lead runners—though he could no longer see them he understood there were two now, as the line of hunters broke into halves, each taking separate directions and then reforming when the best choice had been uncovered—were searching not just for divisions in the grass through which one could move but for dry stretches of earth, dried perhaps by the action of wind and hard-baked in the heat. When they found one a sense of enthusiasm passed along the line. Travel over these bridges was fast and sure.

At other times there was no choice but to pass through mire and the men worked slowly then, deliberately, their legs becoming thickened with the rich smelling green-black slop up past the calf and even the thigh. Deeper than that and they backtracked, as quickly as before and without, Henry thought, any sense of failure or discouragement; until new passage was found, new runnable crust. Before darkness they had come to higher ground and the jigsaw maze of water and earth had given way to reliable soil that was dry and sharp to his feet. After miles of flatness even the tiniest elevation was notable and made for. Henry grabbed the limbs of a small tree as he scampered up the hill, the dead and swollen trunk coming free under his weight and rolling over, half-submerged. At darkness they slept.

Henry's dreams were exhaustion. He awoke, though, somewhere in the deep quick of night and knew his body was still strong, ready for activity, ready if need be to begin running once more even then. An indiscernible shape came between him and the starlight, high up past the scattered clouds, and for just a moment against a clear patch of sky he saw the great white bird again, moving silent and straight.

On the next day they rose at sun-up and continued their hike, fast but not running now. Henry understood that there had been danger in the lowest lands, the ongoing marshes that were neither land nor water, and that the first necessity had been getting clear of them before night fell. He wondered whether the fear of those miles of uncertain land came from a spiritual sense of their indefinablity, of the unstable combination of flowing water and trustworthy soil; or whether the danger were quite literal. The landscape was impossibly level all around him still but they were away from the worst marshes and, with them, the worst assault of bugs. Henry dropped his thoughts and jogged in line.

At noon three hunters flung fish out of a stream so grass-bloated Henry had not even realized it was there. They cooked the silver greasy bodies, ate them down to the bone and kept moving north.

On the next day they flung out another of the enormous silvergreen fish, and ate carefully selected berries from a field of bushes they had come alongside. The hunters were very cautious as to which plants they chose and debated carefully among themselves, peering closely at specimens and crushing them and feeling the small insides between their fingers. Gathering the berries involved stepping down into thick dangerous mud once again and at one point one of the hunters had fallen: pulled out and half-covered in oily black slime he had smelled like a man out of a grave and was the target afterward of much good-natured mockery.

The next morning they awoke as one and gathered in a ring holding hands and began the hunt.

When they hunted the men would draw out their intended motions on the ground with a stake then repeat the gestures on the palms of their hands until the pattern had been memorized. They separated into groups, and Henry saw the leader of his own group stopping to consult his palm as if the imaginary draught still glowed reliably there. In this manner it was possible to cover large distances and re-cross the paths of the others farther on with a startling accuracy. Eventually they were separating for hours, reuniting more than a mile away, expectation on their faces unrewarded by the expressions of the other teams. Then there was a commotion: one of the men had something on a stick.

It looked like a square hunk of charcoal but Henry knew what it was, and what its significance was, even before the hunters started lining up to examine it with fingernail and eye. Animal stool of that size had not come from a deer or anything like a deer.

The hunters inspected the spoor for its dryness, its breakability, for other things the nature of which Henry could not guess. After the formal inquiries were finished several times each hunter breathed in the specimen's musk, showing nothing on their faces but an intense diligent attention, eyes closed and quivering.

They are learning its scent, Henry thought. *They are memorizing its body.*

The spoor was old and they went for high land again, building a fire at twilight and the men falling into a prolonged discussion. The water in leather sacks was keeping well and Henry found that if he only drank when the other men drank he did not feel its parching absence in the way he had when first coming to the island. Already the way Europeans drank seemed to him banquetish and wasteful. When Henry thirsted, which was often, he held the thirst inside him like a tight little ball, neither fighting it nor letting it dominate his thinking. Like hunger, it spoke but was not spoken to. And when the black wet tip of the water sack came to his lips it was an experience unlike drinking had ever been; then the little ball of complaint inside him vanished for a while, and when it returned it was smaller than it had been before.

He began to feel through this that there was a general way of living he had missed. Always in his memory he had been in want; some fundamental part of him, even when well-fed, simply began thinking on how next it would eat, drink, find sheltering warmth. With the hunters he treated hunger as they did, like a fatigued muscle, neither as an indulgence nor a perpetual, unfillable need. All day long they hiked again through the dominating grass and when they stopped he tried to lift this mouth, this need, out of him and leave it, leave it behind him like a stone.

On the third or fourth night the animal was close. New spoors had been found, one of them only a day or two old and adorned, Henry noticed, with a bright sharp pebble. The big animal had eaten something that hurt it: the scent of blood was in the stool and the men reacted excitedly to this. The next trail, though, seemed to show it healed, and a sense of new awareness went through the party that was powerful even in silence. This animal bled but without great concern. It moved fast, for they had been trailing it actively for a day and had not seen it. Henry thought he sensed in the men a new emotion: not fear, but awareness.

The next morning they hunted without eating. Foot-markings had been found, first widely separated, as if the animal walked though the air, only now and again lighting on its nonnative element: then close together, a furious scrabble discovered around a pinkish toss of feathers. Henry peered into the sun-covered distance and something black and lean moved out of the grasses there. He pointed excitedly and the others looked, some of them saying a word. The shape was amorphous, like nothing so much as the sliding hump of a whale. With all his soul he wanted to run after it but the hunters made gestures and repeated the same word to him, but quietly, and Henry did not understand his mistake until the bear reemerged, a hundred yards farther on, and turned and eyed them once before sauntering in an undulous gait back into the green face of the land.

By evening a second bleeding stool was found, only this time the men gathered around it with hesitance, touching at the blood and wiping it between their fingers as they had the berries, one hunter touching a bead of it to his tongue. Their faces showed consternation.

The next day Henry woke confused. The sun was over the horizon entirely, but the hunters were not in motion. They sat crouched around the cooled ashes from the night's fire, discussing, listening. It was as if they did not want to speak too quickly, to make an assertion that would dishonor the totalizing silence of the place. After Henry had listened for a while Achtu-brother-boy turned to him and drew a large cat shape in the dust, its belly protruding.

"It's a female. You're saying she's pregnant."

The men returned to their discussion. Henry felt the sharp pierce of the dilemma, both spiritual and material. The discussion came to a close.

By midmorning they had begun to make their way back south, recrossing open spaces of grassland over which they had already come. Henry saw looking to the west how far the land actually extended, mile upon mile green and brown going out toward an unreachable horizon. The land here was not death, as he had been told. The land here was life, such an uncountable vast stretch of living that it roared like a second sea. The hunters took a different path this time as they headed back and at midday they crossed flower-fields so vast they could not be taken in by a single sweep of the eye. Henry had to turn himself around like a drunken man simply to take stock of how far the colors went, of the constant and almost unbelievable drone of bees passing through multitudes of blossom. He walked into the softness and felt his body passing through colors like wading in a stream. King George Skanondo blocked his way.

Henry stopped. The others were waiting as well; they had heard something. Then he heard it, too: a thunder, growing out of the earth instead of the sky, like an inversion of nature's process. There was higher ground nearby and they rose up on it to watch the herd of small clay-red horses running past like an unbroken a river of muscle. Henry craned his head. Dissipated, yes, in some places; like a crowd of people pressing down a lane, so that more collected here, fewer there: but the line of galloping animals was not broken from one horizon to the other.

That night under brittle stars there came a wailing sound, the lamentation of a lost, maddened spirit. It brought Henry out of sleep and he lay listening to it until his heart itself worked the sound, chewed it like food and pumped its through his veins and his musculature. The wail was repeated, drifting through the dark.

Next to him the hunters lay, eyes wide. He could feel their intensity, the unified focus on that sound. And there was something in him as well, emerging from and eclipsing the hunger, the exhaustion, the rejuvenation. Beyond it all he felt a new consciousness, a willingness and a passion for the hunt.

With the morning came a second commotion. One of the men had been away from camp already and returned, gesturing strongly with his spear end. They followed him.

The prints this time were obvious, and for the first time Henry could recognize them as *cat*. These pads were wider than the female's had been, and heavier, leaving deep-pressed marks in the earth. Little divots had been scratched in front of each imprint, the claw-points reaching almost an inch beyond the paw.

The Walker. The Grass-walker. He flexes his hands.

That was how Henry began thinking of it then, as the excitement of the quest passed once more into them, until it was a kind of urgency: *the Walker.* They were following the shadow of a creature that haunted these lands, this world flat and dimensionless as infinity must be. *The Walker*, a kind of sentinel spirit. In his strong-tired mind he imaged it watching them, taking shape in the startling white clouds, or in the free leaves that came soaring, unbounded, and skittered the tops of the grass where they stood quivering in the wind before being lifted once again.

The Grass-walker. He is all of this. And we are close.

The lead runner saw the fresh spoor first. Not an hour old, green and stinking. They had turned against the falling sun and come back entirely past a location where they had slept once before, having described an enormous circle, and continued from there following the tracks outward toward the sea. A word was passed down the line of men like a lightning strike. The word was passed to him.

"I know," Henry said, grinning. "The Walker."

He had heard the sea growing louder all afternoon as they hiked east, the sound turning at last to the hammers of true waves, a sound never heard on the islands. For hours, it seemed, the sound was with them, growing faintly louder but disappearing; reemerging when next he realized he had been hearing it again for some time. The slow thump of it had become a tolling.

At the very edge of the land the perpetual flatness rose up in a series of true hills. The sun was close to setting once more and the purpling air showed it to be well past the time when they would normally have camped. There was an awareness among the hunters of the lateness of the hour, a mounting concern. But the tracks each time were fresh, fresher, fresher. They were near now, achingly near.

The Walker, Henry heard himself saying. The word sounded like the tambourine beat in his mind. He said it into the eyes of the men when they looked uncertainly into the sun behind them and their own long shadows on the other side. *No stopping, no camping. The Walker is close. Too close.*

They ascended the sandy hills and Isi, having achieved the top, stopped and lay suddenly flat against the ground. The motion caught every man behind him like a whip blow and they dropped as well, remaining motionless for a full minute before inching forward in an arm-and-leg scramble. Henry crouched low but ran still on his feet, eagerness preventing him from crawling as he pushed his way up the hill. Isi waved him down.

No time, Henry thought, *no time*. The sun was gone behind them, only its remnant light scattering the atmosphere. *Attack now*, he cried with his eyes, willing the raised hand of Isi into a gesture of command. *Raise your arrows and bows. Lift your spears. Strike before darkness frees it.*

But the hand, ignoring him, made a gesture that was not one Henry had seen before. It stayed for a moment in the blocking shape, warning of the need for restraint; then separated its fingers out slowly. The hunters, seeing this gesture, moved themselves apart. Abruptly there was a new energy between them, something unexpected.

"Damnation," Henry spat, and threw himself up the remainder of the hill. He peered over the top, at the place where Isi was peering, at where they all were peering.

They were at the water. The land on the other side of the hills fell away quickly to a long stretch of beach. Henry could smell the sudden saltiness, see the waves landing in the faded twilight. Not understanding, he looked at the hunters for a moment and then again across the shore. He saw nothing save a slow gull turning in the air.

Then he did see. A light, making its way gradually along the water's edge. Encased in glass: a lantern.

A handful of figures walked with it. They had vanished into the gloaming before Henry could make out how many were there, but the one carrying the light he had seen clearly. It was an enormous figure, twice the silhouette of the others. Even from this distance something about it seemed to project an insane good cheer.

Isi started to move and Henry put a hand on his chest. He could feel the others all watching him now.

"Stop," Henry said. "I know this man."

Part Six: Dangbe Python God

Indeed, much of the red soil common throughout the Caribbean arrived there on winds from Africa.

—Janet Raloff

21

Black P'ter had been born Kofi Lioness' Tongue Botay, the middle name from his father, who was *Laughs Holding a Lioness' Tongue*. His father had been a great man: when King Agbangla's son made a marching visit to the shrine of Dangbe Python God, his father, who was called in important circles entirely by the honorific Laughs Holding a Lioness' Tongue, traveled with him, wearing leopard skin and standing, his mother always said, "not three men from the highest."

He did not know what had happened to his father after that, remembering the tall, distant man's presence in his life only up to this particular moment with its famous and often-repeated detail. In his mind these events were connected: he felt somehow that the father hidden under that skin was not a man at all but a swallowed man, like a meal already downed by the leopard but not digested. He knew that the Python could eat a man or a hoofed creature entirely and sit on its meal for days, bloated like a stuffed fat elder, its face all mockery and contentment. Also after dark on nights when there had been a circumcision the women had all to remain safely indoors because a Python met on the road or out in the fields would drive a woman mad with desire and enter her vagina as a man enters a woman, and deposit from its mouth inside of her the seed of a child who if he lived would be half human and half god, a monster with dark skin like a man but slit eyes like a god, too powerful to have in the world and a danger to all who knew him.

Kofi himself had never seen such a creature though once his friend Kwesi Barro claimed to have seen an enormous snake walking on hind legs through a farmer's field, its body rolling and swinging around its hips like a loose vine. Seeing the alarm in Kofi's face Kwesi's sister Halima called Kwesi a *stupidity-speaking never-be-a-man* and drove him away with a switch. Kwesi invited Kofi then to come see the garden she was growing that was all powderblue flowers, every shade of blue she could find in the village. Kofi agreed, and the flowers were indeed beautiful, but the image of the lolling, swaying creature had stayed in his mind.

Kofi was raised by his mother and lived on the coast, where the land was rich and seed-yams and cowpeas grew madly inside gardens and out; you could not keep good things from growing. Ajoku was the Yam god and saw to it that there was always plenty going around. Looking west at the water's edge Kofi saw flying fish leap once and bat against the air as if trying to sail there, a whole school of them; Kwesi told him they were souls of men who became lost in the forest and every so often you would see one succeed and take off into the sky like a bird, which is what some birds were, and sail around the clouds free forever. Seeing Halima's face where she sat warming a bottle of oil Kofi laughed bravely this time and said this was not true, he was not fooled. But once again all night he had dreamed of the souls and their imprisonment, and waking up early the next morning he went down to the water's edge to see if any of the fish were truly flying free the way Kwesi said and as he somehow wanted them to be. On the horizon stood three dark shapes, like wedges.

The men in his village were concerned about the appearance of the shapes, and watched them for several days, but the sails never came closer and soon disappeared for good. After that the men were more relaxed and Kofi was relieved, thinking that as he had been the first to see them somehow the sails were his responsibility, like something he had spilled on the ocean and made what was pretty no longer pretty. At night Kofi lay not dreaming but not awake either, letting the thoughts on these events pass and merge the way he liked to do. He told his mother this time was his *asleep awake*, and in it he saw the flying fish escaping to the horizon and growing larger and larger the way your thumb, if you hold it against things far away and bring it slowly closer, gets larger and larger until it can smudge out the whole moon or sun. He imagined in this way the souls trapped in fish were big as mountains, their fins huge as sails and sticking up darkly against the perimeter of the earth.

Because his father was gone it became Kofi's duty when he was old enough to carry paper to the queen, who by then had eaten the son of king Agbangla and taken a Portuguese lover and surrounded herself with zombi soldiers she had gotten from the interior. Kofi knew this was the way things had happened and he said the words proudly in the hearing of Kwesi Barro, who was now older but still foolish and a storyteller. Kwesi's face lit up and he maintained that while what Kofi had said was true what he did *not* know was that Queen Now-Benin had not bought the zombi soldiers as slaves the way people said but had produced them from her belly, opening herself up with a knife and putting in donkey teeth and sewing herself shut again. This however was untrue.

When the paper came for Queen Now-Benin it was delivered by white men in helmets, which Kofi had not seen before, either the white men or the helmets: but he found the latter to be by far the more interesting. They were made of vermilion cloth with three metal sloping sides, like three dulled spear blades all attached in a ring and sitting in the white men's heads, not good at all for protection but shining amazingly, as if three pieces of the sun had been stitched together and were resting on their brows. Under the helmets the faces of the white men were hard.

He carried the papers on foot across the long distance from his home to the Large Tree of Dangbe, and from there the easy distance to the Smaller Tree of Dangbe. There he rested always for the night as his father had done, walking not running in the morning because he was close enough then to the perimeter of the forest where the flat ground grew high and filled in with dark trees threaded by mist. Sometimes when resting at the Smaller Tree of Dangbe if he arrived before sundown Kofi would eat a little out of the breadbag at his waist, respectfully and cleanly, and watch the gray sheets of mist making their way across the distant wood. There was nothing like a forest in the village where he lived, all the land for miles around was flat with nothing on it or flat with fields of elephant grass; when one saw the forest, with its always-moving mists like living things, it was not surprising that you would be amazed. Also when the edge of the forest was close enough that it appeared to be about halfway to the horizon it was an easy thing to turn toward the sun and follow the edge of it up in a straight line to where Queen Now-Benin lived.

Kofi delivered the paper lying flat on the ground and Queen Now-Benin took all the pieces and stared at them for many minutes, sometimes staring at their backs as well and then again their fronts while Kofi rose to kneeling with his head down and his hand outstretched exactly as it had been when Queen Now-Benin took the paper. Then she would tap twice on her chair with her fingernails to dismiss him, a guard with a dancing scar across one cheek holding the curtain for him, and he would hurry from her palace and run back down the cool steps and down the line of the forest again, sometimes (rarely, but sometimes) feeling a cool wet wind blow out of the trees, the smell of animals, and wondering what lived and breathed and had its existence under those shrouding mists.

This duty he performed for several years until the time when Queen Now-Benin, just called Benin by then, took the papers from his hand and dropped them all and reached under his chin and lifted up his face. Kofi felt stones filling his belly but the Queen's hand held his jaw firm and forced him to look at her. She had very dark smooth skin that did not age on account of all the blood of men she had drunk, and her brow was bright and high; in his panic Kofi thought she was looking at him with a view to taking a bite. But her expression softened and then she was like a man making a pot looking at the pot from all angles before deciding how to proceed.

After that, each time he took the paper to her Queen Benin lifted Kofi's face up and looked at him, sitting back again after lifting his chin and smiling at him, her hands sinking down into two dishes of cowries she had on either side of her chair and stroking at their surfaces.

At the end of the year he was told by the helmeted men to go see Queen Benin but without paper. Without paper he had no reason to go to her and did not understand his assignment, but out of duty he went. The journey to the Far Tree of Dangbe was not as far now that he had been running it for several years, and yet he wanted it to be both longer and shorter. For the first time he saw rain clouds gathering and spilling over the forest, and a strange, bitter wind came across the fields where he rested, wind with the smell of carcasses in it.

Queen Benin, when she saw him, dismissed her soldiers with a hand wave and Kofi knelt in front of her, holding up his hand the way he always did only this time with no paper in it. The Queen slapped his hand away and he felt the stones falling inside him again, in just the way he imagined a pig he had seen once felt when he watched it swallowing muddy stones along the edge of a stream until he believed it could not have moved had it tried.

"Look at me," Queen Benin said, meaning *your eyes are open but you are trying not to see*, which was true; and when Kofi looked for real the Queen pulled apart the lower halves of her dress and showed him her vulva. The Queen's between-leg hair was dark and extensive, bush-like, with little gray follicles mixed in by ones and twos.

Kofi said nothing but remained looking until the dress halves were closed again and the guards called back in. The guard with the dancing scar looked once at the queen and then looked carefully at Kofi, still kneeling.

That night sleeping by the Smaller Tree of Dangbe he had awakened in terror: jackals were loping around him where he slept, their faces wet and desirous. Kofi threw dirt clumps at them and drove them away, running that night even in the darkness back to the Large Tree of Dangbe and home.

After that the Portuguese man Benin was present in the room whenever Kofi delivered the paper, standing a little behind the queen in his ceremonial jacket. He was a small, dry man in European dress whose hands twitched in and out of his pockets. Twice he looked at Kofi as if he might say something. Kofi never lifted his head and the queen did not touch him any more, tapping on her cowries with her painted fingernails to send him away as soon as the paper had been examined. The guard continued to watch him carefully.

When the rainy season had come back around the sails returned with it. There was talk once again in the village, and as a young adult now he was allowed to stand close to the circles of men as they spoke, and listen, though he was not yet allowed to interject. One morning he heard shouting and when he was dressed and awake Kofi saw something he could not believe: the zombi soldiers were there, in his village, like a weird juxtaposition of his official life and his actual life. They were not attacking but simply bringing other men, strangers from the interior, to the water. Families who had stone houses were driven out of them and the captured men were locked up in the houses instead. No one was made to join the captured men, and none of the captured men who were imprisoned in their village were known to them. The soldiers walked through their midst without swerving, as if the people here were invisible to them.

The zombi soldiers kept bringing new men in and putting them into the stolen houses without removing the old men, so that after two and three days a smell started to come up from where the houses were and the sound of the captured men complaining. Kofi learned to stay away from the invisible line of the wind that blew backward from the stolen houses and was full of the smell of those men. Late in the day the wind turned around and then their house was right in the invisible line of the smell; it was so bad inside their house that his mother and his three sisters went for long walks in the evenings until the wind had completely died. That was how none of his family was there when the zombi soldier came up to his house. He and Kwesi Barro were outside eating fruit; the soldier looked at both of them.

"The boy who carries the letters," he said.

Kofi stepped forward. He remembered that the pulp in his mouth was exceedingly sweet.

The man who took him into slavery was named Gaston Jean l'Arcveq. Payment for the slaves had been negotiated with the King of Whydah by means of his caboteer, and a second agreement reached in trade for certain items of metal and cloth, some liquor and minimal amounts of gunpowder. This last item l'Arcveq had mixed with beach sand to a liberal degree so that it would not fire well or consistently, in principle not wanting to supply the uncertain and, he believed, morally incapable empires with anything too potent in the way of assertion.

He was an agent for the French Company of Guinea, competent and precise, and midway across the Atlantic he died of a flux. With him went certain plans for the development of the Dahomey gap as a trading route through the interior, where warring peoples were in regular need of exporting captured men and dispersing their number. The gap, L'Arcveq wrote in his correspondence to the Company, represented a natural parting-place between twin dense forests, and as such focused the stream of supply outward toward the transmittable seas. That last phrase, *les mers transmissibles*, had been one over which he labored carefully, along with the image of Dahomey as a kind of narrows through which human waters could be rushed.

A moderate man, L'Arcveq had ordered the establishment of a shrine to the local gods in the operating port. This was being constructed one mile north of the gap, where thinning vegetation had been leapt at too quickly as the most promising route and much energy wasted before the gap itself had been discovered on subsequent trips. The shrine was then slated to be moved south to where it would stand in greatest visibility, but with his death the structure was abandoned and later moved over an old well to serve as a leverage system for raising water. During the days and then weeks onboard *Le Rire du Soleil* Kofi and the conquered interior men were brought up on deck to be washed off with vinegar, to eat burning pepper out of wrapped paper tubes, and to dance. The ones who would not dance or, as the days and then weeks went by, could not remember what was being asked of them were flicked at with knives tied to the ends of short strings. Periodically a robust redcheeked man who chewed unskinned tubers with one hand would turn a brass cannon toward them and light the fuse, watching for fear in the dancers' faces and laughing convulsively when the charge popped harmlessly into the barrel.

Kofi remembered the time when he no longer knew who he was. His old self, what he had once in his own mind called his Mmuo Spirit, left him and fluttered off in the shape of a fish. He watched it lift into the sky and be gone, and what was left instead chained into the hull with the others was empty inside, an unassigned slate. The hollow that had been him danced and ate the pepper and felt the stings of the whip-knives, danced trying to keep its feet from coming down on the sharp shackle edges, danced and ate the pepper out of thin paper tubes. But it was empty, relievingly empty. The thing that danced was as unoccupied as the spaces to the left and the right of him in the hold where living men had turned to corpses against whose rigid sides the dancing thing was close-pressed. When he arrived in the New World, blistered and close to madness, he weighed less than one hundred pounds.

L'Arcveq's second in command, selling off the surviving men to an arm of the West India Company at a holding island, had given him the name *Pierre*. At Port Royal his new christening was further corrupted to *P'ter*, pronounced like *Pierre* but containing the *t* sound inserted by his British master whose French was clumsy and imprecise. The British master had a French wife whose family owned the plantation and French children and French servants, the latter of whom who were regarded differently than his slaves, over whom they had authority. His wife teased him happily over his "*moitié-Français*" and by listening to them teach each other in the redundant, casual tones of the foolishly affluent P'ter came, without effort or intention, to learn both languages at once.

The British master was baby-bald on top with long thin golden hair that hung around his ears and down past his collar, and in the evenings he would sit in a chair of thinly carved wood on the enormous porch of his house and smoke dried marijuana leaves from his crop and suck the soft pulp of mangoes. One day a ship appeared in the harbor. P'ter had seen it but thought nothing of it, as he thought nothing any more of any object in his world that was not immediately in his hands or being arranged by two other men to balance on his shoulders. This lack of mentality afflicted all the workers in his team with the result that when the bell that sounded the call to cease never came they continued on long after the usual hour, standing up in the cane fields uncertainly only when the sky overhead turned the color of tangerines and blood oranges.

When P'ter and the group of six he was with returned to the slave quarters by themselves a man was standing there. He was the largest man P'ter had ever seen: he had a chest like an oak, a huge red coat over shoulders that were double-strung with pistol braces made of rope. The man's face looked wider than P'ter's fully spread hand. In his left fist he held the British master's head.

"Who comes with me?" he said.

P'ter laughed. He was thinking that the British master's head looked so small by itself, hanging sideways from its golden hair and without the brightly clothed torso and belly it usually sat on. He laughed and laughed. The air was suddenly crisp to breathe.

Onboard that night the huge man brought the rest of the crew up on deck and had them stand in a rough circle with P'ter in the middle. The lights from the flaming plantation were visible on shore, quiet flashes in the dusk. The men on the ship began clapping and spitting into their hands, though P'ter did not understand why.

"No more than three," the huge man said, standing above them all on the forecastle. P'ter had not stood on a ship since the crossing, and the sudden motion of the water made his legs tremble.

The first one came toward him fast, whipping a cloth around P'ter's head and punching him in the throat.

P'ter pulled off the cloth and the man in front of him jumped and danced a little on his toes, making the others laugh. The man was barefoot, wearing a shirt with horizontal stripes and canvas leggings that stopped just under the knee. P'ter did not know if he were allowed to speak; he opened his mouth and the man swung a second time, striking him fiercely across the cheek.

There was a cheer as P'ter stumbled backwards, rude hands stopping his fall and thrusting him back up. The dancing man came at him from the side now, his head cocked and watching with one eye only as if examining a problem with very small pieces. His right hand moved fast, hitting twice or three times before the torso pulled back, the left staying cocked and ready.

P'ter had never hit a white man and there was the taste of iron in his nose and mouth before he understood he was to defend himself. He was down on one knee with his hands in front of his face, feeling the broken lips pulse warm fluid into his hands, the dancing man pushing P'ter's palms backward into his own face as mockery and kicking with his foot at P'ter's exposed ears. On the last pass something let go inside P'ter and he came up fast, butting his head into the dancing man's chin. The man's eyes rolled a little and he swung stupidly into the air before falling backward in a daze. There was a cheer from all sides of him and someone else hit P'ter: a bare heel kicked into his belly and sent him down. He got up faster this time and began swinging at the much larger, much slower man who had kicked him and who had a full, thick beard only under his chin, cut away strangely on both sides. P'ter hit him in the face and the man hit back and P'ter was amazed that the man was still laughing, laughing even as he received blows that made his little blue eyes blink and swell. P'ter began laughing too and when the third man came at him he broke him down like a matchstick; then he went back to the dancing man who had rallied himself and came in swinging fast, and let the other man tire himself out swinging, the freed thing inside P'ter flying and dodging his swings, and when P'ter saw his chance he struck the man once, twice in the eyes, and then grabbed his skull quickly by the greased pony-tail in back and drove it down into the deck.

The crowd erupted catcalls and applause and P'ter could see money was changing hands, even as the fat laughing man spat blood on the deck and backed out, replaced by two more who looked like brothers. P'ter was on them before they had fully entered the circle.

He defeated every man who came at him that night, and in

the end he was pulling them in from the crowd, taunting sailors in French and in Edo, swallowing a chipped bit of tooth at one point, his or someone else's, and not caring. There was something inside him spreading from his torso out past his arms in glorious fibers and he thought it was his life.

Afterward the enormous man who had freed him and who watched the fighting with a broad, happy grin put a hand on his shoulder and asking for his name called him *Black Peter*, amused apparently by some coincidence.

"Black Peter and White Paul, twin prophets of the Indies," the man rumbled, smiling close with his wide nothingness-centered eyes, and in that deeper blackness P'ter felt the first fear, what he hadn't felt when grabbing the sweaty arms of three white men at a time and kicking and hitting and being kicked and hit. His soul dropped into those eyes and he thought he saw something that looked like the giant man loved him now and always would and something else that looked like insanity.

Time was of no use onboard *Arrogante*, where seasons meant simply a correlation in the tides and the storms, months had only the most shadowy of existences and the distinction between days was a memory. Holding the British owner's pocket watch in his hand and peering at its ever-circular motion P'ter found that minutes still existed; he walked inside of minutes, then, not fearing but wondering some days what his existence would be when the watch stopped finally and he was left only in the instant.

At the last minute a man will choose to preserve his existence, the British owner had said to his wife, on an evening when the marijuana did not calm him and he had been having his memories again. The British owner had fought in a war, P'ter did not know which one, and often at night he wept uncontrollably. *Even if he dies at sixty seconds, he will choose fifty-nine more.*

Events flowed into one another like the ribbony water they bailed from the jollyboat, clear and cold on nights when the rain came, blood-sopped when a prisoner was being taken and sprang suddenly into life after feigning submission and needed to be clubbed. At such times P'ter was always the first one in. He learned to fight rapidly and intensely and forgot nothing: where to strike a man's knee to make him fall, where his head if you wanted to insult him, to stun him, to make him stupid for a moment or forever. He learned to read the human skull like a nautical chart, covered in guesswork islands and known landmasses. From the captain himself he learned how to plan an attack on a galleon: a raid which was fast and had always three escape routes attached to it; a full-out assault which was slow and at which the men worked, sweating and pushing each other into battle like men lifting sugar sacks; a sidelong pass which disabled the enemy but left him floating and lost no lives. He learned how to swing a cutlass so that the arm did not throw it but carried it over, the edge an extension of his shoulder's motion; learned again how much strength was needed to frighten a man, to bleed him, to scar him, and to kill him if killing him were possible. He learned subtler work as well, no less vital. How to read the surface of the water: how many waves there were, and of what shape, and in what funnel and at what pitch they fell, and how highly they crested, and whether they foamed whitely at the crest or receded, still dark; whether there was a second wave series, which almost always there was, smaller and running against the obvious motion or in some separate fashion, and what this told of weather to come.

By the end of a year—or two, or five—sky merged with sea and he lived in both, the earth inessential and his birth in it forgotten. A fire ran through his liberated muscles that challenged the sun. He imagined he must be visible as a beacon, that the spirits of the men he was going to assault and the ships onto which he would force his way must be seeing him already, growing closer and more imminent, a lighthouse of destruction.

When he was ready for more subtle forms of swordsmanship he received a rapier in one hand and a dagger in the other, learning the ancient *attack of two teeth.* The men who were good enough for this art practiced using long wooden sticks and the loser receiving a beating; before long he was never the loser. When he was ready for more subtle forms of navigation he learned to read the color of the sea-skin in order to judge not just depth and the proximity of land or of reefs, but of reefs that did not discolor the water because they had not had time to build up shallows on their interior sides. He learned the quartermaster's work, the second mate's, the first: how to feel the needs of the ship and its responses, its urgings toward open sea or its shyings away from a double wind. His skin stretched across the yards, his raw bones formed the sloping prow. *Arrogante* was his soul.

Then one day they abducted a load of slaves from a small plantation on Barbados. After P'ter's own liberation Whitepaul had sold every member of the stolen men who would not join him, all of them standing and staring thoughtlessly at the planking under their feet as they were hoisted from one damnation and licensed to another. P'ter found that he hated them, even those he had lived with for years: men shattered and undone, men who could be shown freedom and whose wills were too womanish now to reach for it. For such creatures he had no pity.

The teams they had taken since he came aboard were mostly black, though crimson and yellower skins appeared in their numbers, once even the snowy arms of a white woman who had fallen in debt. Always Whitepaul made his offer. Those who had the will to freedom took freedom, and the agony of it; those who had not he treated like untransformed chattel. This team was entirely African, a purplish stream. P'ter went above to the forecastle and watched as the doubly-stolen men were loaded onboard, like a fantastical preacher examining his former community.

"Kofi!" someone cried. P'ter looked: a girl, thin almost to disappearing, hidden by the shuffling bodies. Through the starvation and the years still he recognized her: she was Halima, sister of Kwesi Barro. P'ter took her to his quarters and she said nothing but wept on his bare shoulder as he held her, her body so thin and trembling it was like holding a doll. He lay down with her and she kissed his face, the fierce unbroken grip of her hands holding onto him, he doing nothing but holding her only. P'ter had participated many times in the attacks on European merchants' wives; now, holding this girl and doing nothing, he realized with a silent cry that this was the first sexual experience of his life.

"Don't let them take me again," she whispered to him in Edo, and he slid his lips across her eyes. "I will stay with you. Here."

"You cannot live here," he said. "No woman can."

"I am strong. I can be strong as a man."

"No man can live here either."

Halima wept hotly, gripping at his chest as if to pull him into herself.

"Kofi."

"Kofi is dead," P'ter said to her. "I do not know him."

Halima stayed on *Arrogante* after the others were sold and while she was there the undifferentiated flow of lost time condensed into days again. P'ter became aware of the distinction between morning and evening and the numbering of the hours, and three days were no longer the same to him as eleven or ninety; each had a character and a reason, and at the end of a week sleep seemed a shame and he went to it anticipating the dawn when once more he could see her there. At night they slept together in his berth rolled into each other like one careful body. Other times he awoke alone, and looked for her and found her hidden in a wrapped blanket on the floor.

The *Arrogante* sailed north and west and when P'ter returned to his cabin one night to find two crewmen in it he threw his weapons aside and beat both of them, still fully armed, until they coughed great mouthfuls of bloody spit and begged him by the Articles to let them apologize to his honorable and lovely wife. At the end of that week he put Halima in the jollyboat and rowed her ashore where the blue smoke of settlements could be seen and gave her the double-ended sack full of food.

"I will bury him," she said, meaning himself.

"He might have loved you, had he lived," P'ter said.

"If I see Kwesi again …"

P'ter shook his chin. She would not see Kwesi again, any more than she would see the world that had been, back across the waters; any more than he would see the world inside himself that had once lived and flowered there.

22

Henry stood in the center of the community, in the gathering space under the newly made roof. The whole People were there, arranged in a circle around the three fires, into which scented herbs had been cast. The elders were first, women and men, then concubines, then the bonded men, then the unbonded men and women. Closest to Henry and occupying her own space of authority was the Caffekey's wife, now Caffekey, along with her children, one of whom would one day be holy; and the hunters who had returned from their quest.

"It's Whitepaul," Henry said. "Captain Quirinius Whitepaul, a British man, a criminal and a thief. He's alive, and so are some of his men. At least four, maybe more. Maybe many more."

Daylaylo translated, listened for the comments of those in front, repeating them to Henry with his face expressionless, watching.

"His people are warriors," Henry said, his voice hot. "You must believe me. These men kill for their living. They do it for …" He faltered, unsure. "They have pleasure in it. The pleasure of an animal. They are a danger to everyone."

Daylaylo listened and spoke.

"Tom Kit is not afraid."

"*It's not a matter of being afraid*," Henry snapped. "They have a cabin lantern and are walking it back and forth across a beach at *Everglade*." He used the People's word. "It's a wrecker's trick. To bait a merchant in close. You see? From the water it looks like a vessel at anchor, on a long anchor tow. Others will think there is deep harbor, and run themselves aground."

"Is this his plan? To sink ships?" Daylaylo asked. Henry found himself listening to Daylalyo's voice but watching the Caffekey, her newly ancient face.

"No. That would gain him nothing. He just wants to draw a ship close, stall it, and attack. Then he will kill the captain, the mate, and take the ship over. Make it his."

"How will he do this thing?"

"He will have to bring it close enough to board but prevent it from foundering. They will strike when they see the ship lose its ability to turn."

"His four men will hurt *Espainia*?" someone mocked.

"His men are not like ours," Henry fired back fast, speaking partly in the People's tongue. "There are many of them even when there is only one."

Henry stopped and gripped hard against his anger, struggling to convey the intensity of what he knew. The faces looked at him calmly but blankly, listening and not understanding. "They strike fear. They move quickly, they kill one or two quickly, the leaders, to paralyze the others. Then the ship is theirs. It can be done."

"He has a boat to reach deep water?"

"He must have. Some of them must have gotten away from *Arrogante* in the longboat. They were smart enough to save a lantern. They will not have forgotten weapons."

Henry looked around, his breathing steady and thin.

"Damn it!" Henry cried. "Don't any of you hear what I'm saying? I spent whole years with these people. I know who they are. No one is safe if they are still alive."

"Starfish wants to kill this man," Daylaylo said.

It took Henry a moment to realize the friar had spoken in English. Slowly Daylaylo translated his own words for the others. The crowd looked more carefully at Henry now, examining.

"Yes," Henry said, after a moment. "Yes. I want to kill him."

Daylaylo reacted not at all. Henry fought to relax his own muscles.

"Tell them we have everything he looks for," he said slowly, to Daylaylo. "Food, slaves, clean water. If he gets a ship, he will come south again, the way he always does. The People burn fires, eventually they will be seen. They are not safe."

"He has never come here before."

"They are not safe."

For a long time there was silence. Then the new Caffekey spoke, her voice strong and audible. When she spoke she did not look at Henry, as if addressing her question to the air; it was the first time he had heard her speak for herself.

"This man Starfish saw was in *Everglade*," she said, using the People's word. "With bears and ghosts. My hunters saw only a light, flickering on a beach. Starfish has perhaps seen also a ghost."

There was a murmur following the words, low and serious. Henry felt himself being closed off from their discussion, from their number. He looked at the dark faces.

"I need warriors," he said. "I need help. Men who can fight."

The Caffekey faced the air.

"My warriors do not fight against ghosts," she said. "Only Starfish can kill this spirit."

There was an assent among the men. Henry could feel them questioning their beliefs about him, beginning to speak and gesture among themselves. His legs were starting to weaken. On the way back to the island he had driven himself too hard, too quickly. It had taken almost a day to convince the hunters of the importance of what they had seen, that this was a sign from the panther itself; another day to hike back through the wastes and another to repeat the long trip in the canoes. Slowly he sat down on his haunches to hide the quaking of his legs.

But someone else was standing. Henry looked up.

"I go," the man said.

Henry looked at Tied Sticks, the furious joy of his face.

"The Caffekey has spoken," Daylaylo said.

"The Caffekey is dead," Tied Sticks answered, loudly. "I go with Starfish."

Fire moved through the seated men, licking and hot. The Caffekey looked at the air.

"Cervos-brother-son stands with Tied Sticks," one said, rising. "The man-Caffekey would have wanted men to stand."

"Let us end this," another voice said.

"I too stand," came a third. "I honor the Caffekey who is a woman. But the Caffekey who was a man makes men stand."

"Dishonor," someone said. "These are not warriors."

"The warrior who sits is dishonored."

"Whitepaul does not yet know we are here," Henry cut in. He could feel the shifting of forces among them, younger ones beginning to rise without speaking, faces afraid either to stand or to sit. "I don't believe he knows exactly where he is." He paused, turned to Daylaylo. "Tell them. Tell them what I am saying."

Daylaylo looked at him, his face a solid thing. He translated.

"If I am right," Henry said, "if I am correct about what he is doing, then his men are not prepared for an attack. He does not expect danger from the land. If we strike after dark we can have some down before the others know we are coming. But we need many warriors, at least three to his one. It is the only way."

Henry waited for more words to come but when they did not he sank his head again, signifying that his comments were concluded. Daylaylo rose.

"Stand up, Starfish," he said. Henry hesitated a moment.

"In any matter where life can be lost," Daylaylo called loudly, "the laws of the People say that the one in favor of action must announce his intention, truly and fully. You must say what you want to happen and you must say that it is you who wants it to happen. If you are not willing to do so your words have no weight. If you are willing to do so, then you must carry the weight of your words, and what they result in, always."

Daylaylo spoke to them all in their own tongue but his face remained directed piercingly at Henry, his eyes on Henry's eyes, the voice no longer speculative or warm. Henry's blood swam thickly inside him and he tried not to swallow. The expression on the Spaniard's face had something in it he had never witnessed before.

Henry looked around.

"I, Starfish, say here and now that we must attack and kill Captain Whitepaul and his men. I say that it must be done quickly. Days have already passed since we found him, and more will be required to return. He has found a beach that is the right shape for his plans, and I think he will stay there. But I cannot be sure. I say we decide tonight, this moment." He gritted his teeth, seeking a word in the People's tongue. "I know you have lost many in battles. I know some would like to hide now, and hope this place is never found by white men in their ships. I say you must be ready to be found. I say we decide tonight who still has *man's spirit.*"

There was a cheer: Tied Sticks and his men raised tilted fists, showing the bundled fingers in the gesture that signified the refusal of an open hand. Henry sat down and Daylaylo, having translated without taking his eyes off Henry's, remained standing. He spoke loudly to all the crowd and then reiterated in English.

"I, Fray Juan Batiste de Daylaylo; I, Man-in-tree; here and now call Starfish a liar and a taker of life. I say that he himself bears black will against this sea captain, and wishes the taste of blood only to satisfy his own desires. I say he puts the new arm he has been given to evil use. I say not one life among the People shall be wasted to feed the shameful hate of Starfish. Further I call him coward who is not able to defeat his own hate, but lets it turn him into itself."

Daylaylo sat fiercely, spinning himself away. He would not turn to let any part of his vision fall where Henry's shape would be in it. Henry felt the blunt power of the refusal, the threat of being made nothing. Suddenly he hated the apostate Spaniard; he hated the freakish and primitive people among whom he, a modern and the son of an aristocrat line, had been flung. And too he felt a pain, a leaping pain in his soul like some netted animal.

"Juan," he said, but the fixed countenance was away from him and unmoved. The darkness folded him into itself and Henry hated again, the hate moving in black wet tides through his veins and over his gut. He stood and left the congregation.

She was there as he had known she would be, not resting on the reed mat but seated on the ground behind it. Cautious, Henry thought, but not of me: of what I am doing. He had not seen her in the general gathering but he knew without hesitation that she was aware of everything that had happened there, was aware, before he had gone through the speaking of it, of everything that had happened even in the forbidden territory up north and the vision he had seen.

Henry flung himself down on the moss sacks and spoke to her, but she would not answer him. Only she remained seated where she was, looking at him, watching him as if to be aware of the minutest change. She did not resist him, remained listening as he tried to explain to her what he had done in the ghost lands and why he was going back there again, and what he would sacrifice in order to make this second journey. She told him that men do not make a second journey to that place; that the journey is only undertaken once in a season and only by men who are ready; that unprepared men must not see too much of the spirits or of their world, because it can become attractive to them, a vortex into which they are pulled, against their own nature.

She told him of the dangerous nature of ghosts, that some are mighty and stay on earth to achieve great purpose, while many are hurtful things. She told of temptation lights that beckon to men, seducing them over cliffs, and how always when this happens a man feels that the desire for it, the choosing of ruin, is his own.

She told him that when a man travels to the ghost lands he sees there the truth of his life, but that also he may see traps, walking dreams. That living men have energy of which they are unaware, they are repositories of force, and that only dead men who do not die can see clearly how great is the surfeit of a living man's power, and seek to drain him of it, for the cold nights flap the hollows of their flesh and the wind howls terribly through their bones.

Yet she had not spoken. Instead she cried for him, and rose and blessed his spirit and covered it with her own, like a blanket; and blessed the earth where he walked, that it might never lose sight of his feet, and left the hut.

In the morning Daylaylo was at his door.

"The People have decided," he said. His eyes, like the Caffekey's eyes, were fixed at a slight tilt to his head, so that no part of Henry's countenance would come within his view. "Tied Sticks will lead one warrior canoe. A second will be occupied by hunters who consider you blessed. A third by those people, neither warriors nor hunters, who consider you friend. You have not many warriors, but enough."

"All right," Henry said, but the Spaniard continued without stopping.

"The remaining men, whose number is the greater, still oppose you and your plan, and reject the welcome once offered to you in this community by the former Caffekey and his wife. They say you have traded poison food for good. Should you return you will find no home in the World. No such rejection falls on your men."

"That I…that only I …?" Henry's mouth was tight.

"*Starfish is not welcome in this shelter*," Daylaylo barked out, speaking as if literally to the hut in which Henry stood. "Starfish is not warmed by these fires. Starfish is not fed at this table. Starfish will leave the World. Starfish is not among us."

And Daylaylo made the shrieking sound, a wailing scream, high and terrible, the sound of skin being threshed. The Spaniard turned.

"And you, Juan?" Henry managed.

Daylaylo stopped. For a moment Henry thought he might turn: then he realized the other man was scraping his feet.

"I too reject you," he said.

23

A man was standing by the water.

"You go for her. To be free of her is still to go for her. You want to be free of her."

"No."

"Then you go because you know her *nickaleer* will die. You want to see him die. Perhaps you want to cut him up yourself."

"He will certainly die. But that is not why I go."

"Then you go because you wish to break every law, to find if there is any law you cannot break. To find a place where you cannot be a god."

"What do you know about me?"

But she came and put her hand again on his arm, not ashamed of what she had said. She was not the interlocutor but herself now. He felt the trembling, the not-warrior in him and he did not dare look.

"I know I am nothing. To you. To anyone."

"You are not nothing," he said.

"Stay then. Stay."

"For what."

But she could not answer.

"You know what it is with me," the man said. "Do not touch me. Do not look at me."

The woman wept.

"Do not cry for me. A concubine's tears."

"Stay."

"I have been great."

"There is no reason for this. A stranger's battle. No one but you sees a reason."

"I have been great."

But she could not answer.

"Learn yourself," the man said.

When the man had left the woman remained looking at the bright water. In her head she was listening to a song that the concubine mother had taught them all when they were children. It was a beautiful tune, but sad, about a girl made of rain. She listened for a while, rocking herself. She did not know just whose voice this was, speaking in her head, singing its song of woe.

24

Coming through the tall grasses again a chaos of mosquitoes met them, dropping down in nets so heavy they altered the afternoon sun. Henry saw the insects blackening the sweat-thick back of the man running in front of him. This native was heavyset and slow, his breath puffing audibly though he struggled to muffle the sound. Whenever Henry broke stride long enough to swipe a hand over his own forehead or the base of his neck it was like wiping away a second, writhing skin. He jogged badly in place, letting the cloud tear at his body.

When they made it to the beach again the *Arrogante* men were gone. There were no footprints and no sign of activity unobscured by the erasing power of waves. The trip up had been long once more, with the hunters in his canoe—Ajapeu, Isi, King George—wanting to repeat their time-taking rituals and Henry felt frustration come over him, a feeling like the reopening of a cut. The heavy man in front of him went down to the waterline and Henry followed suit, staying in the curl of sea breeze to avoid the blackflies. But there was nothing.

A temptation light, Henry thought, his breath coming brittle. *A setter of traps.*

As they turned down the beach again the others were waving to them. A warrior in Tied Stick's party had found something, just south of where they started.

When Henry got there the sand drawing was upside-down and for a moment, looking at its great bloated eye, he did not understand. Then he went around it to where the gondola was and saw the whole.

"It's a balloon. A dream of his."

Henry walked down to the water, crouching in its cool rush until his breathing was slowed. Tied Sticks came up from the treeline, his expression stone.

"It's good," Henry said, when he could speak. "It means he doesn't know anyone is here. He isn't expecting us."

Henry looked at the seascape.

"They need a spit of land to attack from, somewhere without much surf. We know what to look for."

The twins were peering at his mouth, waiting for a discernible sign. Henry drew in the wet sand.

"Half go north, half go south," he said. "Stay in the water, no footprints. See? Come back here …" He drew the sun setting. Tied Sticks called out to his followers and Henry started running lead in the other direction.

At sunset they met again, mirthless and silent, and crossed over the sandy hills to camp in their lee. Henry could feel the burning thing roiling inside him, the wanting thing, and he knew the tense fevered expression he had once been startled to find peering through cabin mirrors had once again come to his face. He could feel the muscles around his cheeks and mouth, pulling it backward as if to expose the skull. And he remembered the wooden mask Black P'ter hung on his cabin wall: lacquered and thick, the mask was rimmed with jutting carved feathers, all explosion and animal fury. Only the mouth had been painted white, every other inch the deep ochre of a devil.

Was he giving himself to this devil? The red screaming face swayed before him, stepping out of the thickening dark. P'ter had taken it from a group of slaves who had somehow carried it secretly, as if they were transporting a weapon that would avail them against their captors. Now the demon seemed free, roaming in Henry's consciousness, a force both familiar and nightmarish.

Vaguely he felt that something had not been realized that should have been realized. But the devil mask was dancing before him and distracting his mind; it buzzed like the insects; he was thinking and not thinking of something else.

"Of course," Henry said unconsciously, and began to ascend the tallest hill. Two hunters came with him and a warrior whose name he did not know, the People falling into alignment immediately and without instruction. Henry mounted the hill and a sea breeze lifted his uncut hair.

"There," he said.

A mile north of where they were crouching, the spark of a campfire shone.

The first group was sitting together on top of some dunegrass. Henry lay down flat when he saw them: three figures, possibly a fourth, crouched around the upward-flapping light. The warriors were on either side of him, blending correctly with darkness and even the sound of their bodies mixing with wave sound and night sound. Henry was amazed at their coordination. The skill of the hunters, the communion that synchronized their motions, was dwarfed by these. Tied Sticks' followers were a unit, speaking neither to him nor, almost, to each other, save for the brief authoritative enunciations Henry took to be signals along the chain of command.

By the time Henry had crawled close enough to make out faces the warriors had completed a circle around the campfire. Henry peered madly into the flicker-light, but already knew the captain was not among them. He recognized one of the sailors, a hornpipe player named Parrish, but the other two were stooped over the fire, cooking something on stakes. In a crazed exhilaration Henry stood up and walked into their circle.

As soon as Henry rose the pipe player turned, his pocked face going blank. For a moment he regarded Henry with neither malice nor comprehension. A gray slice of something was clamped in his teeth.

"Roojman," he said at last, smiling on bird flesh and uncocking the flintlock that Henry saw only then had appeared silently in his left hand. Tied Sticks stepped out from behind him and swung a cane machete at the man's neck, severing most of the shoulder and stopping at the spine. The blow, severe as it was, did not kill and the heavy-set man rose staggering to his feet. Henry saw the quick, soundless movement of shadows as the other two crewmen rolled silently backward. Parrish stood in a kind of daze, his boat jacket gone black down one side. He turned to see what could have happened to his companions and then, realizing for the first the extent of his injury, pried the flintlock out of his newly unresponsive fingers and raised it with the other hand. Tied Sticks swung a second time and hit the gun, knocking it into the sand where it misfired with a blue flash. Two figures came over the piper and closed his mouth in quick, efficient motions, like the skinning of a fish.

"Don't shoot it," Henry said, when a hunter stepped into firelight and lifted one of the undischarged pepperpots. "He can hear us."

They stamped out the fire in sand that was clumping up red. In the darkness Henry closed his eyes against nothing. He would think nothing, feel not at all; he saw only the African mask, the screaming face, and above it now, rocketing into the sky, the *Jolie Rouge* like a slash on the clouds.

You can create yourself again. You can make yourself right.

"There," Henry whispered. In the distance, down by the water: the cabin lantern.

Roojman.

Henry worked two unfired pistols into his belt and jumped at the side of the hill, skittering down it on the soles of his feet like riding a wave.

When they made it to level ground the grassy tumble gave way to hard-packed sand. The warriors began running truly then, again with that uninstructed unity of intention, their feet nimble against the pattering surface. Henry ran as well, desperate to keep pace. In the referentless dark he had the sudden inescapable sensation that he was not charging the lantern at all, but rather sitting immobile while the distant fire assaulted him, rocketing closer and closer with a meteoric precision. The lantern was closing in, not they: it was a flung weapon, a fireball, an omen. The image of Parrish with his neck split and his arm hanging lifeless nauseated his mind and he erased it violently. He himself had not committed the act; he had dwelt with lethal men but never partaken of their crimes. To the world into which he had been spat by some foul providence he had never belonged. Yet repugnance, genuine and extreme, crawled sickeningly over his brain.

Whitepaul. Now you will pay for me.

Henry ran, his blood up, his body strong. His heart kicked high in his throat. The lantern was almost within distance.

And abruptly into his mind came the shape of the constellations, the night he had seen them when the Caffekey died: he saw the lights whirling themselves from their familiar patterns into others, wild and obscure. He saw Libra, Aquarius, dissolve into the broken-winged bird that distracts the fox, the story that had been so alien to him he had refused to allow it a place in the heavens. And in a moment of terrible clarity he understood, he pieced together the sky-code his father had sought for years to decipher. The star bird's story was not alien, not strange: it was the story of the Christ. They were all the same story, told all over the world; the story of sacred martyrs, those who sacrifice themselves in order to save men from their own blood-loving Gods.

Henry skidded to his knees. The warriors nearest him fell too, looking furiously around to see what had interrupted their rush. They were just out of sight of the team at the water's edge.

"Stop," Henry whispered, his voice low. "Stop this."

Tied Sticks, landing next to him, stared wild-eyed, his legs positioned for leaping.

I have created this moment, Henry thought to himself. *This is mine.*

Juan, he thought. *I am so sorry.*

"Whitepaul!" Henry shouted, standing up absurdly and crying over the thunder of the waves. "They're coming for you! They're…"

But Tied Sticks pushed him down furiously and gave the scream, and the men flew, vaulting forward and lifting spear and hawsing iron and hatchet.

"…coming…"

There was a discharge of powder and Henry saw a glowing steel ball pass through Tied Sticks' torso, bringing a puff of sand up where it hit earth. Captain Whitepaul turned the rest of the way to see what he had shot and Tied Sticks' lifeless body crashed into his legs, the huge Britisher heaving it aside without changing position. He dropped the spent pistol and was taking aim already with a second gun, the other hand holding the cabin lantern high.

Henry watched, paralyzed, the amazing composure of the captain's motions. A third warrior closed on Whitepaul's side and the captain wrapped a broad arm around the man's neck and threw him bodily across the beach, sidestepping the foolish thrust of spear.

Shrieking, two hunters had one of *Arrogante's* men down and were pounding their blades into him, wasting time with the already lifeless corpse. Henry saw Black P'ter fire a round through the cheek of one hunter and out the top of his head, then grab the shaft that was being aimed at him and swing it like a club, knocking the second man back. When he had battered the other enough to disorient him he flipped the spear around and drove it into Isi's belly, sitting him down into the surf like an angler.

After the powder was gone there were fist blows, struggle. A final discharge came from somewhere down the beach, a greenish burst. Henry listened to the dimming thunder in himself, each beat of the landing waves. The heavy flintlocks he had drawn sagged uncocked against the sand. The lantern approached him.

"Roojman!" the silhouette roared, grabbing him up by the back of the neck. "If ye be he…!"

A great fist tangled in Henry's hair and hauled him around as if to convince itself of his reality. Then it straightened him up for the rest of the company.

"Roojman lives!" Captain Whitepaul bellowed. "My boy lives!"

Henry looked around. There were ten of them, easily, far more than they could have taken even with surprise. Whitepaul's officers: Hooker and Angel and Benjamin Oldham; the Irishman and the Squire; others he did not know. Black P'ter returned from the surf's edge where several of the hunters now lay, Ajapeu sitting upright like a child musing on a book. Henry watched the edge of a wave topple into the corpse's lap and fill it with foaming water before turning his eyes away.

"Roojman lives!" Whitepaul cried again, and embraced him hard. The gold skull tumbled against his face. Whitepaul had affixed it to a chain and wore it around his neck, Spanish coins now wedged into its eyes. "And ye saved us from destruction, did ye, lad? Did ye, my own?"

P'ter looked carefully up and down the beach before examining Henry.

"The boy wears native," he said.

"Eh?" Whitepaul asked, pulling Henry back to inspect him for the first time. "Now boy, have ye gone and turned savage in so short time?"

The captain shook him hard.

"I lived…I was with …"

"Aye ye did, ye did," Whitepaul clucked, finally releasing him with such vehemence that Henry staggered. "Roojman's the clever one! Red Man dresses on him! He knows where to find it on these islands. Eh?"

Henry looked at the faces in the lamplight: faces out of the dark dream of his life. They watched him with a silent eye.

"How come ye with these, monkey?" the Irishman asked. With one foot he kicked at the unmoving body of a warrior.

"I couldn't …" Henry choked, still facing Whitepaul. The mad captain beamed.

"Heard his cry just before the wild ones made for me. Heard your warning, boy. Saved me, this one did."

"Was it Roojman who cried out, then?"

"Oi, damn your soul, my Roojman," Whitepaul hissed, going to the Squire and pushing him hard. "My Roojman saved us all. You'll love him for it, you will."

The men were silent. Henry could feel the strangeness of his dress, the markings across his body.

"You'll welcome him back to us," Whitepaul shouted, his bleeding fingers wrapping into fists around the lamp handle. "Eh? Will ye? *Eh*?"

Oi, they said then, the spectre-men, and a chant went up. *Roojman. Roojman.*

Henry heard the word echo from the soft hills.

"This one still lives," P'ter interrupted, pushing a cutlass tip into the soft flesh of a native's ribs. Henry looked: for a moment King George Skanondo seemed to meet his eyes, but it was delirium. Henry said nothing.

"Don't waste a powder on him," Whitepaul instructed, pressing his foot into the fallen man's neck and grinning brightly at Henry as he waited. After a minute King George fingered the sand as if to inspect it and lay still. A sailor whose face Henry recognized but whose name he had never known came staggering into the light, his striped shirt dark around the belly.

"Bastards," he hissed. "Native…Adams and Eves …" He was still holding the removed arrow in one hand.

Whitepaul examined the sailor's wounds with his fingers. When the sailor knelt down and vomited a thin bloody stream the captain took the bandana off the man's head and, grabbing the scalp roughly, kissed it. Then he plucked up one of Henry's pistols and shot the kneeling man behind the ear.

"Get his rings," he said to anyone, coming and taking Henry under his arm and pulling him in joyously like a prodigal.

In the morning the last sons of *Arrogante* built a driftwood fire and ate white shredded horse meat burned onto sticks. Henry could see the evidence of their previous forays, antlers and small rib cages buried haphazardly in piles and being worked over by flies. They had had no trouble surviving. The bodies of their slain fellows they rolled into the surf until they were gone but the dead People remained, naked and half buried, spread out randomly over the tide-washed sand. Henry swallowed nothing, seeing and willing himself not to see the faceless humps of the twins, bare and exposed to sun; the wide defenseless back of Tied Sticks, his powerful limbs disappearing under wet drifts of sand.

"We had a day of it, Roojman, in the teeth of the blow."

Whitepaul was grinning between bloody gums. Something had been cracked inside his mouth during the previous night's battle and he worked at it as he ate, spitting red into the fire. "My lady gale came at us with a bitch's tongue, heeled us full over. That's when we lost you, my lad, and other hands too. But old P'ter, my nigger—eh? my right hand—old P'ter is not troubled. Nay. He puts her out to sea, and runs with the greater wind."

Henry looked at the captain's broad, scratched face, impossibly risen before him. He knew what Whitepaul was describing—how he, the captain, obliterated by drink, had allowed his ship to stray into a gale; how to every other hand onboard had fallen the responsibility of salvaging impossible chances out of his deadly irresponsibility. Yet the captain squinted in enormous mirth as he spoke.

"Like a king's mare we rode it, Roojman! And the blow followed us…followed us, hear me…it was tied to our masts. She baited us, dogged us, hour, hour, hour. Now her mind is set on snapping rudders. Now she gnaws on the stays. Every bank, all the whitewater in hell, she sends at us to down us. But we do not down. We do not down. My beautiful *Arrogante* ran with it. Our mainsail broke and fallen. Our foresail in ribbons. We were a devil ship then, my Roojman, running sea behind us and looking like the spirit of the storm. But at full sunup we were still afloat." His voice dropped into whisper. "Do ye know what came *then*, boy?"

Henry watched the great wide face close on his.

"*Gulls*," Whitepaul rumbled, his breath fetid. "A haunting of seagulls, Roojman. A *haunting*."

The captain gestured obscurely with his bone and meat, as if drawing some mystic emblem.

"Staggering from my cabin came I. Eh? The fo'c'sle two-quarters full, men and cargoes, splashing about. A company of gulls—flapping, white as knuckles—gulls in the companionway, *inside*, Roojman, so that holding fast, and feeling her list, every mate and man is faced down by those staring demons. Do I lie?"

Nay, 'tis so, the others assented. They too had witnessed the strange visitation.

"One caught me with his eye," Whitepaul leered, "to curse me with his eye, eh? How I spat at it, boy! But the imp just stood, perched on a locker, with that black water risin and fallin... and risin ..."

Whitepaul flipped the rib into the flames and wiped his hands across his coat.

"When I saw that eye I knew my *Arrogante* hadn't an hour left in her, calm sea or no. I made for deck ladder...imps everywhere, set on every line...making not a sound. But watching...watching...as if every mate's soul was their food. These who loved me most had the longboat lowered. And over we went."

Whitepaul spat and grinned that empty mirthless grin at the sun, looking into its hot white extremity without closing down his eyes.

"She turtled like a child's toy, Roojman," Hooker added, with genuine remorse. "It was a pity to hear her groan. We rowed hard to get free. And many a crewman followed her down."

Henry saw the image in his mind. A sinking ship the size of *Arrogante* was like a clutching hand as it went under, vorticing the fluid around it into a vacuum pool.

"*Oiyay*, and not a few bastards grabbing the oars." Whitepaul huffed. He made a swinging gesture to demonstrate how he had dealt with the struggling sailors, an hour before under his command, who would so far presume as to cling to the lip of his escaping craft. Henry felt a sweeping, bilious sensation pass through his frozen consciousness. The image of the old steersman hacking at his own men, steadying the tiller as he did so with one jovial leg, swam up before him. And in desperate understanding his soul cried out that this man *was* the *Arrogante*, Whitepaul *was* the ship he rode: a bulk of violence and passion, driving down eternally into the murk.

"What happened to the birds?" Henry said. Whitepaul punched

him in the ear, knocking him from the log where he sat.

"Demons they were! White demons and eaters of souls! They had their feast, Roojman, and flew back to their hell. To their *hell*!"

To hell, the others chanted, thick hands beginning to slap at soiled breeches. *To hell.*

Whitepaul reached down and grabbed the starfish necklace, snapping it off Henry's neck.

"What's this, then? Some pretty shells on my boy? Eh?"

He pitched the thing into the fire. Henry saw the five-legged creature land between two logs, beginning to blacken and curl. "Get the damned Red Man paint off him," Whitepaul muttered.

Angel pushed him down to the surfline and into a falling wave, grabbing fistfuls of sand and thrashing them across Henry's shrieking body. Henry swallowed wavewater, heard himself hollering inside the icy wetness. When they came back up his skin was bare and red. Angel put a hand on his lower spine and shoved him to the ground next to Whitepaul. The captain was crying.

"I am glad you live, boy," he wept.

Henry could say nothing. In the company of these men all the changes that had happened in him were vitiated, made hollow; he was child again, his mind blank and unusable. His consciousness returned implacably to the state that held it on the first night on the island, before the World, before Speaking Owl, before his wellness and his indifference and his revenge. The red form of the jacket closed around him like an animal and he felt the hard broken cloth against his cheek. He knew what it would have been like to be strangled by the man, to have his own life literally crushed.

"But we lost a pretty ship when *Arrogante* went under," the Irishman lamented.

"*Oi.* E'en so."

"A large ship, and lovely. Quick in a wind. Not a frigate, but proud as a frigate. And strong in the line."

"*Oiyay.*"

"And now the mad devils have made us miss our appointment. The slaver has passed us."

"What slaver?" Henry asked, abruptly. His body, still puckered by the frigid water, was half covered in sand. The *Arrogante* men looked at him as if a carved figurehead had spoken.

"Spanish slave ship, lad," Hooker said. He tapped a copper

spyglass condensed into one pocket. "She looks to be searching the coast. She was coming on well before darkness, closing at good speed. A brig. South America bound, or I'm a fool."

Abruptly the numbness of Henry's mind lifted. The awakening sensation was like a sensation of pain, like the passage from immovable torpor to sudden unbearable heat. He saw the scattered, bloody beach on which they sat, birds flapping and landing on the warrior's bodies. He saw the rude sun making its way relentlessly up the sky.

"I know where they are," he said.

"*Oh do ye*?" Whitepaul answered, and swung out his meaty fist. Henry ducked and stood up. The captain looked amazedly at him, as if his hand had passed through a shade.

"They're looking for settlements. Indians."

"We know their business, monkey," P'ter said. "We only wanted to relieve them of their vessel."

Henry looked at the breed of men before him. Hooker, his face still intelligent, but thinned now like a melted candle. The Irishman, ill-looking, bitter, perhaps carrying yellow fever. Black P'ter and Whitepaul, unchanged and unchangeable.

"There's a village on a small island south south-west of here," he said. "They burn shore fires at night. A slaver can't miss them."

"And what will they find there, lad?" the Squire asked. "More of your screamin' friends?"

"There are natives there. Many. An entire community. Chaining…chaining them all will take time." Henry waited.

Whitepaul's wide face was looking at him curiously. In his expression Henry could see clearly the two parts of the man's soul: the one that rode the surface, full of bluster and illogic; and the second one, underneath, that saw opportunity and evaluated it with relentless precision.

"How far?"

"A day. Just over."

"That's a hard trip in a longboat," the captain mused.

"We don't have to travel in the boat. There are canoes, enough for all of us. They're thin and fast. I can show you where."

"*Pyratae* in canoes," Hooker smiled, warming. "Now *this* is fresh."

25

Marces Albenix stood at the top of the rise and turned his back until he was once more facing the sea. *Legenda Aurea* was moored there, in the calm just beyond the reef, sternboats anchored at the land's edge where the convenient beach ended in a thick cover of trees. As he watched three pelicans sailed closely over the green water's surface, their wing tips almost touching.

"I want you to know that I understand," he said to the sky.

Behind him a man knelt on the ground. His wrists and ankles were tied with rope that ran also across his belly and large wooden oar had been slid behind his arms so that they were kept forcibly bent. It was not possible for him to straighten himself into a standing position.

"Can you hear me still?"

"I can hear you."

"Perhaps you would like a drink of water," Albenix said, narrowing his vision down to the trim edge of his fingernail. "Clean water, I mean. I can have some brought to you."

The tied man said nothing.

"It is important to me that you understand my position."

Albenix turned.

"I do not wish our relationship to be merely a...*perfunctory* one. In many ways I need you. Oh, it seems a hollow sentiment, hollow. But it is still the nature of the case."

The *comandante* crouched and looked carefully at his prisoner.

"I have been charged with the survival of divinity in a new world," he said, with feeling. "A *new world.* Without such actions as I take, this novelty, this ..." he gestured around himself. "This playground of the nations...would be a bauble. Its destiny would remain unrealized."

The *comandante* waited a few moments before straightening up again.

"Holy Mother Church needs this power. The world has seen to it that she must. And power cannot be given into her hands by weak men. The men God loves. It must be attained by the ones He hates."

The prisoner coughed, spitting something into the grass. His breath rattled in one of his lungs. Albenix seemed to consider the gesture as if it had been a reply.

"What is the image of God's face?" he asked suddenly.

The prisoner breathed, thin, painful.

"I...have...not seen it."

"I wonder," Albenix mused. "How did it appear to the money changers in the temple? The scourge, the whip, wielded by the Savior's hand—that too was the face of God. Was it not? How did it appear to them against whom his fury was addressed? Are we not constrained to say that this too must have been a beautiful...a glorious face?

"Consider my situation. I am a money changer, taking these little coins down to Havana. Taking others up to *Augustin*, there to work the corn. Unknown by even some of my own soldiers, I am sent by *Junta de Guerra de las Indias.* I am sent also by Madrid. Many men make me up. For them all, I come.

"And I expect to see wild ones. I expect that; the outside lands are thick with lost souls. But also I find you. A disciple. Yet not a disciple. Nowhere in your possession an emblem of your faith. Nowhere a book of prayer. No masses held for these *incipientes*, no instruction, no remission of sins. Nothing about you tells me what you are...what you admit to being.

"Brother," he continued, after a pause. "I ask you now directly. Do you believe in the flesh? You know the man I mean: the seed of David."

The tied man was silent.

"Why will you not profess your faith, I wonder? Is it dried up inside you by the endless sun of this world?"

"Finish your work," the tied man said.

"I assure you that I will," Albenix pouted, looking almost hurt. "But you do me an injustice. I have become fascinated by you, brother. Will you not confess to me what it feels like to be inside your soul? Even now?"

The *comandante* lifted the tied man's face up gently and looked into his eyes. The left one had gone red.

"You vex me, my brother, you vex me," the *comandante* said. "My *conciencia.* By your office you are bound to love Him."

"I have loved."

"What, though?" Albenix said loudly, dropping the limp head as if suddenly he held a disgusting thing. "A phantom of your brain? The Risen One is *this*." He grabbed the soft muscle between the tied man's shoulders in a studded glove. "He is meat, true meat. He is not airy fancies of a sun-blinded dreamer. Again."

This last word was spoken to two officers who stood behind the tied man. One was darkly haired; the other had a freckly child's face and his expression was blank, like a parchment from which all the words have been rubbed clean. They unstoppered cruets and poured the clear vinegar across the kneeling man's back where the whipmarks flared red.

"You wonder who I am," Albenix said hotly. "You think me unholy. But the house of God has many rooms: and one of them…let it be only one, still that is a room…one of them houses *me*.

"Listen to me now. Is there not assurance in this? The common lot…the horde of man…who can say of this one or that one for *certain* that he shall be saved? Scripture informs us that few are chosen. *Few are chosen.* I think on those words, my brother. At times I feel that all my life those words have been at my side. *Few are chosen.* Some days they ride in my mouth. Some days they rest behind my eyes, and I see them only…or all things I see must pass them first. *Few are chosen. Few are chosen.*

"There is an economy to the Lord's table. Think again of the horde of men. This one, that one? In whom do deeds shine so brightly as to certainly, without question, attract the winnower's eye? Even a paltry mess of cripples overwhelmed Him in His day. If a dozen broken men taxed His mercy, what then of the thousands? What of the crowds who will rise for the threshing? Think of them, rising like crops to await the blade. Their numbers appear before me, brother, their concept—their *concept* stays with me—a plague, an infection of the brain. *Few are chosen. Few are chosen.*

"But the man who works God's violence." The *comandante* paused. His spirit had grown passionate, as if in this he had come to the *demonstratum* of a well-established claim. "The executioner. The black hood amongst the brown. *This* soul is remembered. *This* stands out loudly. The crucifiers were the first to be relieved of their sin. Is it not then a surety to be a hangman of God?"

" …things…honest …"

The tied man whispered with difficulty. Albenix leaned down.

"... provide things honest...in the sight of men ..."

"What if through my lie the truth of God has abounded?" Albenix retorted.

"He rebuked the wind...and said unto the sea, peace ..."

"I came *not* to send peace, but a sword."

"He that hateth his brother...is in darkness ..."

"But what I hate, that I do."

"Doest faithfully whatsoever thou doest...to strangers ..."

"*But those mine enemies, which would not that I should reign over them, bring hither, and slay them before me.* Mother church requires I exist. She requires my labors so that *she* may come unsullied to her dominance. Is there anything achieved in a million-souled Peace? What have the cattle done toward straightening His paths? Will lambs forge their own pens?"

The *comandante* came low again.

"Listen to me, brother. We are told to shelter them, but not *how*. They would have no shelter if it were not for men such as I. Men who take on the burden of violence. Men who lovingly accept the mantle of His hatred. Can you begin to understand the extremity of my sacrifice? We embrace the despite of the Mighty, so that the Mighty will be praised. We break the spine of the passive, that His passivity be supreme. We are the Scapegoats of the Savior. We give away everything for a place in His kingdom, including our place in His heart."

The tied man stretched his arms wide against the oar, trying to relieve his shoulders. His face was constricted. The *comandante* rose and walked slowly, meditating.

"On my ship, brother, on my cabin wall, I have mounted the head of a large animal. None of them who serve me have seen it. None deserves that beneficence. I myself pulled it from the sea.

"My family, I can tell you, was from Guipuzcoa. When I was very young I felt the calling; the call made to Zebedee's son. The call to which the whole heart responds, unopposed. But my family did oppose. They wanted me to marry.

"There are no coincidences in life, brother. I had achieved excellence in Pamplona. At the end of my studies I was to wed. Instead I packed three breadbags with meats and left for Montserrat. My plan was an innocent's plan. I would travel to the

Shrine of the Black Virgin and cast myself before Our Lady.

"On the way I believed—I confess my vanity—I believed I had begun to come closer to Her. During the struggle, begging…yes, begging…sleeping in streets or in filthy styes, I had moments… moments of closeness. The door touched, even lingered on. But unopened.

"All this time my family believed I was engaged in courtship. How could I explain to them the power of the call, the voice that was consuming me like a wound? How could I explain the She that was like a fire-hot metal the gripping hand cleaves to, unable to release what consumes it?

"And then came the day. My father received word of the young lady's family. She had married elsewhere, and his fortunes had been overpassed. He came for me physically. I was living with the Benedictines then, wearing a pilgrim's garment. He thrust me out into the yard. He beat me until I felt my own defecate drop down the skirt of my cloak. And behind us, eyes averted, the monks chanted their morning Office.

"For many weeks I was unable to speak, to coordinate my hands. Yet the pain I felt, the humiliation, were as nothing. The great suffering was the loss of Her, the sense that it was Her holy hand that had rejected me, struck me out like an item edited from a list.

"I was taken home, left in a cousin's estate. When some weeks later I saw myself in a mirror I believed I was looking at something dead. Some repugnant form, slunk from a sepulcher. I loathed myself then, brother. Had I presented to majesty this? Had I dared offer this offence?

"In time my father repented of his excesses; he put me to work in a fisherman's crew at San Sebastián. One morning a squall blew in off the bay where we were. It was a small affair, but our labor was delayed. The owners had long been engaged in a competition with another family, and their survival hinged on a single night's losses.

"I remember we were pulling in baskets of *macabi*, black, slithering things whose mouths opened wide in the poisonous air. I was aware of nothing. Not hatred, no. Not revenge. My soul was a wire basket and each day was water falling through it.

"And suddenly the *piola* I was turning—the *piola* I gripped in my palms—pulled away from me with such power as to burn the skin. I looked down stupidly at what had happened just as the fishermen started shouting. A mammoth creature had broken the surface, brother, not a dozen leagues off. Something blue and holy, fixing me with the knowledge of its eye.

"All the men worked the one line; a deep water fish, it had come strangely close, as if seeking to cast itself onto our gaffs. After a long struggle they pulled it up and, watching the fishermen beat its skull with wooden hammers, I began to emerge from the cloud into which I had been flung. I saw bright red spill from the beast's open mouth, and the color was a bell in my mind.

"They tell me I knelt by the great marlin and embraced it. That I ran my hands along the snout, weeping and feeling the little hooks. I cannot say. All I knew was my happiness had been achieved.

"Could She have shown me more clearly my *eximia ilustración*, o brother? Could She have demonstrated Her desire for my life in any way greater than by bringing me this like offence—this freak—this thing that was both fish and weaponry?

"The bleeding eye looked at my own. *I am her church*, the eye cried, *spiked and militant.* Live flesh, brother, riding on blue wings. One in being with the natural sword.

"The fishermen saw in me only a mad child, delirious. They threw me aside with some laughter. They were very happy about the money they would have. Then they removed the insides from the creature and strung it on chains. I remember the silver belly swinging about in the morning rain. I lay on the deck, curled on myself. My forehead rested in the red and black wash that rolled slowly against the bulkheads.

"I was born that night, my brother. Born and swallowed."

Albenix mused quietly for a long while. A land breeze came and moved warmly through his thickly curled hair. Then he walked over to the tied man and slapped him across the teeth.

"*Priest! Where is your cross*?"

"All burned and gone," the tied man answered. On his back bright green flies had started to gather.

"A friar who burns his redeemer. You are farther gone than even I can forgive."

The *comandante* dug the ground reflectively with the tip of his boot. Behind him the two soldiers remained at attention, the dark haired one faintly bored. The other's face showed nothing. He might have been staring at a plaster wall.

The prisoner's hips were beginning to give way and he knelt at an absurd angle now, like something melting in the sun.

"I could leave you here," the *comandante* said, after a while. "I could leave you these secret pleasures, these freedoms you have created for yourself. These women. These children.

"But you would have to do something for me. You would have to do something for me. A small thing. A small thing."

The *comandante* leaned close to the tied man, opening up his shirt and producing his necklace. The thin crucifix was hammered silver.

"Kiss His feet," he whispered, close by the tied man's ear. "You need not speak. You need not believe. Simply kiss them. Once."

Juan Daylaylo opened his eyes. The left one was swollen and bluish and came only part way up. He struggled to focus on the object before him.

"Kiss Him," Albenix whispered. "Kiss him sweetly."

Daylaylo moved once in his confinement, his body seeming to disagree with itself. For a moment his torso leaned forward, bobbing against his rope binding. Albenix opened his lips slightly, watching the motions, the cross held excitedly in his outstretched hand. Then the motion stopped.

"Love is not made out of lies," Daylaylo said, drawing back. He began to weep.

The *comandante* stood up.

"Garrote him," he said.

The expressionless *teniente* removed a short but enormously thick length of rope from a satchel at his side. Without looking at the face he wrapped the unpliant length once around the tied man's neck and began to pull. The method was designed not to suffocate simply but to compress the vertebra of the neck until they split. The tied man's tongue was forced gradually through his clenched jaw, his face bent backward toward the sky.

yet he was not kneeling among them. He was not tied to an oar with no feeling in his hands or his arms, needle pains swimming behind his eyes. He was not feeling the sad frenzied desperation for air and the blood pressing like a purple-red thunder against the inside of his head

Rather he stood in the middle of a high-grassed field. It was twilight, the thin rind of sun visible on the horizon, within moments of its final disappearance. The sky overhead was purple with clouds, revealing the first stars in clusters. He could feel the cool breeze that had crossed thousands of miles to caress his skin. The land around him was grass; the land went on forever

Child, *someone said.*

Juan looked: a man wrapped in black cloth, blacker than mere darkness, a velvety absence like midnight. He was kneeling on a wooden cart with wheels, his legs and arms bent uselessly behind him. As Juan watched the man rose, lifting his wheeled cart under one arm. Juan saw the muscular swinging of his limbs. He came with authority

There, *the man said, standing at his side.*

Juan looked and before him was an enormous lignum tree, gnarled by time, its trunk wider than three men could girdle and its branches wrapping the sky. The root of the tree was eons, its bark the skin of patriarchs. The hovering breeze left him and ruffled the tree's leaves instead and there, seated high in its branches, he saw the Panther: its sinewy form slung over the flesh of the branches like a throne. Its pelt had become star-filled and in its jaws hung the spotted deer, kicking. Juan knew

Lord, *he said.* I am not worthy to receive you.

The sun was gone and the cat's eyes met his, its eyes turned to twin shining moons. With a remorseless thrust of its head it broke the animal's neck

"*Ya está*," the *teniente* said. The *comandante* came forward and looked at the tied man as if he were leaning into a well.

"Did he not mutter?"

The *teniente* said nothing, looking at nothing and Albenix drew closer, staring into the corpse's expression as if something about it eluded him.

"A confession, perhaps," he said to himself.

Albenix removed the leather glove from his left hand and with his bare fingers slid the wafer between the motionless lips.

26

The cook was making coffee on deck when he heard the voice. For a moment he stood where he was and listened, his brain, somnolent in the repetition of duty, having difficulty with the emergence of the new. Around him the galley air was thickly laced with scent: the coffee itself, sour and vaporous; the odor of chained men in the hold; the cookstove, still hot from the flamed sowbelly the crew had taken and the saltiness of it congesting around the tarred smokehole. He waited until the sound came again: *haloo-o-o*, from above.

He returned the black crumbles to the paper over which he had opened them and, wiping his square stumpy fingers on his shirt, climbed to the empty deck. There was no one. Aft by the sweeps he even lifted a secured canvas with one foot, making angry sounds at whoever might be underneath because vaguely he felt he was being mocked, before the sound came again. Finally understanding he peered over the side.

In the distance, past the brightly colored shallows, he could see the green-gray edge of the island. At first he thought one of the transport boats had returned, but no, this was not that. It looked like a narrow sliver of wood in the water, with a white man whom he had never seen before standing in it. The boat was so tiny that the figure had a foot on either side of its hull, like someone balancing on a rope. The cook leaned over the bulwark and stared as if at a dream.

"*Qué carajo quieres…?*"

"*Nosotros deber haber un sermón antes de somos por*," the man shouted back. The cook's face hung with a natural stupidity. Really it was a miracle if the fool could even stand up in that tiny bit of wood. The first wave would swamp him.

"Everyone has gone ashore." He pointed toward the green and brown hump in the distance. "There!"

"I wonder if you have an opinion," the man called back in English, using his hands like bullhorn. "Which in the Pardoner's Tale deserves pardon?"

"*¿Cómo dice?*"

"I said, which person in the Pardoner's Tale deserves pardon? For I smell a Lollard in the wind, quoth he. Now hearken me!"

"*What, damned...what do ye say?*"

The man standing in the tiny boat began to sing.

For well says Solomon, in his language,
Bring thou not every man into thine house;
For harbouring by night is dangerous.
Well ought a man to know the man that he
Has brought into his own security ...

"Are ye mad?" the cook shouted. "Are ye sea mad or an Englishman? I tell ye the captain ..."

But his slow brain was picking up speed. Outside the edge of the slaver's shadow something had moved. Low, close to the water.

"*Virgen Maria,*" the cook said, running to the larboard side.

"Listen to me, you bloody stupid spig!" the man on the thin boat was hollering. "I'm over here!"

But the cook was looking at a vision emerging from the shadow where it lay. In the vision was a black man, muscled and large, lying flat on the water as if he had slept there for ages. On his bare chest, one in each hand, twin axes were crossed.

"*Ladrones,*" the cook whispered, then shouted. "*¡Ladrones!*"

The vision seemed to be roused by his voice. In an impossible motion the African rose and threw an ax into the ship's wood, pulling himself up by its handle. The second ax hauled him halfway up the hull and by the third he was over the gunwale.

The cook turned to run and slipped headlong into a deck lamp, shattering it and falling gracelessly to all fours. He looked back and the black man was fully boarded now and dropping lines over the rails. There were other men rising, filling her fast.

"*¡Ladr ...*" the cook cried again and the word was crushed down into his larynx by the brass end of a cutlass. Several shift-men emerged from below, armed with utensils and jackknives, their voices a uniform shout. The attackers launched themselves.

When the fighting was ended three Spaniards stood physically shaking in the center of the deck, their hands raised and empty as the marauding crowd circled them wolf-fashion. One of their member in sea boots and formal naval clothing begged this way and that, desperate to confirm his defenseless position. He could see nothing to give him hope. The attackers were a blur of male faces, mouths laughing, wooden clubs jabbing at his rib and spine and cheek.

Then they broke apart and through their center came an enormous man with a golden ball slung around his neck on a chain. The prisoner stopped his supplications, looking at this figure in disbelief.

"How far to land, boys?" Captain Whitepaul boomed. He leaned into the closest Spaniard's face as if preparing to bite. "How far?"

"Mira, hay dinero puede tenerlo, tom…"

"No Santy-ago talk with me, lad! Speak like a man!"

"You can see," a second Spaniard stammered. He was very thin and the shape of his bones emerged at wrist and jaw and along the broken edge of his nose. "Mile. Two mile."

"Swim it," the huge man said.

The Spaniard swallowed, seeking the word. "S …s …"

The crowd leaned close.

"S…sh . . *arks* …" he managed.

The captain turned toward his ring of companions with a great red-cheeked happiness.

"Oh-ho!" he bellowed. "Thank ye for reminding me, *peso*!"

He drew a dirk and dragged it across the prisoner's ear, splitting the cartilage.

"Now you'll swim faster, won't ye, boy? Eh?"

With one arm Whitepaul hauled the writhing figure toward the gunwale and, when the Spaniard's ankles collided with the railing, flipped the rest of him over like a sack. The officer and the other man, seeing the attention taken from them, charged an empty part of the railing on the opposite side and vaulted it.

The crewmen clapped like a satisfied audience and began spreading out over the ship.

"Square rigged, with a fore-and-aft for good measure! Deep keel, with a Spanish wheel on her! A large ship she is. Now we sail!" Whitepaul stopped. Black P'ter was standing in front of him. The captain put his hand out on P'ter's bare chest, as if to read his intention through his heart: *the boy.*

27

Comandante Albenix walked slowly down the line of resistors, examining each as he passed. When required, the nooses had been slung up over tree limbs but the method was found to be so unreliable—one native had slipped entirely down and choked instead in the dust—that he had ordered his men to erect a makeshift gallows from wooden beams brought in from the ship. Only two structures had been possible, given the limited materials, but it was found that three ropes could be tossed over one beam and two over another and thus a total of five souls accommodated at any given time.

Had they been a Catholic tribe, Albenix thought, he would perhaps have allowed some to stay, but once resistance had been shown there was nothing else for it. Word of hesitation spread rapidly here and was no means trivial in its effects. And resistance there had been. The old woman had fought them by throwing a pot of live coals at one of the soldiers when they were affixing the chains; and Albenix, watching carefully, had come to understand by the way the others regarded her that she was in some sense a leading figure. That made her disciplining especially relevant.

The old woman's neck was thin and hard to tie correctly into place but when it was done Albenix gave the order and the soldiers kicked out the log on which she stood. She did not die at once and he had one man grab hold of the knees and pull downward for a time. Then they unloaded the bodies of the old woman and a few male resistors and put them with the rest.

Albenix went down to the water and surveyed the progress. Some of the Carib he had previously loaded had fallen ill; these number would make up partly for that loss. Some difficulty was always to be expected, and he tallied the additions in his mind and counseled himself to be satisfied if he arrived in Cuba with three-quarters the figure he had originally proposed. He could make speeches there, explaining the settlements in Nova Spain with a romantic flair; he was familiar with the court. He returned to the hangings.

The soldiers had gotten around to the girl. She was short enough that the rope intended for her had to be undone and lengthened before it would reach her neck. When the nooses were on her and another two men on the second gallows Albenix signaled a halt.

He walked slowly along the roped figures, stopping when he was in front of her. She was pretty, really, in an uncultured kind of way. She had small, understated breasts and an evenness of feature, that animal curve of flank that one did not often see. No devil's markings had been inked across her skin. And something was there in her eye: she was looking at him not, as the others did, with hatred, but with a kind of intense and unflinching scrutiny.

"None of you speak my tongue," Albenix said. "Yet some of you have spoken the holy name. From this I must conclude that you have been given the true word and thus have no excuse for your rejection of it. The mad friar did you a great disservice. Before him, you might have been considered innocents."

The natives, when interrogated, had been able to produce a kind of de-elevated Spanish, a strange bastardization that seemed to contain fragments of English and even Latin. It sounded like the mother tongue spoken mockingly, where every mouthful was an insinuation. Worst of all was how they repeated the name of the savior, pointing at him and his soldiers all the while. The effect had unsettled his men, the less robust of whom had grown frightened at their having disciplined a Franciscan. Seeking to quell the chill Albenix had drawn out the crucifix and shown it to the natives but gotten no coherent reaction. Some nodded, as if waiting for him to do more; some responded not at all; others gestured insistently toward the trees, explaining something to him that had no explanation. In time he had stoppered their mouths.

The girl's hair was pulled behind her ears by the noose so her face showed clearly like a male's. Albenix examined her. He realized then why her expression was unusual to him: she was looking at his eyes. Not into them, not challenging, but *at* them, as if seeking something there in the physical objects themselves.

"You are different," he said. "Even your features are distinct. Your skin, your hair. Not at all like the others."

The *comandante* leaned close and smelled slowly the sweat of the girl's cheek.

"Such a fighter," he whispered. "We have that in common. You resisted better than many of these boys."

He put out a finger and touched the girl's upper lip, the small dent that led to her nostrils. His cabin boy had dissatisfied him; indeed, the child had come at him the week before with a sheath knife, so that Albenix had broken him and with a heavy heart lowered his body into the sea.

His hand began to drift down the rope-circled neck.

"Were you the friar's special one, I wonder? Did he show you certain things? Perhaps I could consider …"

There was a noise from the encampment. Figures were moving around them, slipping through trees. One figure moved fast, passing branch after branch as if it rode an invisible mount.

"Hang them," Albenix said, drawing his flintlock.

Something came closer to the edge of the wood and Albenix leveled his gun at it and fired. He waved the spent barrel through the smoke and a charging shape hit him from behind. He saw the ground come up too fast, felt the collision he could not prevent and pushed furiously to his knees, flinging away his tangled scabbard. Whatever had struck him was gone again into the underbrush.

"Do it, do it now …" Albenix shouted, shaking his barrel to clean it and bringing out a new bag of powder.

The soldiers stood transfixed for a moment and then one began kicking away the logs on which the natives stood, one man's legs swinging out in a futile attempt to strike his chest. The other soldier came forward, looking into the foliage. His face was death-white.

"We're damned men if we stay," he broke out suddenly. *"Es la fantasma del fraile …"*

"Que le den por culo a tus fantasmas!" Albenix cried, trying to force the man away.

"*Somos culpable hombres*! He has come for our souls …"

The noise from the village center had risen to discernible shouts and the soldiers turned slowly around. The village behind them was on fire.

"*Comandante …*"

Albenix looked. His landing party was in a battle, being struck by a crew that had come from nowhere. Dressed in rags, the impossible force was brandishing cutlasses with relentless enthusiasm, cheering and laughing like children at a game. In a dreamlike moment Albenix saw one of his best swordsmen sit down as if to rest, removing his helmet. The inside was full of blood.

"*Conjuror*!" Albenix hissed. "A black cleric ..."

There was a gentle sound and an arrow appeared in the neck of the panicking man beside him. The young soldier dropped to his knees, as if suddenly fascinated by the earth. A moment later and this time with no sound whatsoever the second hangman sat down as well.

Albenix looked at the bodies leaking a red creek over the soil and then turned and ran into the foliage himself. He started in one direction, stumbled, and took another, crashing into the underbrush with outraged leaps. His mouth was gritted into a fantastic grin, the pine and creeper and shag-pines whipping at his cheeks and his eyes like scourges.

Henry knelt down with Speaking Owl and embraced her small form. She seemed tiny in his hands, as if there were nothing of her there, and he gripped her more solidly to impart reality to that thinness. Her naturally dark skin was flushed with running and the sweat shone all across her, in the bruised hollow of her throat, across her shining wet cheeks. Her long hair lay wild like a horse's mane after a panic. But she was not panicked; she was only breathing hard.

"Owl," Henry said, and gripped her hard again. "Owl."

She said his name and when her eyes met there was an imperative.

"Yes," he said quickly. "All right."

He went around behind her and pulled through the remaining ropes that bound her wrists. The rope was wetted with her perspiration and when he finally had it off it hurt him terribly to see the swelling where the fibers had been. He threw the bundle away into the leaves and lifted her wrists gently as if to offer them back to her.

"Hide in the woods," he said, looking into her eyes and sending his message that way, the words he spoke only for his own ears to hear and to help him. "Far away from here. The slaver is not the problem." She placed her numb fingers over his mouth to show she understood.

Already, Henry thought, *already she is stronger than I am.*

"Someplace of ours. You understand? One of our places."

He slid the feather out of his ear and put it in her hand.

"I will come for you," he said. "Go."

Only he hadn't spoken the last word, she had spoken it to him, with her eyes: *go*. She disappeared into the trees in the direction of the island's center and he backtracked, coming in close to the area where the fighting was and then cutting hard north to ascend the first hill. From the top he would be able to descry how the contest stood, who had charge of the village and who had charge of the brigantine. He pushed quickly through the underbrush, startling a flight of pink-legged birds, their shrieking number sailing into the air.

There was something at the center of the grassy field that was the crest of the hill: something that knelt with the sea placid and gray behind it, with its hands tied back and its arms bent. Henry went to it. When he was close he saw the hair, the jaw, the up-cast face.

"Oh, John," he said. It was not warm to the touch but not cold, not sea-cold as he had been afraid. They had beaten him without removing his shirt, tearing through the fabric until it hung in wide patches. Henry knelt and put his cheek next to the dead man's cheek and slid his arms around him, the body feeling strangely soft, his mind throwing up no defenses to protect himself from the reality of what this was, what this would always be.

"Oh, John," he said, and the hot fury erupted from him, he cried aloud and gripped the body, the cries spilling and spilling from his person as if to add some tiny measure of heat to the place where it had been lost.

When the racking was done Henry found himself with his head on the dead man's breast, smelling the still-living scent of his body, the odors of life that had yet to leave him. He raised himself back up and stood.

"Go to God, Father Juan," he said. "Please go to God."

He untied the feet and hands and laid the body out across the ground. The muscles resisted this change of position but Henry eased them until the body lay, no longer a grotesquerie but simply a death, and slid shut the eyes.

Go.

Smoke was beginning to cover the village and obscure the images of running men. Three soldiers of *Legenda Aurea* closed ranks with their backs to each other, one of them holding out a pike with an ornamented head, as if baying a hog. He shouted into the flaming obscurity, thrusting forward the tip of the lance and sweeping its edge in ineffectual motions. The other two had swords drawn and were wiping frantically at their eyes to avoid being jumped. One man's face was darkened by power: his musket had discharged improperly and blown fire at him badly enough to force him to drop the weapon, at which point it was lost in the melee. The other man had a set, determined expression, not bothering with the soot-black sweat that was gradually filling the lines in his forehead and around his eyes like charcoal etching. He had killed two men already, both of them Carib; the second one came at him completely naked, his uncut penis flapping madly as he ran with green mud smeared across his face. He brandished some sort of knife and the man had shot him and then dropped the pistol and run his sword through the exposed belly, letting the knife fall harmlessly high over his left shoulder before the attacker died. The sword had stayed lodged in the falling body, though, and the second man came at him fast, swinging a club at the end of which was tied a sharp stone. That man the soldier had strangled with his hands.

The retrieved sword was red at the hilt and almost black at the point, and the look of it continually circulated his own blood and his own sense of immediate power. He did not feel intelligent, nor brave, nor calculating, even. His mind was only a single impression symbolized by the sword, an impression of his own capacity, like a darkness beating inside his well-tuned soul.

"*¡A los barcos!*" he said, and in a circle of three they began moving through the spread-out bodies backward in the general direction of the water. Once they were out from the cover of the grass-roofed buildings a sea wind blew and the smoke that made everything into a chaos of quick-moving forms dissipated almost at once. The soldier looked up and in the new clarity saw something leaping towards him, something that had followed their progress from on top of the roofs themselves. He drew the smaller flintlock and pulled the trigger but the charge did not speak, and in the next instant the man to his side who had been once more wiping his eyes received a blow from some kind of weapon that severed part of his head, spattering the man with hot liquid. He swung his sword at the figure and it danced back into the smoke, both hands up and giving him the fig.

"Go back in. I'll have him."

The two remaining soldiers closed on the shadow. The one with the pike stabbed furiously and terrifiedly, and so did not see the second figure that came from behind him and inserted a thin long blade carefully and with precision into the open space between his metal chest plate and the armpit, puncturing lung and heart in a simple, almost surgical gesture. The lanceman fell and the one remaining soldier found himself confronting two enemies now, the dancing, apish one with the candy-colored scalp trying to distract him while the other, weirdly tattooed with Egyptian figures, walked sideways around him and sized him up like a patient man evaluating a problem. The soldier gripped hard the bloody sword and shouted a wordless noise at the thinking man, bracing his legs to prepare for the charge. But the tattooed creature simply walked sideways around him and then continued walking, as if having lost interest.

The soldier looked behind himself; the capering figure was gone as well. For a minute he peered frantically around, and above, waiting for the trick. But there was none. The brigands had simply left.

He paused the length of three breaths and then bolted toward the longboats.

It wasn't until the baby palm in front of him blew open in a shower of fresh green that he understood why they had let him run. For a moment he turned and tried to tell how far away the man with the slingshot stood, one arm cocked high, his tattooed companion watching skeptically at his side. Then he started to run again, dropping his weapon. For just a moment he could almost see the water.

Albenix stopped his headlong flight when he spied the girl. It was an interior pool, shaded on all sides by trees, and for a moment some strangely unaffected part of his mind compared her to a great painting, a Velázquez or a Murillo: *Girl by the water*. Then he saw who she was and drew closer.

She was dipping her hands up to the wrist and running her fingers over her face and hair, wiping away dirt. For several minutes Albenix watched her. He saw the way her cupped hands carried water, a still, glimmering cup of it suspended between them; saw the way the water, lifted to her forehead, ran in lines down her cheeks and across her neck and down through the space between her breasts. Her hair was water-slicked now, so black where the streaked sun found it that it showed hidden tints of blue. Her skin was brown and smooth like an unpicked fruit, a kind of tropical curiosity sprinkled in cocoa. He watched the water gather and spill from her lap.

Then the wrists themselves excited his curiosity. Yes, they were red; even through the darkness of her skin he could see he had hurt her by binding so tightly. The idea gave him a strange warmth. She dipped her wrists again and cringed and he felt a stir inside himself, almost shameful, at the sight of her cringing. He could feel the chafed skin, the helplessness of the rope. His genital began to stiffen.

"*Hola de nuevo*," he whispered, emerging from the gloom.

The girl gasped and tried to rise, and *Comandante* Albenix forced her back down. After a small struggle he impaled the ground through the fabric of her dress with his sword so she could not run. Then he held a gloved hand up to his lips and nose, scenting it carefully.

"I am glad, you know," he said, stepping a little around. "I am glad I was prevented from lifting you on the gallows. That would have been wrong. Truly."

He reached down with one hand and for a second time took hold of the girl's chin. She pressed her eyes shut, dark lashes against little folds, her angry mouth tense.

"You cannot stand to look on me? You, who gave my men something to remember you by. My men." The *comandante*'s thought seemed to stray. "I wonder how you managed it? This trap so cleverly executed. This magic you have wrought for that black cleric."

He released her and the girl turned inward, struggling against the blade.

"You will learn to look on me, *criaturita*. In time. First I will regain my ship. Then we will look on each other much. Then we shall see each other truly."

For a moment he seemed to be thinking. Then Albenix grabbed her hair in a sudden fury and twisted the girl's head sideways. The redness where the noose had been stirred that strangeness in him again, almost shameful. He felt the erection beginning to throb.

"I have tried to be true to the Word in my life. Can you understand that? I have labored... *labored* as a secret Benedictine. Though none of them know me, none of them...though none say masses for me, though none are aware they have a disciple outside the monastery wall, I have kept my fidelity. I have avoided all women, honoring the *regula* in myself. Tell me, is this what it means to taste seduction?"

The girl gagged out involuntarily as Albenix hauled her head back. With his free hand he began unlacing his breech-front.

"Is this what seduction means? Is that what you are doing to me now? Ruining my soul? Is this your victory over me? Is this it, serpent? Is it, Eve? Eve? Eve? ..."

A shadow was on the ground. Albenix dropped the girl.

"I don't know you," the English boy said. "I don't know anything about you."

Albenix looked at him, amazed. Physically he did not seem more than a teenager. He was shirtless and his skin was whipped red around his chest from a race through the undergrowth. The empty hands were at his sides. No weapon.

"Daylaylo's ghost?" Albenix asked in Spanish. "Or another of his serving spirits. A tiny thing."

"Go away from us. Go away from her."

Albenix rebuttoned his breeches almost casually. In the same motion he unclipped a belt loop at his side and slid out a pearl-handled knife.

"My English you will forgive," he bowed. "I would not have expected your master to summon *un inglesito*."

Stepping forward, the Spaniard began drifting the blade in front of himself, slowly, as if testing the air.

"Tell me then, child-familiar. How did he do it? Do spirits live on this island? Little boys and girls? Or, your master, did he conjure you two only?"

Henry took a step. The leafy ground crackled under his feet.

"It is a bad thing when friars turn wizard, no? A grave sin," the

Spaniard asked, almost lamenting. "*¿De acuerdo?*"

Albenix' free hand was up now in the position of a formal fighter. He wagged the knife foolishly a moment and then restraightened it. "In Madrid there is no need. We let the priests do as they please. Nuns. Altar boys. Rich men's wives."

Henry took another step. The shadows in his peripheral vision turned by a degree. The sun was low enough here to blind.

"I don't want to fight."

The Spaniard made a tragic face. "It is bad how far a holy man falls." His eyes darted to Henry's feet. Henry watched: the mouth was speaking, but the eyes were careful, measuring. "When he falls, it is to the pit."

Then the eyes moved for real and Albenix leapt, feinting a jab but kicking out instead at Henry's ankle. Henry saw the move coming but failed to avoid it; for a moment he was on the ground and the other man maneuvering to straddle him. Henry rolled spastically, trying to break free.

"I have learned new things this day," Albenix said, retaking his position as if the victory were too simple a thing. A small leaf was in his hair and he plucked it aside.

"Please," Henry said. "I'm not with the others. You don't have any ..."

"I have had a...what is the English...*un hallazgo*? My country comes here looking for new lands. But I am the explorer. I have found new land."

The *comandante* swung again, real but not expecting to make contact. Henry escaped the swing but felt the fear of it sailing through him.

"Please ..." he tried. His heart was leaping.

"I have this discovery. I may not be the man I believed. You know, I think I am a much better man, child-familiar. I may be a saint."

Albenix struck viciously and cut into Henry's bicep. Henry made a noise against the sudden pain and the Spaniard looked evaluatively at the blood.

"What is a saint, after all, yes? But a man who looks...how is it...a man who *looks carefully, yes*? And could not I be such a man? Tell me now, and I may let you go. When you look at me. Do you see *saint*?"

Henry looked at the face, knowing it was a trick, the same trick Benjamin Oldham used when he made pebbles disappear under bowls: to direct your opponent's eyes and take them away from your hands. He knew it was a trick, that all the other man wanted was a moment's distraction, but instead of expecting the blow Henry looked at the man's eyes and saw suffering in them and the *comandante*'s hand came in close, serious now, and the sharp tip sliced him lengthwise across the belly.

Henry cried out in terror and shame and stumbled backward. Speaking Owl, from her position by the water, cried with him. Her voice came to him not so much as an expression of sympathy as part of his own voice, his own cry. Albenix examined his knife edge a second time. He seemed to be considering whether to taste it.

"Think of what it means, to hurt for a saint," he said, not even bothering to look now. He was coming forward, seemingly lost in his own meditations. "This hurt…to hurt for the saints…is holy, yes? So you may be holy as well. Look at me."

Henry looked, and again he had fallen into the trap: the Spaniard was in front of the sun and in the instant Henry instinctively looked at the fiery ball he caught a blue spot in his eye and the Spaniard rushed in. Henry scrambled pointlessly away and something hard knocked him back. He ducked the blow that was coming at his eyes and instead felt the flat handle of the blade slap insultingly across his forehead. He fell.

"This is an honorable thing. Even for a ghost, a spirit like you. But then, you are not truly this spirit, are you? I see you bleed now, I feel your body at the end of my blade. No. You are no spirit but a strange boy, come out of nowhere. Child of nowhere. Son of nowhere."

Henry was scrambling around on the ground in a circle, his mind empty of reason, empty of all the power and will it had so laboriously gained. The beaches were gone, the canoe ride, the attack when he felt the unstoppable energy of the warriors. He tried to conjure the red mask of hatred, finding it nowhere; these places in him were wasted fires, cold ash. His heart was galloping, wheeling. The Spaniard looped his knife evenly as he talked, seeming almost bored with the exercise.

I'm going to die here, Henry thought. *I'm going to die after all* and, what was worse: *he's going to take her away.* After all he had seen he was afraid still of dying and terribly afraid of the pain, the sticking pain of the knife. But what came next in her life he could not bear. He had brought her to this—taken away all the People's defenses, left them vulnerable and her unprotected. It was true of him, as the People had said. He had been given a second chance and refused it, following his own worst spirit. He had brought ruin where there was love and disaster where there had been hope. Everything that could have been his he had lost. The knife was his condemnation.

And then, with the calmness of absolute conviction, came another voice.

You know.

The words were uninflected, cool as still water inside his consciousness.

You know, lad. Because I showed you.

Henry stopped moving. After a moment, he made a sound.

Comandante Albenix stood where he was. His face drew in and the thick lips pursed curiously.

"Something amuses?"

Laugh, boy, the voice said. *What's this world but a pity? What's a man but a joke.*

Henry rose from the ground, slapping sand from his breeches. He was chuckling to himself, the chuckling rising to a firmer tone.

Laugh.

He wiped a hand across his belly and felt the sting and saw it come away red where he had been cut. He looked at the Spanish commander in his blue and gold uniform, his trim moustaches, his black leather scabbard, and suddenly Henry felt his own face open in a broad guffaw, rising almost to a shriek. The sound was terrible and sweet.

Laugh. And then knock the bastard's teeth in.

Comandante Albenix started to respond and then something came at him so quickly that for a moment he was elsewhere, watching an array of lights blossom inside his head. Then he was on the ground and the figure he had taken for a child was hammering him a second time, a third time and a fourth time in the already-shattered bridge of his nose with a fist that felt like a rock, with an arm that swung like a catapult.

Roaring madly Albenix threw the weight of the boy from him

and rose, but a fist went up fast into his stomach and he doubled over, blowing spit. He realized with amazement there was blood taste in his mouth. The knife was gone and with his left arm he swung out hard but hit nothing; the boy had ducked under it expertly and was bludgeoning him again, blinding him and filling his eyes with ugly light. Albenix reached out for something to grab and the boy was behind him now, kicking quickly and precisely the soft backs of his legs so he fell hard on his kneecaps.

Dazed and kneeling, the *comandante* looked up almost innocently at the juggernaut that was battering him. The trees opened in a breeze and he saw only a figure made out of sun, a hammer god, a man of power flung out of what had been hardly a boy; and when the closed fist feinted one direction and then came against his cheekbone from the other side splitting it open in a shiver of brilliant pain Albenix' thought was *no más papito papito no más no más …*

Henry stopped, his body thudding with energy. Gradually the other man picked himself up from the ground. His face was a startled mass. The *comandante* seemed unable to align his joints; he bobbed a little and tilted on his own legs, like a marionette in the hands of an incapable player. Then with one hand he reached over and pried the long sword from the ground where it pinned the girl's dress.

Speaking Owl scrambled up into Henry's arms and the Spaniard turned toward them, gesturing with the weapon. Henry turned his side against it and covered the girl, staring back madly as if to stay the blade by intention.

But the blade did not approach. Instead the Spaniard waited uncertainly, wobbling like a collection of pieces. Henry realized the man's eyes were pointing in two slightly different directions. Then the *comandante* turned and, fantastically, faced the water. The edge of his sword glinted copperish in the sunlight. He took a step forward and fell.

Henry backed Speaking Owl away from the edge, feeling the tremulousness of her body. The Spaniard, splashing, raised himself up again in the muddy lagoon. He was facing away, toward the collapse of the sun, the blade still held oddly in one hand and sending coherent ripples across the water. He took faltering steps forward, his already lost feet stumbling in silt, and seemed to sit down in the sunset-colored pool. For a minute his torso remained visible there, the head sagging, the sword disappeared under the water line. Then he lay down in the water himself, gradually, as if by intent, like a man spreading himself out for sleep.

When they reached the village again she took the arm.

"I have to," Henry said into her eyes. "He raided an entire landing party to bring me back. He isn't going to sail without me." And then, in answer to her asked question: "I don't know. I don't know."

Henry walked into the open space of the village and felt Speaking Owl disappear behind him into the unbroken line of trees. At once he felt her disappearance and her presence, her languaged eyes watching him, keeping him like the feather in her palm. He willed her unafraid, giving the same prayer to himself.

The World was a chaos. What structures had survived the general burning looked weirdly out of place, like unwetted citizens standing in the wake of a monsoon. As Henry passed them the scent of palmetto leaf was thick. Too damp or too fresh to burn, the greenery had by the proximity of fires been somehow encouraged to open its pores and a rich, honey-like sweetness streamed out in bizarre juxtaposition to the odor of smoke. The bodies lay where they had fallen, some in the ridiculous oddities of death, most in the uniformity of it, the lying-down men, the simply dead.

Henry came out to the terrible victors.

"Roojman!" Whitepaul cried when he saw him. "Have ye grown so eager for a fight, my boy?"

A cheer rose among the bloodied men. Some were already busy with looting the village, assembling piles of stored food. Around their number, seated in threes and facing away, were the remaining soldiers. Several of *Arrogante's* crew had been emptying the pockets of one when Henry emerged. The Spaniard, small-faced with foolish orange whiskers grown to lengthen it, seemed to consider running for a moment at the distraction and then sat again where he had been.

"Roojman, my own. Give him a wrapping for that head. And clean off his belly."

I gave you your life once, Henry said, speaking nothing. *I gave you your life at Everglade.*

"I want my freedom." Whitepaul stopped what he was doing.

"Oh aye?"

"You have a new ship," Henry said. "You have crew. You have slaves and booty. Let me go."

For a moment Whitepaul made an expression Henry had never seen before, a mime of sadness.

"Do ye not love me, then, boy?"

Henry waited until the laughter had died.

"No," he said.

The broad face lost its mockery and something else emerged from it, something dark and serious. The wild unkempt brows pressed together, like bulls in a pen. Whitepaul's mouth sank to a scowl.

"Do ye say that to my face," he rumbled.

Henry could feel the tension among the crewmen now. Still hot from the battle, they were backing slowly away from the invisible circle that contained him and the captain.

"I only ask ..."

"*Say that again*," Whitepaul thundered, coming closer until he closed off Henry's vision like a cloud. "Say ye that ye love me not."

Henry looked into the madman's eyes.

"I don't love you, Quirinius," he said.

"After what I did for ye," the captain whimpered, unexpectedly. "After saving thee from what kills a man when he still is a boy. After saving thee like a little fish...and raising ye in my home...my home in the sea."

Henry opened his mouth to speak and Whitepaul put a dark boot in the center of his chest and shoved him down.

"Now ye say that ye loves me not, eh, eh, my Roojman?" he hollered. "Now ye slap and spit in my face, do ye? Now ye thinks to leave thy old man, eh, thy keeper and thy maker?" A torn button tangled with his pocket and Whitepaul snapped the thing away, flinging his coat like a missile at Henry's face. "Nay, ye won't escape this schoolmaster without a whipping, my Roo ..."

"*My name isn't Roojman*," Henry shouted, standing. "*And you aren't my maker*."

The sound of his shout echoed impossibly loud, causing a cloud of white birds to rise crying over the village. For an instant Henry stared, believing the power of his words had somehow done this;

then he heard the echo of the report. The prisoner with the shaggy whiskers was pointing an exploded flintlock at Whitepaul, his face quivering with the terror of what he'd done.

For a moment Whitepaul turned and simply peered at the man, who remained holding the spent gun in both hands with his mouth open. Then he turned back to Henry as if the actual physical blow were irrelevant to him.

"Not love me," he said quietly. He lifted with one hand the gold skull away from his chest, revealing half its strange face glistening red. With the other he dipped three fingers under his shirt at the junction of the X. They came up shining. "Not love me. Oi, you say. Oi."

"Captain …" Benjamin Oldham began, his jaw working quickly against itself.

"Oiyay," Whitepaul said, sitting down on the ground. "So he said."

Without any sign from their leader the men descended on the whiskered assassin in a rush. The pig-sticking continued for a full minute.

Henry went to Whitepaul and knelt.

Blood over gold. His life.

"Sir," the crew were calling, as if to disagree with his present intentions. "*Sir! Sir! My captain!*"

But the crimson hand merely waved their cries down. Whitepaul's unfocussing eyes seemed concerned with other matters. He started to lie back and one of the men pushed up a log with furious urgency, letting the huge torso slump against it. For a moment Whitepaul looked at the man who had supplied the gift as if to thank him. Then he took the gold skull in one hand.

"She'll not be there. Nay," he said. "Not that one. There's the damning of it …"

His head rested back on the stump.

"There's the damning …"

Henry watched. The eyes, large and red, looked upward for a moment. They seemed to descry something in the high clouds. *See, see*, the eyes said. *See its grace and its beauty approaching.*

28

To hell, the voices cried, when enough unburned wood had been scavenged to erect a pile. The body laid across it dwarfed the wood and dry leaves were thrown on top, the men dancing as they threw, wide leaves that caught rapidly, the light of the bonfire spreading upward.

To hell in a ship, in a ship, a ship,
To hell in a ship, and you, and I.

To hell in a ship the faster we fly,
And devil take all, say I, say I.

At dawn Black P'ter had the surviving prisoners brought out from the brigantine and ordered their bindings released. With his cutlass in hand he walked the length of them, looking each long in the face.

"Who comes with me?" he hollered.

There was a shout from some and the blessing of blood began: each man thrown in a circle and defending himself from fists and from knees. The ones who refused looked on with hate-filled masks.

"You," P'ter said when it was done, placing the tip of his cutlass against Henry's chest. "Not *Roojman*, I hear it said."

Henry closed his eyes. "The people here called me Starfish."

The deep-skinned man folded his steel back into its rope.

"*Stahhhr-feesh*," he grinned, showing greatly amused teeth. He touched a hand to Henry's heart in the gesture of recognition. "No more slave."

"Captain," Henry answered.

P'ter rounded up his men and his prisoners. In an hour the *Legenda Aurea* moved, catching a sunrise wind that Henry could see but not feel from the distance. After a little work the brig heaved to and slid, freeing itself of the close waters, making directly for the open sea.

The next day was cold and rain moved in quickly from the east, the strong winds of twenty hours before turning into the fiercer kind that bring trouble for navigators and turn currents against the sea-riched beaches of the islands. On the following day the air was clean and glistering, like something baptized.

At the end of the long walk Henry Cote stood at the Rest of the Old One and buried a body, which he put with reverence into the earth. In the next site to it he opened a second mound and laid in it twin handfuls of clumping ashes. When the dissolution was filled in he went into the forest for an hour and returned with two arms full of wildly colored flowers, purples and violets and ocean colors, the greens and bright pink-reds of the listening water before the reef and the dark, stained blues of the ocean beyond. These he laid between the two mounds and in their center, standing over both, erected a wooden pole on which was written

Fray Juan Batiste de Daylaylo Man-in-Tree
Quirinius Nicolai Whitepaul
Free men

And then, under a line that drew them together, an icon in the language of the People:

Father

The young woman standing next to him looked at the unfamiliar words and the one familiar one and turned without condescension and without contradiction, and the young man turned and looked at her as well.

"Yes," he said. "I'm ready."

Epilogue: *Ocuia*

Often during that time the man would be awakened by nightmares and rise, sometimes only bending at his torso like the body of a corpse left unattended; sometimes rising entirely to his feet and calling out in a frightened, childlike voice. At those times she would hold him most carefully, staying away from the hands that fisted and unfisted in his lap, until he grew calm and his eyes, staring out into the predawn air, would lose their inward-looking quality. Then he would return to her, lying down again next to her on a blanket or simply in the grass. As he fell gradually back into sleep she would hold him with her forehead pressed against his, where the scar was, drawing out the dreams that were there and taking them away from him so his softer, interior self could rest. In this way she saw images of the dreams that were in his head: she saw men rising up from what had seemed quiet waters, their bodies soaked through and their hands lifted menacingly to the air. She knew what frightened his soul in this image was the violence of it, the dreadful sunken faces like hollowed-out rock, the flesh dropping away and fingers that were sticks of bone still grasping at rusted weaponry.

But she felt in her own soul the true dreadfulness of his vision: it was a vision of nature reversing its healing course, of old pains returning to inflict themselves fresh, of the past breaking from its appointed time into the daylight of the present. Unafraid she took the rotting men into her soul, she took them in and made them small woven toys and scattered them with her hands, back into the waves or over the trees or out into the lonely outer darkness where they cried like babies and were gone.

On the day when she, the morning sun filling the calm sky above them, stooped and took his head and pressed it close to her own and saw inside the man's dreams not the rising mad corpses but a cloud, a traveling thunder racing over a plain of swept grass, she knew his spirit was healed and the other dreams would return no more. For the sweeping, traveling power she had seen in his dream drew close and was a column of horses, their chests heaving and their powerful hooves sawing the earth like wind.

The People never returned to their World, scattered throughout the islands by the assault. She and he had lived there alone, needing little and repairing only as much as was necessary. At the end of the first year together she had been surprised to see the man crouching down happily and speaking to an animal that had come walking out of the forest. It was something sleek and admiring, that made noises at him as if it knew him. *It's Thins*, the man said, and they had fed the small animal from their food for a week or more before it vanished back into the unseen wood.

They built a boat like the canoes but thicker, more capable of long-distance traveling. Its front space filled with food and utensils for cooking, for scraping, for making fires, and all these things roped down safely, they entered the boat finally when the man was satisfied. It was morning and the lean wooden frame passed quickly through shallows that reflected so brilliantly it seemed they were moving across the sun. The man was happy. Together they rowed mile after mile on the face of the sea.

At one point she had stopped and gestured at something he had not been able to see, a quick-moving form under the brightening waves. The shape, whatever it had been, disappeared but the man continued looking after it, saying something to her and looking longingly, well past the time when it was gone.

When she had been a child her mother was forced from the community of her birth by men who called her a seducing woman. Three of the elders had come to her tent and lit a curse-fire in front of it, taking out her mother's things while her mother cried out and throwing them on the fire. After that they had left that place and traveled, riding in canoes like men, swimming small streams when no canoes would be offered them, moving always south. *What you know already is behind you*, her mother told her, making a dismissive gesture with her fingers. *Throw that to the sun.* One day she had seen an alligator crouching in a sandy pond and when she asked her mother what the animal was her mother had said that the animal was dangerous, yes, but that she must always look for a man with that animal's eyes. A man whose eyes were that animal's eyes was the most dangerous kind of man in the world.

That night wrapped tightly against her mother's body she had dreamed of the man with the alligator's eyes. His eyes were the largest part of his head and the green scaly matter extended outward onto his face as well, until lizard nature and man-nature were mixed. His hair was white, hair a color she had seen in no person other than spirits, and as she watched he crouched down in his sandy pool of time and waited for her, waited with unblinking vision the day when she would return.

In the morning it rained for three days and they could not travel. Then the sun returned and she and her mother had continued moving, covering miles in a day, her mother working hardest not to show the fatigue she felt to her daughter who was aware of it all. There was on her mother's face a tragic expression: she seemed to have lost her sense of purpose and lived now only for moving away. At times during the walking she smiled to her mother, saying that life would be fine for them, saying that many lived as they did, and there were, somewhere, some who would take them in and give them a resting and a belonging place. Yet more and more she became frightened at her mother's unblinking expression, and that night she dreamed that her mother was getting the alligator's eyes.

After that her mother began speaking to herself low and meaninglessly in the mornings and the evenings, her face older than itself, unable to stem her tears as if there were a crack in her person and water were simply running from it. During the day her face became fixed again as they traveled or begged for food or stole, a few times. Then at night she began the chatter again, seemingly terrified of her tears but beyond all capacity to solve them.

On the last night her mother simply pointed to her the direction, as if this information were not already known. They sat by the ashes of a fire where a few late raindrops hissed and her face was no longer her face. The girl had sat by her and cried for more than a day but her hunger grew so great that on the next morning she did the impossible thing: she set out walking on her own, knowing what she needed to do in order to live and to feel, and the greatest sadness in her was not a fear of how she would live or where she would go, but a terrible sadness that after years of trying she could no longer save the old woman with the blank, unloved expression.

Now living with the man she remembered the unloved expression of the old woman who had been her mother and whose spirit had haunted her in its loneliness and its terror for so long, until she had found she no longer feared loneliness, in herself or in others, and then she had been free.

The man did other rituals of whose precise nature she was uncertain. On the first night on a new island he stopped her from building a fire by taking the wood out of her hands and pointing upward. Time and again he pointed to things in the sky and said words to her, laughing sometimes and showing her with his fingers. She looked up and saw the lights and let the man continue to point and explain, and for the rest of the night he was silent, so that when they slept she put her arms up by his neck and held herself against the beating of his chest.

Then at a point where no islands could be seen in any direction and they rowed all day by the orientation of the sun alone he had suddenly stopped, removing from the strapped-down place a sail bag and reaching inside it for something he needed. The object was scarred black with golden bright streaks, affixed to a clattering chain. She could see it was dotted all over with hammered gold, though the inside seemed hollow, as if it held something once that had long since dissolved. With one hand the man leaned over and dropped the ball into the water, and she watched him watching as the thing turned to show a surprising face before descending invisibly into the deep.

When they passed an island large and green in the direction of the setting sun he had indicated no, and she had known already that this was not far enough, for she could see the smoke rising in several places. That had been the last island they had seen with men living there.

Then at the end of the moon she had seen the quick-moving form under the waves again, a watcher of their progress; and, knowing he would want to see it if he could, she stopped his red working arms and pointed to the sea. The shape rose up again and this time he did see it: it became flesh and an animal broke the waves nearby, and the man repeated a word to her again and again and laughed to watch the animal play. Before it descended, blue and lean and dark-eyed, with a powerful stroke of its tail it went sidelong to their boat, and the man reached out and touched the long blue flank. *Dolphin*, he said, his face ecstatic, his hand out as if showing her the moment of his touching. She reached out and placed his hand on the area just over her heart, and he took her palm and pressed it to his own heart so she could feel the relieved life stirring there. The man smiled and Ocuia kissed his silent mouth, resettling herself forward again with the long wooden paddle in her hands and with all that she knew at her back and given to the sun she joined him in the long motion south.

About William Orem

William Orem's first collection of stories, *Zombi, You My Love*, won the Great Lakes Colleges Association New Writers Award in 2000, previously given to Sherman Alexie, Alice Munro, Louise Erdrich, and Richard Ford. His second story collection, *Across the River*, won the Clay Reynolds Novella Prize for 2009. Other stories and poems of his have appeared in over 100 literary journals, including *The Princeton Arts Review*, *Alaska Quarterly Review*, *Sou'Wester*, and *The New Formalist*, and he has been nominated for the Pushcart Prize in both genres. His plays have been performed in Miami, Ft. Lauderdale, Louisville, Buffalo, and Boston, with a staged reading in Manhattan. Currently he is a Writer-In-Residence at Emerson College.

LaVergne, TN USA
13 March 2011
219933LV00004B/54/P

9 780981 949550